Victoria McCombs
Woods of Silver and Light

To my sister, Kaitlyn,
who has both the gentleness of Cosette and the strength of Anika

CHAPTER ONE

"Keep your head about you."

"Attend all the balls you're invited to."

"And please, *please*, Anika, don't swear in front of the king."

Cosette and Rumpel repeated rules to me all morning as if I would turn feral without their constant supervision. "I will do quite fine on my own, thank you." I broke away from their tight embrace. "And perhaps the king finds swearing to be charming."

Rumpel snorted, but Cosette frowned. "I doubt it. Lady Claire, I'm sorry to be leaving you with such a mess." She turned to the older lady at our side who wore a bulging, blush dress and a straight line on her lips.

My eyes rolled but Cosette swatted my arm, causing me to straighten. "I'm sorry I'm such a disaster, Lady Claire. It is not my intention."

Lady Claire stretched the corner of her lips into a small smile and waved her large fan over me. "It's been quite some time since I could help the society. You will be my greatest project yet."

I resisted flaring my nostrils at the word project. Cosette had befriended Lady Claire and, upon hearing how she used to school young girls into proper women, beseeched her to come stay with me once she and Rumpel returned to Autumn Leaf Village. She also invited Lady Elenora to stay with us, and I knew she secretly hoped the girl's fine manners would wear off on me. Lady Elenora was my age and could be tolerated. Lady Claire was a different beast altogether. I didn't know if she needed the small payments we offered her or if my lack of manners hurt her, but she acted as if it was the second.

I had enough projects on hand without becoming one myself.

The village was still broken from the war that ended a year ago, and my farms were failing. My plans for my time involved donning my flax breeches and saving the lands, not forming stiff friendships among the other nobles. But I repeatedly promised to be on my best behavior until Cosette was satisfied enough to leave.

"Farewell!" I waved them away in their carriage with a wild arm while Lady Claire twitched her fingers beside me. When the cobblestone dust resettled and the click clack of the horse was too far away to hear, I announced I was going into the village to check on the farms.

With a disappointed shake of her head, Lady Claire pulled a parchment out of the pockets of her dress. "Have you forgotten?"

My blank expression answered her, but the silver etching on the paper she waved wasn't a good sign.

"Your invitation. Lord Carson's ball is tonight, and you will be the definition of proper the entire evening."

"A girl playing cards? Would you look at that!"

I ignored the newcomer's remarks while cursing under my breath. Unless Lord Nevins was bluffing, a skill he was undoubtedly adept at by the hefty stack of tokens tucked by his arm, my hand would lose. I kept my elbows close to my side and thumbed under the corners of my gray cards, bending them up to peek again. The corners were permanently bent from months of playing, so my hand pressed against the top card to keep it flat. Beside me came the rhythmic sound of fingers tapping against the table as the third gentleman pondered his hand. Hallow and deep it played, dum dum…dum dum dum…he threw his cards in.

Jolly good. Only two of us left. The previous card did me no good, and I silently cursed again.

"Another one?" The low voice of my opponent came, mocking me. He knew I had nothing. The victory would taste sweet to him. I sucked in my chest as the last card was flipped over in the middle of the table. Heads swiveled from one side to the other, looking for a reaction from either my opponent or me, but I wouldn't give them the satisfaction. My head stayed down as I peeked at Lord Nevins. The final card brought little hope, but at least now I had a small pair to my name. That might do it. *Blast, I should have tossed in rounds ago.*

Invitations for tonight arrived a month ago, and Lady Claire trained me ruthlessly in preparation, not only for this evening, but also for the countless invitations that followed from families on either side of the Westfallen/Vestalin border. She would be dismayed to see me now, blue tokens in hand and ignoring the dancing beyond these doors.

I laid down my hand and hoped for the best outcome. My opponent might be bluffing, but it wasn't likely I'd beat him.

Lord Nevins, to his account, showed no great joy at winning as he shook my hand respectfully. "You had me worried there; not many can do that." He twirled his mustache between two fingers as his other hand stretched over the table, bringing his loot close.

My disappointment was difficult to mask. "You are a worthy opponent."

A new voice came. "Did well for a girl, I'll give her that."

My attention swept across the room to the speaker. Roughly twenty people squeezed together in the oval room, most holding glasses or a cigar. My hair would be stained with the thick stench of their smoke in the morning, and Lady Claire would know I had been at the cards again.

Through the smoke sat a man older than me who I thought made the remark. "And what do you mean by that?" I asked him squarely.

His voice fumbled, not prepared to be questioned. If he didn't want me to comment, he shouldn't have spoken so loudly. "I only meant...that is, you are a girl, and can't be expected to know the cards as well."

"Is there some magic on these cards that only a man's eyes can see?" I asked with annoyance. Most of the lads smirked, but the man I was staring at looked uneasy as he shifted sideways.

"I was wondering when we would get some attitude tonight." Lord Byron chuckled. He was a kind man who meant no disrespect by the comment; I had been known to speak out vividly when insulted.

The man held his cup close to his body and shrugged. "Surely we've all been playing longer than you have; I guess that's what I meant by it."

I squinted my eyes at him. "Aren't you the man I beat a month back? Took several pretty coins from you, if I recall."

The man next to him laughed, but he shook his head. "That was my brother; he came home in quite a fit over it."

I grinned. "Glad to leave an impression. And I'll have you know, I've been playing cards for years."

As the lads chuckled, Elenora passed by the doorway and gave me a disapproving shake of her head. She proved a loyal companion over the year I had been here, but she couldn't understand my love for the cards. She chalked it up to my 'rough upbringing' as she called it and avoided the topic. I knew her father had lost a great deal to the cards when she was little, though few played at such high stakes anymore.

"How is it that you've been playing for years, when you've only come here a year ago?" the gentleman next to me asked.

"I was taught how to play by some boys in the village."

"What's this, you lived in a village?" another asked as he placed two chips on the table.

I sighed. It felt as if each time I played my past was brought up by curious gentlemen who couldn't wrap their head around a strange girl. I laid my hands with my cards on my lap and crossed my legs. "That's right; I came to the

Wateredge Manor a year ago when my family acquired the title."

I didn't offer any more information, but the man slowly nodded his head. "I recall now, you took on after Lord Gregory." A man next to him coughed, and another drew his mouth in a thin line. This was a sensitive topic he'd unknowingly treaded into.

"That's correct," I confirmed.

Another cough. "Thomas, will you raise?"

He was bringing the conversation away from Lord Gregory and my estate, which was a smart move. The man who held my title and lands before me died during the war with no direct family to pass the lands to. His cousin should have inherited the land, but the late king of West-fallen gave the title to my family instead as appreciation to my sister for her work in the war. It was my lucky break out of Autumn Leaf Village, but I hadn't been received warmly. Lord Gregory was well loved, and many felt I cheated my way into his manor.

They might be right, but it wasn't such a great prize as they believed. The floorboards in the manor sagged, rail-ings were rotten, windows missing, and many tenant's lands had failed to produce a generous crop in years. I spent the long year in tedious work fixing up the home and helping the farmers in the fields. This past year proved a more frustrating learning experience than I'd anticipated, but I was desperate to keep my lands. Many around me had to sell chunks of land to the king to keep afloat due to the shortage of workers.

More than half the boys had gone to war, and many hadn't returned.

Wateredge Manor rested on the boundary line between

Westfallen and Vestalin, our allies. While no bad blood stirred between our countries, the war had left a bitter taste in everyone's mouth. Only four countries fought, but the whole land felt the sting of battle.

My sister and her husband brought relief from the war, spinning straw into gold for the king to provide the resources to bring the fighting to an end. That act awarded us this estate in the first place, however unqualified we were to run it, and my sister and I moved across the kingdom to live here. I only had a few months with Cosette filled with working in the village and healing the town before the letter came that Mama was ill and Cosette's tender heart pointed her home. But not before inviting Lady Claire to the manor.

I hated admitting it, but I did need a few lessons to navigate the social waters, and I'd greatly misjudged how much socializing nobles did. Friendly alliances with the surrounding nobles boosted my status, and as much as I detested it, their business was crucial to my survival here. That meant participating in these horrid gatherings and playing nice.

There wasn't much to complain about at the balls. I wasn't one to turn down free food or a chance to make some money at cards, but the secret reason behind the multitude of events is what made my stomach churn.

With the end of the war, many nobles sought their own alliances, resulting in a land-wide scheme to send off eligible children to other countries to make friends and secure their parents' place, should another war break out.

Consequently, the ballroom was stocked with maidens hiding their faces behind bright fans or oversized hats and all-too-eager gentlemen filling their dance cards. They were all searching for marriage. Luckily for me, not many looked for a match inside the card room, hence my inclination to it.

"Very well done!" Lord Byron clapped as I revealed my hand. Finally, some luck wandered my way. I grinned and collected my winnings. I promised Joshua, a kind farmer who was a tenant of my lands, that we'd buy a few pigs at market this year; this money would serve that purpose.

I'd only made a little money when taking in account the cost of the tokens, but it was enough.

"I think I'll call that a night, gentlemen."

They tipped their heads at me as I turned in my tokens, gathered my money, and left. I had to brave the ballroom at some point.

CHAPTER TWO

lmost two steps out the door, a hand appeared on my elbow. I cursed as I correctly guessed who it belonged to.

"I've been looking for you, Lady Anika." Freddy's cheery voice pierced my ears, a sound several octaves too high for a man his age. His wide glasses, which I'd first thought made him look smart, rested on his long nose, and he kept his head tilted up slightly as if the glasses would roll off his face if he held it at an appropriate height. His hair shone like polished wood and his cheeks sunk in.

Freddy was another reason I enjoyed the card room; he didn't dare go in it. I had no trouble believing he'd been pacing outside waiting for me to come out.

His cold hands rubbed my skin as I pulled my elbow away. "Good evening, Freddy. I was just on my way for some air."

"I'll walk with you." His voice seeped with enthusiasm and my feet hesitated, but I regrettably couldn't find a decent excuse to free myself from his company. I should have said I was on my way to get a refreshment, which would surely take less time than a walk outside.

He walked beside me while we crossed the room to the back doors, and the band played a familiar jig as we passed.

They say Count Branson throws the grandest parties, with lavish food and the most expensive band around. If I had an eye for such things then I might be impressed. The room did seem larger than most, and fine decorations overpowered the space. The band, however, sounded just like the one from last week at the York's party, and just as the party the week before as well. If this band was more expensive, I couldn't tell the difference.

The only difference to indicate that this party was more expensive than others were the performers set up in low balconies in the room, three along the inner wall. One held a juggler, another held a violist that Elenora had gone on and on about before coming, and the third held a magic performer. If his magic was real or fake, I couldn't tell, but if it was real, it was the first sign of real magic I'd seen in this part of the kingdom. Most people ducked their heads or furrowed their brows at the first mention of magic or their Gifts, and none seemed willing to speak on the topic: one of my most peculiar findings upon moving here.

Elenora gave me a joking wink as we walked by, and I tried to grab her to join us with as much delicacy as I could muster but her hand masterfully slipped from mine. She'd tease me about my evening stroll with Freddy later. The poor chap had been attempting to court me for months.

Elenora had a slew of suitors at her beck and call, but my luck gave me just one. Freddy. The idea of handling a court of interested men sounded less exhausting than my alternative. Short of physically pushing him away, the art of telling Freddy I wasn't interested was proving quite difficult. The manners Lady Claire taught me weren't doing the trick.

"It's quite beautiful out tonight," Freddy said as he pushed the door open for me.

Lanterns illuminated the night sky, with occasional fireworks blasting over the hedge and filling the air with brief color. The gardens extended from a stone pathway before bursting in all directions and spanning the side of the house, covering almost as much ground as the building itself. They blended into the front courtyard where our carriages lay waiting for us to depart. A brief part of me debated walking there now and ordering the driver to take me home, but I knew I'd never hear the end of it if I left Elenora here.

Fireflies lit up in patterns throughout the garden. The fountain trickled quietly, the sound almost masked by the music behind us. A few streamers wrapped around pillars of benches and overhangs in combinations of purples and greens. Count Branson really spared no expense at these things. He boasted two nieces who he was eager to marry off, and I wondered if tonight's spectacle was to entice suitors.

As we came upon marble stairs leading toward the shrubbery, I hiked up my thick red dress and descended the few steps.

"You have beautiful ankles," Freddy said. I dropped my skirt and whipped my head back around to him. His face remained unfazed in the flickering light.

"Is that really an appropriate thing to say?" I marveled at his candor. It rivaled my own, but we wielded our bluntness differently. He shrugged, obviously seeing no problem with the comment. I peeked down to make sure my ankles were properly covered as we continued walking.

What made ankles beautiful anyway?

I counted in my head, wondering how long it was appropriate to stay before I could excuse myself. A year ago, I would have walked away with no problem, but Lady Claire was training me with relentless determination, and her manners wore off on me a bit. Still, polite or not, it felt wrong to let Freddy put so much of his focus on me.

"You know I'm not interested, right? You shouldn't waste your time on me."

"Oh? Is there someone else?" he asked, with no disappointment showing on his face.

A small laugh escaped my throat at the thought. "Most certainly not."

He made an odd grunting noise in the back of his throat. "I find it difficult to believe you don't fancy anyone."

"I fancy people, just not in that way," I corrected him. He kept his eyes on the smooth cobblestones as we strolled toward the center fountain where we could stop for a moment then walk back and part ways. I would owe him no more than that.

He sniffed as he scrunched his nose to push his glasses up. "Most girls like someone, whether they admit it or not."

"I'm not most girls."

"That's why I admire you, you're strange," he said.

"You're strange too," I whispered under my breath. Just as he was leaning down to ask what I had said, a new noise cut through the air. My head perked up toward the direction of what sounded like a distant shout. Someone was having a jolly time.

Another cry came and I corrected myself. From the ballroom the noise would be masked, but it didn't come from the party. The noise echoed from the other side of the tall hedge. Curse my short height.

The second-floor balcony door burst open, and six figures threw themselves over the railing. The hedges hid their landing from me, but I knew that wasn't a short jump from the balcony to the ground. The darkness hid distinct features from me but they moved with a stealth befitting a cat in the night and the silence of a mist.

I sucked in my breath. Intruders.

Forgetting about Freddy, I ran toward the hedge to see the creatures who jumped from the manor. It was lucky we came out on the north side of the gardens, or else we would be too far away to get to the intruders in time.

I rolled the front of my satin dress up in my fists and stepped up on the wooden bench, giving me enough height to barely peek over the box hedge.

Each jumper landed safely and hoisted bags upon their shoulders as they joined a few others on the ground who came through the open servant door under the balcony.

The nearest one spotted me, and I thought I saw them wink but I couldn't be sure.

There were ten in total, each dressed in dark clothes with wolf masks over their faces. I couldn't be sure of what lay underneath, but by the body size it looked like only a few were male, and the rest were female. One of the males let out a laugh as he dashed off toward the east.

Count Branson's home sat on an open field, with scattered trees surrounding the horizons. The livery sat on the opposite side of the manor next to a small keep, while behind the manor ran nothing but soft grass that muffled the feet of the cloaked figures as they fled the scene. They ran in the open for a minute before the darkness and coupled trees took them from my sight.

I brought my eyes back to the balcony where a second figure stood dressed in a gown watching the figures with her hands on her hips. I couldn't identify her, but I thought her to be one of Count Branson's nieces. Moonlight bathed her hair, dark like mine, and showed her chest as it rose and fell heavily. She didn't say anything but stared for a few moments before she disappeared back into the home.

"The Silver Raiders," Freddy breathed next to me, almost making me jump. I forgot he was there. He had climbed on a bench next to mine to watch, though unless he'd run, he didn't get as good a look as I did.

"Who are the Silver Raiders?"

"No one knows, but they ambush the rich and steal a portion of their money."

I stared into the tree line, trying to find a hint of movement. All I saw was the slight shake of trees and a bird take flight.

"Well," I said. "Finally something interesting happened at one of these blasted things."

CHAPTER THREE

Adrianna, who turned out to be the figure from the balcony, rushed into the ballroom in a dramatic manner to tell her tale with great animation.

"I fetched my golden broach and was about to leave when they burst through the doors! Filthy lot they were, and they started going through the desks; it took them a good few moments before they saw me. No thank you, but yes, I'll take that." Her mother stroked her hair and her sister offered her a plate and a glass of red liquid, which she took. She fanned her face with her fan, which she periodically waved toward people, bringing a crowd in close to her.

The music stopped, and word spread that the Silver Raiders had come. A few, like me, knit their brows at the phrase, but most eyes lit up with knowledge.

Adrianna continued to tell her story to any who would listen, how when they saw her, they pushed through her bedroom window to the balcony and ran off. The tale grew more dramatic each time until they almost attacked her. I doubted that. She looked calm when I saw her standing over the balcony watching them run off. Very different from the girl I saw now, draped across a chair with her fan tapping her forehead.

Word got out that Freddy and I saw them as well, and we were beseeched for our tale. Adrianna didn't look pleased the attention shifted, while Freddy stuttered too hard to get out a good sentence.

I sighed. "Yes, we saw them, but there's no more to the story than that. We barely saw anything before they ran off."

Count Branson came to the center of the room and put up his hands. "I assure you, everyone is safe." He rubbed his hands on his slender stomach as he turned his bald head around the room. "There is no danger here. Please," he gestured to the band, who hesitantly started back up.

The crowd took a few steps away and split off into smaller groups, but it was clear the topic of the Silver Raiders hadn't left anyone's tongue. Elenora appeared at my side and pulled my arm, leading me away.

"Are you alright?" she asked, pulling on the end of her blonde, braided hair in concern. The large freckle by the corner of her thin mouth twitched as she sucked in her lip.

"Yes, I'm fine, truly. But I've never heard of these Silver Raiders. Have you?"

She turned up her nose. "I wish I knew more, but I've only heard of them recently. I thought they just ambushed carriages, taking some money. I didn't know they broke into homes. I wonder why they did it with all of us here; you'd think that'd scare them off." She glanced out the window as if they might break in again any second.

I glanced at the window too, but my expression was more of interest than worry. "Where are they from?"

Her face lit up. "That's the most interesting part. It seems they are from the Woods of Silver and Light."

"The what?" That seemed like an unnecessary long name for a group of trees.

Elenora smiled wide and lowered her voice to hardly more than a whisper. "It's a fascinating forest west of you. It's neither in Westfallen nor Vestalin territory; no one dares claim it. The Woods are where magic lives. All sorts of creatures and powers dwell in their trees, including the Silver Raiders."

"How have I not heard of the Woods before?"

"We don't like to talk about them. No one who goes in ever comes out; the magic is too strong."

Perhaps I've found the reason magic is a taboo subject here. I hadn't realized such a place rested near my lands. "The raiders didn't look magical to me."

She shrugged. "They must be, to survive in there."

"I heard you saw the Silver Raiders," a new voice came. I turned to see the man who sat next to me during cards. His light hair paired poorly with a yellow vest and I could almost hear Lady Claire's disapproving clicks now. Despite his odd coloring, he had a nice look about him: wrinkles by the corner of his eyes, dimples in his cheeks, round eyes, and a slight tremor in his stance—not one of nerves though, but rather of excitement.

He came accompanied by another fellow, who carried no tremor in his step or wrinkles by his eyes, with features that were softer, almost unreadable. Two freckles made a path from the corner of his lip to his right eye, brown in color as his hair. Everything about this gentleman was darker than the first: darker skin, darker hair, and a darker, navy suit.

Beside me, Elenora straightened and fixed her gaze on the man in the yellow suit as slight color filled her cheeks.

I looked back to the gentlemen. "Yes, I did, but I'm afraid there's nothing to tell." Their shoulders sagged at the lack of a story. In her corner, Adrianna still soaked up her attention.

"Anika, do you know Lord Berkley and Sir Christopher?" Elenora introduced the gentlemen to me, identifying Berkley as the man whom I played cards with.

Berkley nodded toward me. "This is the girl I was telling you about, who plays cards and curses like a pirate."

Christopher's eyes brightened as he stuck out his hand to me, which had two freckles identical to the ones on his cheek. "Ah! I was hoping I would meet you. I've heard quite a lot."

"Nothing too bad, I hope?" I gave his hand a firm shake.

He smirked. "Depends on your definition of bad. My mother would have fainted at some of the stories."

I could only imagine what he'd heard; numerous silent rules had been broken during my transformation from a village girl and into a proper lady, and sometimes I still caught people whispering about some of my antics. Elenora came to my aid, always the faithful friend, though I suspected Christopher intended his remark as a compliment. "Yes, Anika is unique, but she's smart."

"I don't doubt it," Christopher said. "Good thing those Silver Raiders didn't come any closer; I bet you could've given them a run for their money."

Elenora coughed. "Well, we're all lucky they didn't

come closer." She then turned to Berkley. "Will you be at the Thames birthday ball in two weeks?"

"I will; we both will!" When he smiled, it was large enough to stretch from one side of his face to the other. Behind him, the clicking of heels came, making us all turn our heads to see Freddy with a slender girl by his side.

"Anika, are you sure you're alright?" he asked me, looking down through his glasses. He was taller than both Berkley and Christopher, but if Christopher straightened up his height might rival Freddy's.

"Honestly, I don't know why everyone keeps asking me if I'm okay. I was never in any danger."

A hint of smile played on Christopher's lips while Freddy stammered. "Right, well I just wanted to be sure." The girl at his side glared at me as if I willed Freddy over with my own power, then placed a porcelain hand on Freddy's arm to steer him away.

"Sorry your romantic walk in the gardens with Freddy was cut so short," Elenora mocked me in a quiet voice.

I shushed her. "You know it was no such thing. I do wish I knew more about those Silver Raiders, or that forest."

"You don't want to," Berkley said, his round eyes widening. "There's something very unnatural about that forest, making all kinds of sounds at night. And the way it's always lit up, as if stars live in its branches, it's not right. It'll bend your mind if you get too close, lure you in and you'll be lost forever."

Christopher laughed. "That's not all true."

"You should know," Berkley said, until Christopher placed a hand on his arm to stop him.

He meant his words to frighten me, but they only

strengthened my resolve to learn more about the trees with stars in them and the raiders who wore masks of wolf fur.

I'd always found these parties to be dull; turns out all I needed was to walk in the gardens to find a mystery.

My curiosity was only heightened when Lady Claire met us that night at home. She waited in the front siting room with a small lantern lit for reading purposes. Her thin glasses perched on the end of her nose, and her long robe was tied around her waist. Her skin was light and her hair was full of grey curls, which bobbed as she looked up in surprise at mention of the Silver Raiders and the Woods of Silver and Light. She set down her book hard.

"You stay away from them, miss."

"I didn't say I was going to go there." I put up my hands defensively, trying to stay back so she couldn't smell the smoke and alcohol in my hair.

She clucked. "I could tell what you were thinking. You mind me, don't go in those woods. We don't need any of that dark magic here."

CHAPTER FOUR

Someone was here.

I set my glass down with a slow hand as my ears strained to identify the source of the noise. My breath blew out my candle so the only light in the kitchen was from the half-moon that peeked through the smudged window. My eyes took a moment to adjust to the darkness before I eased open the door and peered down the hallway.

It was empty. But I swore I had heard a sound.

Still alert, I snuck toward the front hall. After two steps I heard it again. A soft creak that could only be made from timid footsteps walking past the sitting room. That spot was especially creaky, as I should know from the countless times my own feet had attempted to sneak past Lady Claire in that very spot.

There was someone sneaking in my house.

Thoughts of dark magic roamed through my mind, but I pushed them away. I shouldn't have stayed up so late with thoughts of those cursed Woods. This was nothing more than a thief looking for money to line his pockets with, something that would be hard to come by here.

Now wishing I'd brought the glass of water with me so I'd have a weapon, I crept closer to the sitting room. There were definite footsteps moving about.

The intruder had a light of sorts that they carried about with them, casting dim shadows along the wall. As they turned, their own shadow danced across the floor and I paused at its size. Blast. I need a weapon.

Here was where my months of bluffing at the poker table were put to the test. "Stop now or I'll shoot you," I yelled out.

A clatter made me yelp as the light went out. I darted into the room in time for a figure to ram into me with sharp elbows and a swift kick to the stomach that sent me sprawling to the ground.

Pain rippled from my side. With a low grunt, I hurled myself after the thief who dashed toward the front door. My hand collided with his heel and he fell flat against the ground with a growl. He was faster than me though, so before I could scurry after him he'd gotten up again and thrown himself out the door and down the stairs to where a horse waited.

With a flick of his wrist he untied the horse and they were off.

Curses left my mouth as I clutched my throbbing side and watched him leave. At least, I thought it was a he, but from the loose clothing and little time we had, I couldn't be certain. He was taller than me, but practically the entire kingdom could claim that.

Unless he'd left his calling card somewhere, I'd little

hope of identifying him. I could only hope he didn't take anything.

The night made it difficult to see much, but the room looked to still be in order. Perhaps I'd caught him on his way in before he had a chance to grab anything. This room held nothing of value to me but there were a few trinkets of Lady Claire's that she'd be livid to lose. My stomach turned. I'd rather face an intruder again than Lady Claire's wrath.

A new thought came to mind that made me forget about the sharp pain in my side: if he came looking for something specific and he didn't get it, there was a good chance he'd be back.

My heart thumped against my chest as I fumbled for the steel lock.

Strange, it doesn't appear broken. Either he had a key, or someone let him in.

My face washed of color and my body went numb. How did he get in the manor? My eyes scanned the dark room, but if anyone else was here, they stayed hidden. Somehow, that man had access to my house.

If he came again, I'd find out who in my manor let him in.

"Lady Anika?" Lady Claire stood behind me with her hair in curls and her night robe pulled tight across her body. She held a tall candle in her hand as she peered at me in the darkness as if I was up to no good.

I pointed to the door and spoke with a voice that still shook. "Someone broke in the h-house."

I expected her to gasp or clutch her chest as she does so often when I do something improper. Instead she held the candle closer to the door. "It doesn't look broken."

I blew into my hands to calm myself and rubbed my thumbs across my chin. Lady Claire shook her head and turned, but she didn't retire. She went toward the sitting room.

"They were just in there," I told her. Without replying, she picked up her book and opened it to a page, holding the light close. The top of a paper stuck out from the rest. It was yellowed while the rest of the pages were white, and shorter. Unless the night had made me lose my mind, there was a letter in that book.

Lady Claire grinned and snapped the book shut.

"Thank you, Lady Anika. All appears to be fine, so let's return to our chambers."

She crossed the hallway with calm steps and went into her room while I stared after her, unable to shake the feeling that she had something to do with the nighttime visitor.

As Joshua and I rode in the carriage, I mentally went through anyone from my household who would have let an intruder in and if Lady Claire was up to something suspicious. If it wasn't for last night's odd encounter, I'd say she would never, and I doubted Elenora would either. That left the workers. I couldn't afford much, and most of the money I did have went back into the land so we would survive these next few years. But Lady Claire and Elenora brought some of their own help, and I couldn't account for their morality.

And who would they be letting in? Even as I sat next to Joshua I wondered—*was it you who broke into my home?*

"Something on your mind?" Joshua asked as he placed a

hand over baskets of vegetables we were bringing to trade with some neighbors. He was a hard-working farmer on my lands, and I got along with him and his sister well. The money I made from poker last night would go to buying pigs for their farm.

"Nothing to bother yourself with," I replied. The spot on my side had turned to a nice blue bruise that ached as I twisted in my seat. All the bumps in this road weren't helping, either.

"These pigs will really help us get on our feet! I know Marty wanted new crops instead," Joshua went on.

"I agree with you, for this year that is. Next year we can focus on the crops."

"If we are still here, that is," he sighed. I wished he wouldn't talk like that. I didn't like being reminded that we might not have enough money to pull through.

I came here as the war was ending, and as a result my first few months were grim. Families eagerly waited for their husbands and sons to return from the war, but the ones who did were so damaged that they had changed. Two farms down from Joshua lived a man who lost a leg and spent each day since swinging on the porch in front of the house, staring off into the distance as he clutched a rusted sword. The war raged on in his eyes. The farm past that was still waiting for their son to return. It had been a year now; he wasn't coming home, but the mother refused to give up hope. She still spoke of him as if he was on his way home. I couldn't decide which family I felt worse for.

There were other stories that broke my heart too. A man on the edge of my lands returned home to find his wife had died of hunger, and his baby daughter had been taken in by his neighbors. So many families dream of their husbands coming home and pray for their safety, but they lose the strength to survive themselves.

Here the war touched each person, and I felt selfish somehow for not being affected by it. My childhood village remained unchanged by the terrors of war. I wondered if it changed after I left, when some men didn't return home.

My heart didn't break often, but it broke for these people. While devoted to making a new life for myself here, I also worked tirelessly for the lives of the crippled and those who were lost in the village who had little hope left.

The carriage came to a halt suddenly enough to make us both lurch forward in our seats and zucchini roll from the baskets.

"What was that?" I cursed as I picked myself back up and stuck my head out the window. "Williams, is everything—" My voice trailed off. There was a carriage ahead of us with gold trimming and gold wheels and a brocade pattern along the sides. It didn't move, and it was clear to see why.

Silver Raiders crawled atop.

They stayed quiet as they swung open the doors, ducking in to rummage around. Ladies screamed inside. My head pulled into my carriage and I tried to open the door, but it held fast. I put my hand through the window to open it from the outside but yanked it back in when it touched someone else's hand.

A wolf mask appeared in the window as someone yanked on the door.

Joshua breathed fast, but he didn't make any noises. He pushed himself against the seat and folded his hands as he prayed. I searched myself for a weapon, grabbing a heavy zucchini so at least I'd have something to throw.

The door opened, and the figure stared at us. I could see their eyes, female eyes, by the look of the body, as she peered through her mask. She turned her head to her friends then back at us.

"You're not nobility," she said. I was right, she was a girl.

"Well, no, I'm not…" Joshua stammered, but I kicked his leg.

"What's that got to do with anything?" I asked as I waved my zucchini around as a warning. The nose of her mask tilted down as she studied the zucchini.

My brown hair was pulled into a loose, ineloquent bun, and I wore a plain shirt and the long trousers of a man. Lady Claire had a fit when she first saw me in pants, but I pointed out how much easier it was to work in them, and she let it be so long as no one with a title saw me in such a condition. I was grateful for the pants, even more now, as they fooled the Silver Raider into thinking I was a farm girl.

She blinked. "Where'd you get such a nice carriage?"

"Ours broke, and our lady was kind enough to offer hers as we transport vegetables to friends." I gestured to the baskets of vegetables that had stayed fairly put together through the ordeal. The Silver Raider eyed them, then us again.

"That was nice of her. We're sorry to bother you." She pulled back and shouted to the others that we were merely farmers. A few of them came to the window to look and confirmed her assessment.

Joshua breathed a loud sigh of relief. I put my hand on his shoulder. "Stay here." I dropped my zucchini and jerked the door back open to run after the Silver Raiders who were still congregated around the other carriage.

"Who are you?" I asked.

The girl who had come to my window turned around and lowered herself in a bow. "The Silver Raiders, of course, here to provide for the less fortunate." Her mask didn't move as she tipped her face forward to reveal a black ribbon tied in the back holding it in place over a tight, black scarf that covered their heads.

There were about ten in the group, once again mostly female, and each wearing dark shirts with pads strapped to the elbows, long pants, and flexible shoes. They had gloves over their hands and the mask bore a long snout and rubber nose wrapped around the full head.

The Silver Raider's heights varied: some were as short as me and one was almost as tall as the carriage they stood by. The ladies' screams continued as a Silver Raider stepped out of the carriage with a small bag in hand.

"Those are my grandma's jewels!" A lady yelled, though I couldn't see her face.

"Then you shouldn't be traveling with them," the Silver Raider pointed out.

"You can't take those," my voice shouted, surprising the Silver Raiders. They all swung their heads back to me in unison. I marched closer and pointed to the bag, repeating myself.

A few Silver Raiders took off, but half stayed close. "We do it for you," one snapped, while others mumbled in agreement.

I wasn't sure what she meant by that, but the one holding the bag stepped closer to me. The ladies in the carriage continued their protesting but none got out of the carriage and the driver, frozen in fear, didn't drive off.

I heard shuffling behind me and turned to see Joshua

who exited the carriage. I should have known he wouldn't stay put.

The Silver Raider approached me. "Is your farm struggling?" Her voice was deep and muffled by the mask. With her standing close, I could see the whiskers built into the snout.

"What's that got to do- "

"It is, yeah," Joshua pipped up. I turned my head and shot him a look.

The Silver Raider quietly opened the bag, reached in and tossed me something. I caught the small object with two hands and looked down to find a golden bracelet with emeralds dotted along the bottom ridge.

"If you ever need anything," the Silver Raider said, drawing my eyes up from the bracelet, "just call on the Silver Raiders. I told you we do this for you." With that, she was off, running down the ditch and into the trees.

I understood now, they stole from the nobles and gave the profits to the poor.

Joshua joined my side, staring at the jewelry. "I reckon we can buy those pigs now."

The thieved bracelet felt heavy in my hand, and I closed my fist over it. "It's not ours." I walked over to the carriage and knocked on the door. Three ladies sat inside wearing day gowns. One cried heavily, while a second wrapped her arms around her, and the third stuck her head out the other window, talking to the driver. I slid my arm through the window and showed them the bracelet.

The girl brought her head back through the window while another snatched the bracelet. "Thank goodness we got this one back."

"We should have gotten them all back; granny will have my head," the first spoke through her tears.

I tipped my head at them and retreated, not wanting to be recognized. I doubted they could see through my faded clothes, especially with their attention so focused on the bracelet.

"Pity we couldn't have kept that," Joshua mumbled as he held our carriage door open for me.

"It would have been wrong. Can you tell me, are we still on my lands?"

Joshua nodded, and I cursed. It was one thing when the Silver Raiders invaded the party of a man I hardly knew. But they were ambushing people on my own lands.

"Something must be done about that."

CHAPTER FIVE

*A*lone farmer stood in the distance, but I kept low to hide from his sight. I abandoned my horse a while back with a friendly man who, after seeing the coin in my hand, promised she would be well taken care of until I came back. The sun barely peeked over the trees to my left. With luck, I'd be back before dinner and Lady Claire would never know.

Some old maps in my library pointed me in the right direction, and I hoped the faded pages remained accurate. When my sister was here, the library had been cleaned and well-tended to, but dust had already begun to settle in her absence.

My mission was clear: find the Silver Raiders and force them to stop stealing from my lands.

A small blade hid in a sheath at my right side, ready to be gripped in a moment if needed. I purchased the blade a month ago at the market, lured in by the blue hilt, and was grateful now that I did. It boosted my bravery.

A cotton bag hid in my deep pockets, stuffed with wool

so the coins wouldn't make a noise and give themselves away. A handsome bribe, if it came to that.

I wore a simple dress, light enough to move easily in but nice enough to give me a sense of authority when I faced the Silver Raiders. I hoped they were home today and not robbing more carriages.

The Woods loomed in front of me, vast and dark. Even the sun's rays weren't enough to penetrate their thick cover of branches. A grain mill lay to my right, marking the end of my neighbor, Lord Hughes's land. He was a nice man, from what I heard, with three grown sons to his name. His lands were, unlike mine, prospering, and I knew most of that came from the success of his mill that sat by the river flowing from the Woods of Silver and Light. Maybe there was magic in the water coming from the trees.

If there was magic in these Woods, I hoped to find it.

My plan could have been better thought-out, I admitted that. The Woods were larger than they appeared on the map, and I couldn't see the end of them. I sucked in my breath as I continued closer. Now almost upon them, my mind picked up things that it couldn't from a distance. The howl of an animal, the chirp of an unknown bird, the abnormally large leaves.

A small blue light flickered from inside, and I thought my mind must be playing tricks on me. Either that, or the Woods really did hold some kind of magic.

The Woods weren't like normal forests, overrun with vines and thickets and bushes that made it impossible to walk through. The floor of this forest was neat, with low grasses and blooming flowers, though I couldn't fathom how the light reached the ground to nourish the plants. Different colors erupted from each direction: a patch of yellow flowers here, red ones there, purple climbing the tree.

The trees grew thick; whether it was from years of uninterrupted growth or from magic, I couldn't say, but they banded together in a line, creating an obvious starting point for the forest. It was clear this was where the Woods began, and they taunted me to enter within their borders. Here lay the boundary of Westfallen. Beyond this, the land that no one would claim.

I hesitated on that line. I saw no path to enter the Woods: my first warning that I wasn't welcome within. Another animal noise came as a low vibration that almost turned my feet back and led me away. I gripped my knife. I would keep my people safe. No Silver Raiders could disrupt my lands.

The first step proved the hardest, but once I had committed, I found the next step easier. I never let my guard down though, and my hand never left my blade. After thinking about it I decided to unsheathe the weapon, feeling safer with it clutched over my chest.

Step after cautious step, I wandered into the dark unknown. Branches hung low and roots jutted high. Subtle streaks of shimmering light flashed occasionally through the vines of the trees as if magic coursed in the wood, spiraling along the base and stretching to illuminate the leaves. Each time it happened my head snapped toward the light to study it better, but it never stayed lit for long. Only long enough to settle on the tips of the leaves and leave a few sparks floating down before disappearing all together. Sometimes the color was blue, other times it was green, but usually it was a bright silver as if stars lived there.

Now I knew why they called it the Woods of Silver and

Light. It was beautiful, but the unknown of it all sent shivers down my spine. I twisted the blade in my hand as I carried on.

I knew it was foolish to think that I could find the Silver Raiders in a forest this size. Honestly, I assumed they would've found me by now. I wandered on for what felt like hours with no sight of a creature besides myself. Many noises came, stopping me in my tracks each time as I faced the direction of the sound. I was certain there were animals in these woods. I could hear distant rumbles and howls and chatters, but if the animals knew that I was in their woods, they left me alone. For the time being, anyway. I had no guarantee their generosity would last.

Each minute that passed brought me further from my sense of direction and my hope of finding my way back out again. Now, my main hope rested on finding the Silver Raiders and praying everything sorted itself out from there.

At this point, as long as I made it out without being eaten, I would consider this trip a success.

A twig snapped to my left. I dug my left heel into the ground and twisted my right foot to swivel toward the sound. I barely got a look at the tall trees before a hard object, tougher than a hand but softer than a blade, struck me against the back of the head.

My eyes rolled up and then blackness settled in.

CHAPTER SIX

When I woke, I knew something was wrong; I couldn't move my hands. They were bound behind me with a rope that dug harshly into my skin. Now aware of that, I could feel my feet bound as well, but not to each other. I sat on a chair with one leg bound to one post and the other leg bound to another.

Well, I wasn't dead.

There was no gag in my mouth, nor blindfold around my eyes. I felt something loose around my neck and wondered if I had been blindfolded at one point. From the hallow sounds I guessed I was still outside, but there were new noises now. Distant talking, a rhythmic clanging, the occasional laughter. I slowly peeked through one eyelid to see my surroundings. Grass lay beneath my feet, confirming that I was outdoors. I risked raising my head a bit to get a better look. A canopy of sorts hung around me, with three walls made of tight animal skin and an opening where the fourth would be.

Craning my neck to look outside, my mouth dropped open. The thick trees of the forest still stood, but fewer and far between, offering several patches of clearing where small huts made of wood sat close together. Each hut looked identical to the one next to it except the vivid blanket over the front, marking them from each other.

It was still dark here, even with the fewer trees, but lighter than in the heart of the Woods. It was clear that the Woods were in charge as they cast their darkness through the air and teased with flickers of lights in the background, banishing the sun from shining inside. The main source of light came from lanterns hung periodically through the camp.

Right outside the tent was a large fire roasting a pig. A man sat next to the flames with his back to me, turning the pig slowly. I wondered if he was the lookout for me. I tried to stay quiet so he wouldn't notice I was awake as I pulled at the tight ropes. They gave no sign of loosening.

Other figures wandered the camp in and out of my view, but they were all too far away or too preoccupied to notice me.

A girl appeared from the right side with her arms crossed as she stepped into the hut, surprising me too quickly to drop my head and pretend to be unconscious. Her skin was the color of burnt umber, her hair dark and curly. I stared at her with wide eyes as I waited to see her reaction. She grinned slowly then turned her shoulders to holler behind her.

"She's awake!"

Just like that people came rushing to the front of the tent to see me. The girl came nearer to walk in slow circles around me while others flocked to the doorway like curious wolves to study their food before pouncing.

When the original girl came back to the front, she drew my dagger from her side and twisted it slowly. "Did you think this would save you from the beasts that lurk in these woods?" She tossed it at my feet and scoffed. "You would have been dead before you had time to swing."

The blade rolled to my feet, but my eyes stayed on her. "I survived, didn't I?"

A devilish smile played on her lips. "Because we allowed you to. Don't count yourself lucky yet."

"I see she's awake." A man spoke, and each person turned at the sound. He came from the left, weaving through the group with a second man trailing him. Dark eyes studied me as they stood side by side, one tall and the other with a wide nose and defined muscles.

"So, this is the girl who came into the Woods of Silver and Light with nothing but a dagger to protect her," the shorter man said with a grin. His expression was softer than the girl's, and I decided I liked him better.

"If you hear her accent, I don't think she's from around here," the girl who first spotted me said.

"I'm from Westfallen," I corrected her.

"But not these parts," she shot back. Her hands caught her hips as she leaned against the side post of the hut.

"What are you doing in these woods?" The shorter man asked as he crossed his arms. Pieces of cracked dirt on his sleeves broke off and fell to the ground. His tan shirt was tucked into black pants, and both were riddled with tears. The man next to him looked a tad neater, in a clean grey shirt, but it still carried wrinkles. I wasn't sure what else I expected from bandits who slept in a forest. I should have been pleased that it was only mud and wrinkles and not blood.

I swallowed as I answered. "I came to ask you to stop." My voice came out higher than I had intended, and I coughed to clear my throat.

The man laughed, and he wasn't the only one to do so. I narrowed my eyes at him.

"Stop what?" he asked me, crossing his arms.

"Stealing from people."

"Ah. Have we stolen from you?"

"Well, no," I admitted. "But you've stolen from people on my lands and I won't allow it."

More laughter. I tried not to waver in my stance. I didn't sense any fear here, but the magical forest frightened me more than I wanted to let on.

"And who are you, to demand such a thing?"

"The Lady Anika of Wateredge Manor."

His eyebrow raised and he exchanged glances with the taller man next to him before pulling back his lips. "Yes, I have heard about you. Good things, you'll be pleased to know. Stories of how kind you are to your people."

I was surprised they had heard of me. I hadn't heard of them until a few nights ago, and they were bandits living in a magical forest. I was just a girl struggling to keep her manor afloat.

My arm ached and my wrists burned with the tight draw of the rope. I wished they would untie me soon. "So, will you stop?"

He reached to the floor for my knife, and I stiffened. He glanced at me before he reached behind me and cut the ropes loose. I held my hand out for the knife to undo my feet. He handed it trustingly to me but stepped away so he would have reaction time if I decided to swing at him once I was free.

"Your people are still struggling, no matter how nice you are to them," he spoke as I freed my feet. When I was done, I put my knife back in its sheath, so they knew that I had no intention of using it if I didn't have to. I hoped I didn't, because I knew I stood no chance against them. Each person here possessed twice as much muscle as I could pretend to.

"I'm more than nice to them." My tone came out sharper than I intended. "I put on pants and I work the fields with them."

I don't know why he found that funny, but he threw back his head and laughed. "Every girl here wears pants and works."

I pulled myself to my full height and folded my arms over my chest. The man, who still hadn't given me a name, was average height for a male, which meant he still stood a great deal taller than me. The man next to him was so tall that I had to tilt my head up to look at him, and I didn't like doing that. The girl was tall as well, with slender legs that showed through her tight pants.

The gatherers behind them watched with mild amusement, some wandering by to stop and look for a few moments. The casual reaction to their prisoner made me think that they had prisoners often. I wondered what became of them.

"I'm not asking you to stop stealing from everyone, just don't do it on my lands. My people and I are working together to save our lands, and we don't need bandits getting in our way."

He shook his head. "I don't take my orders from you.

Sorry you came all this way for nothing; good luck getting home."

With that he turned around and waved the crowd out, leaving me behind in the empty canopy with a sense of failure. My fingernails dug into my palms.

I didn't come all this way to fail.

CHAPTER SEVEN

I hiked up my skirt and ran after him. As I did, my money bag bounced in my pocket. Either they didn't find it, or they let me keep it. The former made more sense.

"I don't take orders from you either and I'm not leaving here until you agree to my demands."

Both men turned around. The shorter one grinned. "Where does a lady of the court get such *fire*?"

I held my chin up. "I'm not from court, I grew up the daughter of a tavern owner in a small village."

His eyes widened in surprise, then he chuckled. "Well that makes sense then. What brought you to your position?"

"A bit of magic and some luck."

"We know about magic here," he said as he tilted his head and studied me. After a moment, his demeanor changed. His body straightened and his arm extended to me. "Come, take a tour with me."

He looked at me with innocent eyes and a hopeful smile

that carried no mark of trickery. My fascination of this place caused me to hesitate before agreeing, though even as I took his arm, I kept my senses alert for any trap he might be leading me into. His sudden warmth was suspicious.

Now that we were out of the canopy I could get a better look of the area and found it more enchanting than I had previously guessed. Along with the huts on the ground, I saw forts in the trees, reached by ladders built with ropes and draping down against thick trunks. Some forts started only a few heads above me, but others reached up to the highest branches. A few dangerous-looking wooden bridges stretched between some of them, but most stood alone. The charming homes, both on the ground and in the trees, extended as far as I could see.

We stood in an oval clearing where stacks of weapons leaned against tents. In the clearing next to ours a serene pond glistened with sparkles. As I watched, a small child walked with his mother in tow to the water's edge where they both knelt, cupped water in their hands, and sipped. I marveled as they drank it. I had never seen a clean water pond before but shouldn't have been surprised there was one located in the middle of a magical forest.

"I was wondering how commoners had such a nice carriage. You were the Lady."

I turned around to see a girl with light hair approaching us. I didn't recognize her face, but her voice sounded familiar.

"You're the girl who raided the carriages yesterday."

She smiled. "Along with others. I'm Annabeth." She stuck out her hand to me. "You're the first one to try to follow us here."

"I doubt I'll be the last, you're setting yourself up for a lot of enemies."

"Doesn't matter, she can handle them."

"Who?" I asked, but at that same moment the man interrupted.

"Annabeth." He shook his head at her. She dropped her head and backed away.

I glanced to him. "Are you not the leader here?"

He puffed out his chest. "I am. Everyone listens to me. Even Jack here." He bobbed his head at the tall man next to him, who stayed quiet. Though his mouth didn't move, his eyes looked to hold all the wisdom of a library. I noticed a sheath tied around his waist, but there was no sword in it. His hand rested on the empty lid.

A quick glance showed Jack wasn't the only one with a placeholder for a sword; both men wore one. Had they used those swords to kill before? Did they plan to do so with me? There was much unknown about these men and this camp in the Woods, but my curiosity matched my concern.

My mouth opened to ask the shorter man what his name was, but as if reading my mind, he swept himself down into a bow. "I am the great Ronin Arrows, leader of the Silver Raiders and caretaker of the Woods of Silver and Light."

"Well that seems a little much," I said when he straightened himself. Beside him, Jack smirked.

Ronin didn't look offended. "It's not though; I'm quite impressive."

He straightened his lapel and pulled back his shoulders. Everything these two men did: the way they looked me in the eye as they spoke and shared no sideways glances, the way they waved to others as we passed and let me walk with no restraints—it all carried the bearings of someone who could be trusted. For as long as they were going to act as if they trusted me, I would play their game. Any secret distrust we would both keep hidden. So I smirked and shrugged. "Quite impressive, eh? Impress me."

He looked downright giddy that I asked and bounded off into a tent just to come running back a moment later with a bow and quiver in hand.

"Hold this for me, will you?" He handed me the bow while he strapped on the quiver of arrows. A few children gathered nearby to watch while Jack cleared a space for Ronin to shoot. Ronin thanked me theatrically as he took the bow back, then notched the arrow. He held three of his fingers on the string as he pulled it back to the corner of his jawline below his ear.

"What shall my target be? Please, no people," Ronin said. I looked around for a small target.

"Do you see that tree over there, the one with the ladder on it? Oh, there's two that way, okay the one on the left. It's further. I want you to hit between the fourth and the fifth bars of that ladder." I had to squint to count the bars.

"Easy," Ronin said, as he waited for Jack to jog toward the ladder and keep the space clear of people. Jack called when he was ready, and not a second later Ronin released his arrow. It wavered up and down slightly as it moved through the air. By the time it struck the tree, Ronin had already loaded another arrow and pulled back to fire. Twice more he did this before lowering the bow. He spread out his arms toward the children and gave a dramatic bow.

I narrowed my eyes to see better. Sure enough, all four

arrows had landed within the mark. Not many things impressed me, but the speed and accuracy that he showed surpassed any that I had seen. My experience with the bow was limited to one invitation Elenora and I had received to shoot with friendly lads a month back, and while I mostly watched, I hadn't seen anyone who showed half the skill of Ronin.

Ronin tucked his bow between both arms and waited for my reply. The smug look on his face made me want to hit him. I shrugged my shoulders. "You did it, but I bet you've practiced a lot."

He laughed. "You have a sort of spirit to you, don't you? Bet you stand out among the rest of the court."

"For your record, I haven't been to court yet, but yes I am different."

"You remind me of Cera; you met her earlier. Don't tell her I said it though, she likes to think herself unique."

Jack rejoined us and together they gave me a tour of the place. I wasn't sure why they were being nice to me, but it was clear that we posed no threat to each other or ill-wishes, and I found myself relaxed in their presence. More relaxed that I had ever felt among the lords and ladies at the balls. For a moment, I allowed myself to pretend that this was where I lived: in the dark woods with sparkling lakes and houses built in trees, wearing pants every day.

"What's that one?" I pointed to a large golden tent. It nestled back in the trees where it should have been dim, but the fabric of the tent seemed to glow, so that even the shadows hid from around it.

"Nothing. Come, you should be getting back home. You don't want to be traveling through these woods at night." With a sudden change of temperament, Ronin sharply led me away from the glowing tent and out of the Silver Raiders camp.

He escorted me through the Woods and to the front tree line where I had come in while I pondered the strange tent that made him drive me from the camp. He talked as we walked, clearly keeping the conversation from the golden tent.

Once at the edge of the Woods, I assured him that I could find my way from here, and he took back off into the dark trees. The sun was low on the other side of the sky, and I knew that I had no hope of making it home before dark.

I was right; it was dark well before I was home. Lady Claire sat in her chair waiting for me. Her hair was in pins and she wore a thick shawl though the night wasn't cold. She turned up her head when I came in and set her book to the side. "You shouldn't worry me by staying out so late. It isn't right for an eligible lady to be out after dark on her own."

"I'm sorry Ma'am, I was just at the farm working and lost track of time."

"I figured. Your hands aren't dirty though." She peered at me, and I was impressed she could see my hands well in the flickering fire light.

I hide my hands behind my back. I usually came home with half my dress and most of my hands stained with dirt. "I washed before leaving," I explained. She nodded slowly then turned her nose back into her book.

"Very well then. I'll see you tomorrow. You and Lady Elenora have an invitation to the Thompson's for an afternoon ride."

The disgust showed on my face and Lady Claire raised an eyebrow. I ducked my head.

"Right. I'll be ready. Goodnight." I left quickly before she could have a chance to notice the glow of magic that I was sure the Woods had left on me.

CHAPTER EIGHT

"Cousin Alfred said they were strong men who get their strength from magic in those woods. Said he's never been more scared in his life," Matthew Thompson said as he rocked back and forth in the saddle. I rolled my eyes. His cousin Alfred must be very weak to think a band of mostly girl bandits were strong men.

"Your cousin is afraid of horses too, so that doesn't count for much," Christopher said.

The gentlemen we met the other night, Christopher and Berkley, received an invitation to ride as well, making a group of five. Elenora rode gracefully, keeping one hand on the reins and the other holding a petite umbrella over her head to block the sun. I had left my umbrella behind knowing that I would need both hands on the reins to ride as gracefully as Elenora. I could ride easily, but gracefully was another thing.

Christopher seemed like a smart lad, with a straight smile that he gave out sparingly. Berkley smiled too easily.

He was smiling now, looking goofy as he trotted on. Elenora kept her eyes on him, and I knew she had feelings. I couldn't tell if Berkley shared her feelings, but he kept his horse near hers, so I guessed so.

"I heard you had a run in with the Silver Raiders, Lady Anika?" Matthew said as he bent his back to look at me.

"You could say that."

"Was it scary?"

"No, dreadfully boring."

Elenora shot me a look and I turned away. I had meant that this was boring. We were riding on the Thompson's grounds, which consisted of a large field and some pathways through a small walking park. The most exciting thing we saw was a squirrel chase, but they darted away before we trotted too close.

"My brother got accepted into school this week," Christopher declared. He rode next to Matthew, in front of me, with Elenora and Berkley behind me. I felt very caged in.

"That's wonderful!" Those around me congratulated him, but I didn't know why. He wasn't the one going to school.

When asked what his brother would study, Christopher replied, "Agriculture. There are enough brothers in the family that he isn't set to inherit much of his own so he's ready to set out and make something of himself. He's passionate about farming and thinks he can do something with it."

"Have you thought about school for yourself?" Matthew asked him.

"I have, but my time is much too limited I'm afraid. I plan on living through my brother."

"Anika, what are you looking at?" Elenora's voice jolted me. My eyes kept wandering into the distance, watching behind every tree as if a Silver Raider waited there. I didn't fear them, but the thought of Ronin and his Silver Raiders consumed my mind.

Ronin asked me to not tell a word of them to anyone; he said their mysterious presence aided the mission. I turned my head forward and willed myself not to give anything away. I hoped to earn Ronin's trust and protecting his secret seemed like the first step. While I didn't support stealing, even for a noble cause, I desired to know more about the Silver Raiders' way of life, and sharing their secrets hardly felt like the way to earn their confidence.

Each person looked at me with a puzzled expression and I offered an innocent smile in response.

"It's nothing. Just thought I saw something."

"I'M SURE IT WASN'T THAT BAD," MARTY SAID AS she washed the vegetables. I had enough time to ride down to Joshua and Marty's farm after my outing at the Thompsons'.

I helped her set the table, though I wouldn't be eating with them. "It was. It was more boring than you can imagine."

"Christopher sounds nice enough," she said as she peeked at me.

"His head doesn't seem to be empty; I'll give him that." I ignored her looks. I made the mistake of describing him as handsome and now she won't let me live it down.

"Handsome and smart, my my. Will you see him again soon?"

"At the Thames birthday ball in a few weeks, probably. But I'll spend most of my time in the card room making us enough money to get some good pigs." I came back for the glasses to set on the table.

Marty's eyebrows drew down though she put on a smile. "I meant to tell you; we don't need money for pigs now."

"What are you talking about? We need them to keep this farm going. I know we need money for crops too, but we can get by another year if we work hard."

She shook her head and tucked her hair behind her ear before handing me the bowl of vegetables. "No, we don't need money for either. Joshua and I went over some savings and realized we have enough after all."

I furrowed my brow. We spent hours together going through the budgets and how much money they had saved. I knew there wasn't enough money there, not even close.

"Are you sure?"

She bit her lip and tugged at her tunic. "Yes, I'm quite sure. We are fine."

Her eyes begged me not to ask any more questions, and I decided it best to respect her privacy about such matters. "Alright. That's good news, I guess. Means we won't lose the lands this year."

I didn't stay long, but when I left, I took her words with me and replayed them over and over in my mind. Where had they gotten the money from?

There was only one explanation that presented itself forcefully in my mind. Joshua had been with me when the Silver Raiders ambushed us. He had heard what they said about doing it for us, and I had seen the way he looked at that bracelet. I saw no other way for them to get that amount of money in such a short time.

Joshua and Marty had turned to the Silver Raiders for help.

CHAPTER NINE

Dear brother,

How is my mother? Is she quite well?

I seem to have stumbled into quite the situation here and was hoping you had some knowledge that may help me, since you are the one who brought magic to this land in the first place. Have you ever heard of the Woods of Silver and Light? There are bandits living there now, and I'm quite curious about them.

No, you can assure Cosette that I am not running off to join a group of ruffians. I've actually been behaving perfectly. Write me when you can, and give my family my best.

-Anika

I folded the note and slipped it into an envelope. Perhaps Rumpel had some answers for me. The moon was quite high now and my bed called for me to find it. Just as I finished moving the ink back to its place in the drawer, a creaking sound caught my attention.

The intruder was back.

This time I'd have a weapon. Behind the ink and quill sat a dull knife that I gripped before rising to my feet and blowing out my candles. I made my way to the open door before footsteps came from the hallway. They were upstairs.

I ducked behind the door to listen to them move. Their feet came closer and closer until they stopped outside my door.

Then they stepped in.

I bit down hard on my tongue to keep from shrieking. The figure didn't see me shaking from behind the door as they stayed focused on their mission. I pressed myself against the wall while they tiptoed toward the bed.

What could they want from my bed?

A strand of moonlight caught something they held behind their back. A knife. My eyes grew wide as they raised that knife above their head and lunged onto the bed.

They stabbed into a pillow, then growled.

I should have run. I should have hidden better. I should have done something. But instead, when they turned around, they saw me cowering behind the door with fear in my eyes.

They weren't here to steal something; they were here to kill me.

If I didn't protect myself, they'd kill me now.

So I screamed at the top of my lungs to wake up everyone in the house, then I raised my own blade and I charged at them.

They dressed in all black with fabric pulled around their head so only their eyes could be seen, but the shadows and darkness made them difficult to make out. If I didn't find out who this was, they could return and make an attempt on my life again.

My mind still hadn't wrapped around that—someone wanted me dead.

Still screaming, I changed direction and put the bed between me and the attacker. They'd expected to find me sleeping, so they needed a new strategy now. Those moments of hesitation would give me a chance to figure out what I planned to do. I jumped on top of the bed and shouted again.

The first noise came as a door opened down the hallway. The attacker tensed and looked between me and the doorway. The moment they looked away from me, I jumped on top of them and we rolled to the floor. I could have stabbed them, but I had no interest in killing anyone. My only goal was to know who they were. My hands tugged at their neck to free their headwrap, but they jerked away, leaving something in my hand.

They kicked me off them and jumped to their feet. I hopped up to deflect their block, but they didn't advance. Instead they ran to the window, opened it, and jumped through.

The sound of my breathing filled the room, and the knife clattered to the floor.

"They're gone. You're okay," I whispered to myself, but my rapid heart wouldn't be stilled.

"Lady Anika, what is this mess?" Lady Claire stepped into the room with a shriek and shook her head at the messy bed and knife in my hands.

"There was someone in my room!" I shouted, my energy still high.

She looked around. "Are they gone now?"

A shaky hand pointed toward the window. "They went through there."

She studied the window for a few moments with tight lips. Finally, she spoke. "Hmph. I see nothing more we can do tonight, so we will deal with this in the morning. If you are quite done screaming, I'd like to go to sleep."

She put her hand over her chest as if all this was quite too much for her, though her voice remained calm at the mention of an intruder. Without a further word, she headed back down the hallway and into her own room where she shut the door behind her.

I closed both the door and the window, then lit a candle. When I grabbed at the attacker's neck, I pulled something free, and I wanted to know what it was. The small candle flame flickered with enough light to see by as I opened my fist.

A broken necklace and clasp sat within. Green thread was knitted together in an intricate braid like a small snake in my hand held together by a silver lock on the back, with the thread broken at either end. I scanned the room for the rest of the necklace, but it wasn't there. The only clue I had about who tried to kill me was this broken jewelry.

It was an interesting clue, though, and not one I would have guessed.

A woman wanted me dead. And I had no idea why.

LADY CLAIRE AND ELENORA WERE THE ONLY ONES not on my list of suspects, because they were in the house with me. No, I realized, Elenora hadn't come to my room, so it might still be her. But if I had to make a list, she'd be pretty low on it.

Cera would make that list. She hated me. But she had no reason to kill me.

There was no one else I could think of who'd want me dead. I stopped thinking of only women and entertained the idea that a man had hired a woman to kill me, but I couldn't image what man would want me dead, either. Perhaps someone I'd beaten in poker who was looking for his money? He wouldn't find any at my home.

They had failed to kill me, though. So they might come back.

I'd much rather be at home recouping after the attack, but Elenora dragged me out to Edward Thames's birthday ball. At least this gave me a chance to watch people for any signs of hidden aggression toward me.

ELENORA DANCED IN THE MIDDLE OF THE ROOM with Berkley. From the way he looked at her I guessed her feelings were returned. She gushed about him every night since riding, and while I'd be sad to see my friend leave at the end of the season, I'd be glad to stop hearing so much about him. I felt as if I knew every detail there was to know, including the gold specks in his eyes.

Gold seemed to be the theme tonight; half the ladies were dressed in it and most of the room shone with it. Gold cloth covered the tables with gold plates stacked upon it. Golden balls hung from the ceiling, and gold banners lined the walls. I felt like I stuck out with my dark dress and dark hair, but Elenora had missed the memo too so I was in good company. Of course, her hair was bright, so she didn't cast quite the same shadow as I did.

While the men in the room didn't stick to the dress code quite as much as the ladies, there was an excess of white in their outfits.

My gaze found Christopher whose suit leaned closer to cream. He spent most of his time talking with friends rather than dancing and I glanced at him more often than I intended. Right now, he spoke with a blue-eyed girl with big curls. I didn't recognize her, but he seemed enthralled with whatever she was saying.

A blond-haired, brown-eyed man approached me and asked if he could sign my dance card. I held up my wrist to show him that I didn't have one. Most people knew me enough to know that, but he must be new to the area. From his accent I would guess he was from somewhere north.

"I don't like my time overruled by dancing, so I don't have one."

"But you do dance?" As he spoke again it reaffirmed my guess that his accent was northern.

"Not tonight," I said. Not after almost being killed. He grunted and made a comment about terrible manners and rude company, then paraded off.

"I think you are delightful company." Freddy appeared at my side.

"Hello Freddy," I moaned. He tipped his head in greeting then leaned against the wall and watched the people with me. Freddy didn't mind standing in silence, and while it felt awkward, I could deal with silent awkwardness. For two long songs we stood without talking until the girl I'd seen him with a few weeks ago came to whisk him away. He gave me a small smile as if he was sorry to be cutting our great conversation so short, and I waved as he left.

My eyes drew back to Christopher, who still spoke with that girl. Whatever they were talking about must be interesting. I longed for a friend that made insightful conversation; I was tired of pleasantries and meaningless words.

I'd found decent company in Elenora, but she didn't understand me. I scanned the room for her. She'd switched dancing partners but hadn't left the floor. It was a wonder her feet didn't hurt her more. Mine killed me in these shoes. But, I remembered, she was raised in shoes like these, while I was raised lucky to have shoes at all.

I didn't belong here. I didn't like these people, and I didn't enjoy these parties. The loud music, endless sea of people, pointless conversations—none of it appealed to me.

If I didn't want to be here, there was no reason that I should stay. I could leave. Happy with my decision, I resolved to wait in the carriage until Elenora was ready to return home. After choosing a small cake to eat while I waited, I headed outside.

There was a slight drizzle in the air, and the first thought that came to my mind was how good the water would be for the crops. I shook my head, marveling at who I had become. I sounded like the farmers back home, talking about the weather and their crops.

My second thought was to protect my cake, and I hunched my back to cover my treat as I hurried to the front of the house where the carriages waited. With my head low, I didn't see anyone approach me until they were close enough to make my heart jump.

"I thought that was you. Leaving the party early?" Ronin's voice startled me, and I whirled around to see him. My first thought was that the attacker was back to kill me, but my nerves relaxed as he pulled his mask off his face and smirked at me fleeing the party with my dessert in my hands.

I peeked back at the house. The rain kept the people inside, so there was little chance of someone spotting us. "Do you ambush every party now?"

He laughed as he looked through the windows into the Thames home. "Not everyone, but his lordship had something that we needed."

"Money?"

"Well we did take some of that, but no, we were after something else." He patted the small bag in his hands. I asked what it was, but he shook his head.

"Promise you won't give us away?" Ronin asked. Behind him, the other Silver Raiders were leaving. I wondered if they had a carriage or horses around somewhere. It was too far to run from the Woods of Silver and Light.

"I don't feel good about it, but I don't want to return inside. Besides, there's nothing they can do about it now and I guess he will know you've been here anyway."

Ronin smiled as he pulled his mask back on. "He sure will. You look beautiful tonight by the way."

With that he turned and fled the scene, leaving me behind with a soggy cake and a small wish that I could run wild with them.

CHAPTER TEN

*R*onin

The note sat outside my window for me to find when I returned home. If I hadn't wanted a sliver of fresh air coming through for the night, I would have missed the folded-up parchment with the dirt smeared on the edges where Ronin's hand must have creased it.

Suspicions ran through my mind. From what I'd heard, the Silver Raiders didn't interact with nobility or invite anyone into their Woods, so this invitation for me to visit was peculiar to say the least.

They were thieves, bandits, outlaws. What did they want with a lady from Westfallen?

Perhaps they thought they could use me to secure information about potential targets outside these Woods. Perhaps I was a target for their robbery, though that was unlikely. But there must be an explanation for their freely given friendship.

As long as the invitation was open, I would take it. There were secrets hiding in those trees, ones that threatened to hurt my kingdom, and I intended to dig them up. If they planned to steal, I could find out where and warn the nobles beforehand. And if they planned anything more than stealing, I could find a way to stop them.

Since coming to the manor, I'd doubted my place here. But this I could do—not as a lady, but as Anika.

So I strapped on my leather boots and went to the Woods of Silver and Light.

They didn't knock me out this time, a fact that I and the back of my head specifically, greatly appreciated. Cera did insist that I be blindfolded, however. I pointed out that I walked out last time unblindfolded, but she wouldn't budge.

Whatever friendliness they were pretending to have toward me, she wasn't playing their game.

Before Cera blindfolded me, she waved the other Silver Raiders on ahead. "Give us a moment, I want a word." Annabeth shot her a look but Cera shook her head. She offered me a friendly smile before leading the other Silver Raiders into the thick of the Woods. Once they were gone, Cera pulled a blue blindfold out of her pocket. She had a second bandana wrapped around her forehead holding her hair back. The color matched the hilt of her blade, red as blood.

"You just keep that with you?" I asked. My own hand rested on my blade in case Cera had been my attacker the other night, but she made no move to harm me. Instead she gave me a stern look.

"Let's be clear, I don't trust you. I don't know why you've come back, or what your intentions are, but if you are a spy, or here to collect some ransom, I promise you won't get it."

Clever girl. I didn't know what she meant by ransom, but I understood her message. "I don't expect you to trust me. But I'm not against you," I lied.

"You aren't one of us though." She pulled the bandana tight in her hands and twisted it once. "You don't belong with us. You're one of *them*." She pulled her lips back at that word and sneered. "You don't know what it's like to wipe the brow of a starving child. You don't know what it's like to care for a dying mother whose only worry is how her children will get on. You don't know what it's like to spend every day since you were four out in the fields doing what you could do put food on the table." Another sneer and narrowing of the eyes. Deep rooted bitterness seeped in her tone along with a heavy sorrow that could only come from personal experiences. What trauma had this girl gone through? What pain drove her into these Woods and a life of banditry?

There was fierceness in her eyes paired with disdain for me. How much could she see of my own mind?

With a firm voice I replied, "I know more about starving than you think. You forget, I didn't grow up with a title." I could still feel the ache of hunger that my family endured for years.

"You have one now. That makes you different from us. The only reason I'm letting you into camp is because Ronin said you'd come, and you were to be let in."

"Then you'd better not keep him waiting." I put my hands on my hips and closed my eyes so she could blindfold me. She yanked it tighter than necessary, and I suspected she did it on purpose.

If Cera wanted to kill me, she'd do it now. Or she'd pretend to be my friend so she could stab me when I least expected it. She was too blunt with her dislike for me to be found sneaking through the night with a blade.

If Cera wanted me dead, she wouldn't care about anyone seeing her. She'd just do it. She was not my attacker. Besides, my attacker had been wearing a necklace, and she wouldn't be caught in jewelry.

So I relaxed as she led me toward camp. My feet remembered the way back in fairly well now that we weren't far away, but it still took twice as long as it should have. Cera guided me, but not perfectly. I fell multiple times, stubbed my toe, and banged my head on a low branch. By the time the voices of camp met my ears, I'd acquired quite a bitter feeling toward Cera. Relief filled me when the bandana came off.

"Was that really necessary?" Ronin's voice came before my bandana was completely off.

"You're too trusting," Cera replied. She didn't wait around before stomping off toward a tent and disappeared inside.

Ronin sighed. "I'm sorry about her; she can be a tad rough."

"I noticed," I said, rubbing the front of my head. We came in through a different angle this time, between the huts on the ground. The last time I was here, I'd failed to notice how many homes lined the trees, each built with wood and covered with bark and hay and mud. The wood provided a good base, while the rest added protection from weather, though it wouldn't surprise me if the magical properties of this forest kept it safe from storms.

At this point, very little about these Woods would surprise me.

Intricate lanterns hung from branches above, providing light that the trees blocked. Though it was the middle of the day, the Woods of Silver and Light denied the sun opportunity to shine. Instead, these silver light spheres trapped in glass lanterns illuminated the area. Occasionally the light was a different color, sometimes blue, others green, some gold, but the silver outshone them all.

"It's beautiful, isn't it?" Ronin asked when he saw me admiring the homes.

Again he showed no hesitation in interacting with me as he stood close to my side and kept his hands free from his pockets. If I asked, how much would he be willing to tell me? I began with a simple question. "How did you end up living in these magical woods?"

"Ah, tricky question." He turned and started walking as my hopes dropped. If he thought that was a difficult one to answer, there was little hope in him answering my others. Why do you steal? Where will you steal next? How do you move so stealthily?

Ronin gave a reply. "Simply put, we were invited. The Woods of Silver and Light have their own…spirit of sorts. They saw our need and invited us within their borders, protecting us from others who live in these trees. At first it was me and Jack, then we started recruiting others for our mission. They were nervous at first but after they saw the beauty of this camp, they were willing to live here. Most were from struggling or broken homes, so they had limited options."

I waited but he didn't say more and my question still felt unanswered. "How did the Woods invite you exactly?"

His eyes twinkled as he turned his head back to look at me. "A chap needs to have some secrets."

"I see you came again," Jack interrupted my interrogation with a chipper voice as he walked toward us. His loose, black shirt was tucked into his pants, allowing me to see the tattoo on his arm—a circle design that I didn't recognize—and his belt. The sheath wasn't empty today. His sword swayed lightly as his hips moved.

Perhaps he'd tell me things that Ronin wouldn't. "Jack, why did you and Ronin come to live here?"

"I just said I need secrets—" Ronin started with a faked offense, but I ignored him, crossing my arms and tipping my head down slightly as I tried to order Jack to answer with my eyes.

"We were offered a safe haven here, and we accepted," Jack replied with his deep voice.

"By who?" My questions continued. They had a funny way of answering without giving a real answer.

Ronin held up his hand to steady Jack's free tongue. "That'll be enough of that. Do you want me to teach you to shoot? You mentioned it last time."

So there was some mystery as to how they came to the Woods that they didn't want me uncovering. I looked between Jack and Ronin. My guess was Jack would be the better one to squeeze information out of, so I resolved to find him later and get it.

There was something about these Woods that drew me in, a warmth I didn't find outside the borders of the trees. The free spirits, the laughter of the children, the playtime by the clear water, the floating lights—it all created an atmosphere that I found difficult to resist.

Was that the spirit Ronin spoke of? Was it calling me too?

But along with the warmth, there was also something that I didn't trust.

It was a prickly sensation on the tips of my fingers that made its way to my heart to warn it of this feeling. It was the darkness of the shadows that moved as the lanterns floated overhead to remind me that some things remained to be seen. It was the all too eager smile on Ronin's face and the way he asked nothing of me.

There was light in these woods, but there was also darkness. And from Ronin's expression, there was a chance he didn't see it.

Or, he was very good at hiding it.

I pasted an innocent expression on my face and accepted his lessons. "Fine. I bet I can shoot as well as you by the end of it."

"Careful that you don't," Jack grunted. "His pride is at stake."

Ronin chuckled. "My pride will survive. It'd just show how great of a teacher I am. Come along."

He taught me the best that he could, but I proved a terrible student. It didn't help that we were interrupted often by his friends or curious children stopping by to say hello. The distractions made little difference, though; I was truly a terrible shot. Ronin laughed at me multiple times throughout, which was rather unkind of him, but he made up for it by having patience when showing me the same things over and over.

"Cera's right you know," I said as I struggled to pull the string back. I didn't realize it took so much muscle to draw. Ronin found me a bow with a smaller draw weight, but I still struggled. I tried not to grunt as I pulled it. He offered to find me a children's bow—I was shorter than some of the kids here—but my pride refused him.

As we shot, I took the chance for further questions.

"You are too trusting. You don't know anything about me."

"I know you can't shoot a bow to save your life," he grunted. I moved the arrow toward him and gave a small glare, but he was right. I didn't know I'd be this bad. "However," he continued. "Yes, I am too trusting. But I don't think you mean us harm. Actually, I mean to ask you to join us."

Shock was the fault of my arrow veering to the side this time. "What?"

"I mean it, I see a fire in your eyes that doesn't belong at court. You should join our Silver Raiders. You have a desire to help your people; you can do that with us."

I thought he was using me. I thought he was playing me. I didn't think he liked me. Or was this another game? It was hard to tell with Ronin; the smile in his eyes looked genuine but such blind trust couldn't be real.

I lowered my bow by my side and didn't reach for another arrow. Was he serious? "I am...amused by your way of life. But I can't join you. I don't know anything about you."

Ronin didn't look disappointed by my refusal. The smile on his face seemed impossible to remove. "May I be forward for a moment?" At my nod he continued. "I'd guess you don't fit in among the other nobles. You have the title but you don't have the pompous attitude they possess. Your spirit is more like ours. I see the way your eyes light up at the Woods and by the way you constantly messed with your skirts the other day, I'd guess you're more comfortable in these pants. You can be free here. We wouldn't ask anything of you."

An offer like that was too good to be true. Even if I trusted Ronin, even if his offer was real, there were many reasons why I couldn't live here.

"Now may I be forward?"

He spread out his hands. "Ask anything."

I set the edge of the bow on the ground and twisted it in my hands as I formed my words. "It would be wrong. What you are doing in these Woods is wrong. You steal from people, and I can only guess what else. But I have a manor to keep, and people who are still suffering from the war. The only way I can properly help these people is by working hard, not by stealing from others."

"We aren't stealing a lot; they hardly notice anything is missing." He didn't look bothered in the least at my accusation.

I gave a dry laugh. "That doesn't make it right."

"It makes it okay." Ronin crossed his arms and spoke with a hint of harshness before pulling back and repeating more gently. "It makes us okay." His chest rose and fell with a few breaths as his eyes scanned the lake in silence before he licked his lips and continued. "They sit in their oversized manors and throw lavish parties while we starve. They don't hear our pleas; they don't try to help. Those people that you surround yourself with—they don't care about us. They let us die while they turn a blind eye."

He spoke in the same way Cera had with the same amount of bitterness filling his tone. But there was more anger here than she had, and more pain.

"I don't think you're being quite fair." I could see how

easy it was to blame the people who had money while you had none; it was something I'd done often while growing up. But Ronin sounded like a man unwilling to do hard work, instead taking from the nobles and justifying it with excuses about the imbalance of life.

Ronin set his bow down. "Fair? None of this is fair." His arm reached out and pointed across the lake as if the nobles were on the other side. "They sat in their lavish manors while my son died."

That stopped me cold. My body turned fully to face him and the pool of tears resting on his lids. For the first time the smile was not on his face, but rather an expression of hopelessness.

His voice cracked with pain. "They let my son die. My wife left me years before, when Landon was too young to remember her. We were fine on our own until he got sick. It progressed over a few months, and I knew I needed a doctor's help, but none of the local doctors could figure it out. I didn't have the money for a better doctor, so I pleaded with our lords and ladies to help me. I begged them with my whole heart."

He paused, pulling his lips in. "They said no, and my son died."

Tears spilled from his eyes. I lowered my face to the ground, embarrassed for thinking him lazy. "I'm so sorry."

He sniffed. "You're different from other nobility, but you are the exception. I want better for the people here, and I can give them better. *That* justifies my actions."

It still felt wrong to me, but it also felt wrong to tell him that right now. He asked me to join them again, but I sighed deeply. "I have to think about it." There were still answers here that needed to be found.

"Fine, take your time."

"Ronin, I really am sorry about your son. I would have helped if I were here."

He offered a small smile. "It's okay. I'll see him again someday."

I rested my bow on my foot. "You believe in an afterlife?"

He laughed. "I'll see him much sooner than that."

My brow furrowed in confusion, but Ronin got called off to do some important job before I could continue questioning and Jack took his place with me. He offered to continue teaching me how to shoot, but I informed him that I was a lost cause. I put my bow away, my mood dampened by Ronin's heartbreaking story.

What had he meant by saying he'd see his son again soon?

While nothing could convince me stealing was okay and I wouldn't join the Silver Raiders, I found myself drawn to this place, nonetheless. Drawn to Ronin. If my friendship with Ronin continued, I'd first want more information.

I was so busy recounting Ronin's story that I almost forgot my plan to squeeze information out of Jack.

"Jack, how did you and Ronin end up in these woods? Who offered you safety?"

He leaned against a tree as he twisted his dagger in his hands. The hilt of the dagger had the face of a lion. "I'm not sure Ronin wants you to know."

"He told me about his son," I blurted out, hoping that since Ronin trusted me with that bit of information, Jack would think I was trustworthy enough to have it all.

He nodded. "Then you'd understand why we came here."

"To help people like his son, who others won't help."

"It's more than that," Jack said. "But that's not a story for today. It's a good story, I promise you that, but it's not mine to tell. You'll have to wait until Ronin trusts you for that one."

CHAPTER ELEVEN

The rain fell hard, coating the air with a thick sheet of water. I stood at the edge of the Woods of Silver and Light, staring into the storm. Of course, the rainfall stopped as soon as it touched the forest. I wonder how these trees flourished if water wouldn't touch them.

I didn't have time to ponder it. I needed to get home. I was glad that I wore my pants today; it would make running easier. I took a deep breath then darted out into the cold rain, keeping my head low as I dashed down the path. I should start bringing my horse closer to the Woods, to lessen the distance I traveled on foot. My boots would be soaked through by the time I reached her.

My feet almost slipped several times, but I stayed my ground, flying at my top speed through the rain. Water streamed down my face and into my eyes, making it difficult to see. I tried to wipe it away, but my arm carried more water with it, and I accomplished nothing.

I thought I heard a voice call out, but I saw nobody around. After a few more steps the call came again. I halted, putting both hands over my forehead to shield my eyes as I scanned around. The Woods loomed behind me with open fields on all other sides. I'd seen men working these fields the few times I'd come, but I hadn't thought they would be out in this weather.

To my right, a horse rode up. A man sat on top, calling out.

"Do you need a lift back—Anika, is that you?"

I didn't recognize the person, but if they recognized me then they must be nobility of sort. I was embarrassed to be caught out in the rain in my trousers, but that couldn't be helped now. I could just hope that word of it never reached Lady Claire.

As he got closer, Christopher's features came into view. His dark hair was soaking and pinned against his face, and his clothes hung with the weight of water. Like me, he dressed in common clothes, so it took me a moment to recognize him. He extended his hand, but I shook my head.

"I have a horse up ahead!" I yelled through the pounding rain.

"A brown courser?" he asked. I nodded. "We found her tied up ahead with no sign of a rider. She's already being cared for in the stables."

It's a good thing I came across Christopher then, or I'd be lost without my horse and looking at a long journey home. When he offered his hand again, I accepted, and he pulled me upon the giant horse to sit in front of him. I was grateful for the pants now; both of us never would have fit on this horse if I'd ridden sidesaddle.

We didn't speak as we rode. I doubted the roar of the storm or the beating of the horse's hooves would have allowed us to hear more than a few words. I realized I had no clue where Christopher lived, but I hoped it was close.

He turned off the main road, toward Lord Hughes's estate. I wanted to protest but I was eager for relief from the storm. I'd only spoken to Lord Hughes once; hopefully he didn't mind me showing up soaking wet on his doorstep. Perhaps Christopher had a closer relationship with him than I did.

We pulled up to the grand estate. No matter how much work I put into my home, it would never look as fine as this. Christopher rode right up to the main doors and helped me off the horse. A man came running out of the manor to take care of the horse as we hurried under the balcony.

"I'm not sure we should go in," I said as I shivered. Now here, the thought of knocking on Lord Hughes's door dripping wet didn't feel right. I wondered if it was too late to call the boy to bring our horse back.

"You'll die of cold out here." Christopher's voice shook with his chill. He pushed open the door for me and placed his hand on my back, gently pushing me inside.

If knocking on the door unannounced felt discourteous, blatantly walking in felt both uncivil and beyond rude.

The warmth greeted me favorably, and for a moment I forgot about anything else but the comfort of a shelter. Lord Hughes's estate had high ceilings and a tall staircase that branched off into two directions. Blue color popped out from family crests hanging on the wall and from soft rugs on the floor.

I marveled at the grandness of the estate. I thought the outside was beautiful, but the inside was indescribable. This is what a noble's manor should look like.

"The rain got you, eh?" A voice echoed toward us. My head spun toward the sound sending droplets of water flicking from my hair.

"Lord Hughes, I'm so sorry to impose like this. We really shouldn't have come." I backed against the door, ready to flee.

Christopher cleared his throat besides me. "Anika, you know I live here, right? I'm the second son of Lord Hughes and Lady Isabella."

My mouth dropped open in surprise. No, I didn't know that. Lord Hughes laughed at my shock. "Anika, you are welcome to *impose here* any time that you wish."

"We should go dry off," Christopher shuddered. I thanked Lord Hughes as Christopher led me up the stairs. He showed me to a room where a fire burned and left for a moment before returning with a dress. "None of my sisters are as short as you, but I hope this will fit." He handed me the blue garment. Eagerly, I took it, ready to be warm and dry.

The dress, while far too long on me, was higher quality than any day dressed I owned, and I felt nice wearing it with its long sleeves that flowed around my elbows. I'm sure my sister could identify the fabric; all I knew was that it felt soft and I liked it.

Once changed, I wrung out my hair and braided it. I could have stayed by that warm fire for ages, but I didn't want to be a rude guest. Uncertainly, I ventured out of the room to thank my host.

Christopher waited in the corridor for me. He'd changed into a clean white shirt and simple jacket, and while his hair was still wet, it didn't cling to his head now, allowing the ends to curl up slightly. He pushed off from the wall and smiled at me.

"There's the lady I recognize. Want to tell me why you were in those awful pants?"

"I happen to like them and will put them right back on as soon as they dry," I informed him.

"Fine with me. Do you want to sit by the fire in the main room until they're ready? I've called for some tea."

The taste of tea didn't appeal to me, but I agreed to sit by the fire. Some light snacks were set out, nothing more than crackers and cheese, but I devoured them. It was late in the evening, and I couldn't be sure if the household was asleep or merely giving us our space, but no one bothered us. I tried to look through paintings to figure out Christopher's family, but I couldn't spot him in any of the paintings in the room, so I couldn't tell if this was his immediate family or not. They were all nice-looking people though. He had a strong family line.

"So, what were you doing in the Woods of Silver and Light?" Christopher asked.

I frowned. It hadn't occurred to me that he saw me coming from the Woods. "That's not really your business, is it?" I asked as I popped another piece of cheese into my mouth.

"Easy there, I'm not trying to fight you. Just not sure you know what you've gotten yourself into."

I leaned back in my chair that was softer than my bed was growing up. I could sleep in this chair happily. My arms crossed as I looked at Christopher. "What do you think I've gotten myself into?"

"I'm guessing it has something to do with the Silver Raiders who live in those woods."

I shrugged. He grinned. "Alright, keep your dangerous secrets. But you should know they aren't the only creatures who live there."

He could tell my interest piqued. He peeked toward the entrances to the room before leaning forward and putting his elbows on his knees. I grinned inside, eager to know what secrets he could have that he didn't want overheard.

"Those trees are filled with magic. The very essence of it lives there. Over time, things were banished there. Some magical beasts, some magical people. People like wizards, or evil witches with too much power for their own good. No one could kill them, not completely that is, so they were destroyed, and what was left of them was locked in those woods. Their spirits float through the branches and settle in the trees. They prey on the ignorant folks who wander through the woods, stealing their hearts and disturbing their souls. It's not a safe place to be."

I raised my eyebrows at his seriousness. I'd been through those woods twice now, and no danger came to me. I had heard animal sounds but hadn't seen a creature that could do me harm. I wasn't entirely convinced that the sounds belonged to a real creature as opposed to noises the Woods make. "What kind of sorcerers live there?"

He leaned back, looking unpleased with how little concern I showed. "I don't know them all; my grandpa has always taken more interest in those woods than I have. He says there's a man who can persuade anyone to do anything, even kill their loved one. The stories about him were always my favorite. Let's see, there's a woman who can bring people back from the dead; another woman has the ability to make animals obey her. I think there's one—

"Stop." My skin felt cold by the fire. "Say that again. A woman can bring people back from the dead?"

"Yes, that's right. Well she could, at least. She lost that power when she was defeated years ago. Now her spirit lives in those woods."

I ran Ronin's words through my mind again. Someday soon he would see his son. The thought formed in my mind and caused me to shiver. Was this his plan? Is that why he lived in those woods? Was he hoping she could bring his son back from the dead?

"Can she do it again?"

"Bring someone back from the dead? She'd have to be brought back herself first, but I don't know how you'd do that."

"But it can be done?" I asked him in a serious tone.

He crossed his arms. "Anika, I hope you aren't planning on seeking her out."

I waved my hand. "No. Of course not. I just like a good story, that's all."

"Well you'd love my grandfather then, he's full of stories like that." Christopher went on to tell me more about his grandfather, while I stared at the crackling fire.

I tried to be a good guest and listen to him, but all that I could think about is what magic Ronin had gotten himself tangled up in, and if he was powerful enough to withstand it.

CHAPTER TWELVE

"*I* assume you have a reasonable explanation?" Lady Claire stood in the dining room, catching me as I was sneaking food back up to my room.

"Yes; a very good one. The rain caught me, and I spent the night at Lord Hughes's house as his guest. Christopher invited me in; I didn't impose." I tucked my bread loaves closer to me, eager to flee to my room and devour them. One of Lord Hughes's maids brought me a plate for breakfast, but they greatly underestimated how much I could eat.

The frown on Lady Claire's face deepened as she inspected me. I changed back into my working clothes before riding back home and hadn't changed out of the pants yet. I knew I should have changed before trying to eat. The bread didn't seem worth it in comparison to avoiding Lady Claire's scowl.

"I'll write to him to thank him. Meanwhile, you have a letter of your own." She reached into the pockets of her oversized dress and produced a folded-up envelope which she handed to me gracefully. I grabbed it with much less grace, recognizing Rumpel's writing.

The main courier works fast. I thanked Lady Claire and flew up the stairs to open the letter, praying he'd know something about those woods.

As the letter opened, Rumpel's beautiful handwriting greeted me along with a brief scent of home. I devoured his words.

Anika,

Perhaps we were wrong to leave you. Those woods are not to be trifled with. I've heard many stories about the Woods and the crea- tures that live within, and the people are right to fear them. Even when I had magic, I wouldn't have dared enter the trees, for the Woods have a spirit of their own, and if they decide they don't fancy you, you won't make it out alive.

Please stay out of those woods. They will bring nothing but ruin. As for the bandits who live within, I'd heard of them when we lived there. If they've gotten mixed up with someone from inside the Woods, then I fear for them all.

Your mother is doing well, she's been healing. We all miss you. Write if you find out more about the Woods; I'd very much like to know.

Best wishes,

-Rumpel

Had he heard of this woman who can bring people back from the dead? Were there worse people than her living in the Woods? How long would it be before the spirit of the Woods stopped protecting Ronin and the Silver Raiders?

And who the blazes tried to kill me?

Questions swirled in my mind until my head ached. When a knock came at the door, I flew from my seat.

"Who is it?"

"It's Lady Claire." Her soft voice drifted through the door, waiting for me to open it. When I did, she passed me a large, red envelope with a golden seal which felt heavier than I'd anticipated it to be. My finger slipped under the seal to open the top and I slid out a shimmering paper.

"An invitation to the Prince's ball?" Lady Claire made a thoughtful noise in the back of her throat while I turned the paper over, looking for the trick. "But I don't know the king, or anyone in the royal family."

"Well someone wants you at that ball, and you'd better go. An invitation like this isn't to be ignored."

My blood turned cold at the thought of who could want me there and for what purpose. Perhaps a place to kill me amidst all the distractions of the night.

"Now you better get ready for you luncheon at the Carlstone's with Lady Elenora. I've got to go to the jewelry repair shop this afternoon."

She stepped into the hallway but I gasped. "What do you need from the shop?" I asked.

Her thin eyebrows lowered at my pale face. "One of Lady Elenora's necklaces broke, and I'm to fix it for her."

My entire body went numb and the room felt as if it was spinning. Lady Claire didn't notice my unease as she pulled at the door behind her. "And Lady Anika, do try to behave in front of the king. You wouldn't want to bring any trouble upon yourself."

Then she closed the door, and I fell into my seat. My hands fumbled to open the drawer and look at the broken knitted necklace.

It was Elenora who tried to kill me.

• • •

"YOU SEEM DISTRACTED," CHRISTOPHER SAID, holding his cup in both hands as he stood next to me. We had been invited to a luncheon gathering at the Carlstone's home, and once again Berkley and Christopher showed up shortly after we did. The Carlstones had two eligible sons with no title but a grand inheritance, if what I heard was correct.

A large pavilion was set up outside to block the sun from melting the ice cream they'd set up for us. I'd only tried ice cream a few times, but the soft texture and rich flavor was heavenly.

The ice cream was the best part of the day so far. Elenora talked with Berkley on a bench, and the two sons were at a table under the pavilion with three guests I recognized. A few others were scattered throughout the gardens, but I stayed on my bench by the trellis as I watched Elenora with a close eye.

So when Christopher sat himself on the bench next to me and spoke, I almost didn't hear him.

"I am distracted, but it's nothing to worry you with."

"More about the Woods of Silver and Light?" he asked.

I shook my head but then paused. "Actually, I would like to know more about that woman who can raise people from the dead, if you know anything else."

As Christopher squinted in the sunlight, the two freckles on his cheek squeezed closer together. He'd combed his dark hair to the side with three waves in the top, and a slight curl by his ear. He scratched behind that ear, his hand grazing the curl. "I'm not entirely convinced that you're not up to trouble, but I suspect you'll get into it with or without my help. Come on then." He stood up. I furrowed my brow, reluctant to leave the warmth of the bench but he waved his hand at me. "They have a large library here; we might be able to find something."

A groan came from my mouth. "This sounds like something my sister would do. Go to a library for answers."

Christopher's laugh was pleasant. "I don't know your sister, but she sounds very smart."

Elenora didn't see us as he let one of the Carlstone boys know where we were going before leading me inside to a warm home. The interior was almost as nice as Christopher's but lacking the lavish decorations that set his home apart. It still made my manor look like a pile of rubble.

"Are you really not going to tell me why you are so curious about those woods?" Christopher asked over his shoulder as he pushed open a door from the entry room.

"Will you stop helping me if I don't?" I asked.

He tilted his head to the side as he walked in front of me, thinking for a moment. Finally, he decided. "No, I don't think I would. I'm curious myself. You know, I've lived by those woods my whole life and never seen anything strange from them. But then those Silver Raider's moved into the Woods, and a few of my tenants have expressed complaints. Some are threatening to move if the Silver Raiders get much worse."

"I thought the Silver Raiders helped people like them. Shouldn't they like living so close to their heroes?" I asked.

"Yes, the younger tenants near worship the Silver Raiders. I think it's the scandal of the whole thing that worries the older, more stabilized tenants who don't want to be associated with anything wrong. I heard the king of Vestalin put a reward out for anyone who captures them."

My eyebrows raised. I hadn't known that. I wondered how big of a reward it was.

"Ah, here we are." Christopher pushed open a large door to a room filled with bookshelves and my mouth dropped open. The room was larger than the tavern I'd grown up in. This was going to take a long time.

Only four small windows shed light from one side of the room, making the rest of the room appear dark and dusty. The other three walls were lined with bookcases built into them, and two more rows stood in the middle of the room. To my left sat a stool to help reach the top, but I doubted it was tall enough for me to reach the highest shelf, or even the one below that. I'd leave those ones for Christopher, who would have no problem.

"Not really sure where to start," Christopher mumbled.

"Why do people accumulate so many books?"

Christopher wandered to the right and I stepped to the left to start sifting through the books, though uncertain what the right book would look like. My eyes skimmed over the titles and I pulled out a few that I thought might hold something. After flipping through a few pages, I changed my mind and slid them back on the dusty shelf.

I had little hope that this would provide any answers on the magic that lived in the Woods of Silver and Light.

The darkness about them haunted my mind. I was usually brave, and the idea of admitting fears wasn't appealing to me, but those were the feelings the Woods gave me. Each time I had visited, they cloaked me in their darkness and warned me with their foreign sounds. Even after leaving the Woods, I still felt like I saw flashes of lights floating in the outer corners of my eyes.

I wanted to learn its secrets, better understand the magic inside so that my fears would lessen. Because, in addition to the fears, there was excitement. Part of me was falling in love with the Woods and the freedoms they offered to Ronin's people. It was a strange array of emotions that played through my heart, and I didn't know which ones would win.

My feet shuffled through the library, continuing my search. Beyond learning about the Woods, I wanted to know if Ronin planned on bringing his son back from the dead, along with an evil sorceress.

Shelf after shelf I wandered, peering through stacks of books and plucking out ones that looked magic-filled. Each time I thought I'd found something it would turn into nothing. The time went by like this, with neither Christopher nor I coming up with anything.

Finally, a glimmer of hope came as Christopher cheered. "Aha! Here, I thought Grandpa mentioned something like this." He held open a big black book and I ran to his side, eager to be done with the search. He pointed to a page. "There's not much here, because it's not the focus of the story," he said as I read quickly. The page spoke of a battle, with pictures of horses riding along the bottom.

"It was during the Trade War right before we were born. The war was moving closer to the Woods, which concerned the soldiers because of who lived inside. So, they called on magicians to kill someone by the name of Basiliea who was working with the enemy. They couldn't kill her completely; instead she was chained to the Woods so she couldn't come out and hurt anyone or help the enemy." Christopher pointed to the paragraph on the page. "Then it moves on to continue talking about the war."

"What was she doing to help the enemy?" I asked. I couldn't read very quickly and was having trouble finding the right part.

"She brought their soldiers back from the dead after they were killed in battle."

"And can she be brought back herself?" I looked over at Christopher, who was inspecting the book with a concerned expression on his face. The corners of his lips were pulled in and his eyes narrowed as they moved back and forth across the page. His hand gripped the top corner of the book.

Christopher closed the book and pushed it away. "I don't know how, but my grandpa believed there was a way to bring her back."

expected Cera to stop me, but I made it all the way to the border of camp without seeing the Silver Raiders. My dagger stayed in my hand the whole time as I jumped at the sounds around me. The floating lanterns of the Silver Raider's camp were a welcoming sight. It was late morning, not that you could tell in the dark woods. I expected to see people around—a wandering child or a working mother, but I saw no one.

The men were gone during the day, farming land on the other side of the woods. Ronin explained to me that the men were built better for farming the land and catching food, while the women were stealthier and had the wild spirit fit for the Silver Raiders. So, the men worked during the day while the women watched the children, sometimes watching more children than their own while others donned the Silver Raiders' masks.

I knew why I didn't see many men usually, but this morning I saw none. I didn't see anyone at all. No women, no children. The camp lay quiet. I wandered into the camp, calling out for Ronin. Silence greeted me. It was eerie, seeing the camp abandoned, and I wondered if someone had captured them and received their ransom.

A woman called out from one of the homes in the trees, frightening me. She pointed down a path and I thanked her, hoping she was leading me to the others and not some trap.

The path led further into the woods and floating lanterns guided the way. My hand rested on my dagger firmly in its sheath, ready to wield my weapon if necessary. I doubted my skills with the dagger were much good, but they couldn't be worse than my archery.

Noises came from up ahead. My feet quickened to find the source. As I drew nearer to the sound the trees thinned out until they opened almost completely. A gathering of people stood in the clearing, laughing amongst each other.

Ronin stood on a wooden platform about a sheep's head above the others. Cera stood next to him with her arms crossed and a wide smile, her hair braided back. The people laughed at something, but their attention wasn't focused on Ronin. It was turned slightly to his right.

A tall tree stood with high branches. Attached to one of these branches was a rope that hung down low. The other side of the rope was wrapped around a man's ankles, dangling him upside down from the tree.

As I grew closer, I cursed.

Christopher.

What in the blazes was he doing here?

"Ronin, what are you doing?" I called out over the crowd. He spun his head in my direction and I saw a goofy grin on his face.

"Anika! Join us!" He waved an ecstatic arm.

"Let him down; he'll pass out." I pushed my way through the crowd to get to the platform. Children stood in the crowd, which I didn't find appropriate. None of them looked bothered, and I suddenly worried for what kind of people the Silver Raiders were raising.

"Fine with us," Cera grunted. Her smile lowered at the sight of me.

Christopher hung close to the ground, spinning slowly. A dirty rag tied tightly around his mouth, but he wasn't blindfolded. If he reacted to seeing me, I couldn't tell. All his strength went to attempting to straighten himself upright.

"I mean it, Ronin. Let him down. He's my friend."

"That doesn't make him our friend," Cera scowled.

"As the lady commands." Ronin took out a blade and dramatically held it up to the rope. I bolted to Christopher in time to push his back, so when he fell, he didn't land on his head. It didn't look like a pleasant fall, but I saved him from a nasty headache.

The crowd booed as I untied Christopher's hands from behind his back. I ignored their comments as he turned over and I ripped off his gag.

"Are you crazy?" he asked me as soon as he could speak. I leaned away from him in surprise.

"Excuse me? I saved you."

Christopher spat on the ground then wiped his mouth. "I knew you were mixed up with the Silver Raiders. Do you know how much trouble you could get in with the king? A noble being mixed up with this lot. Do you want to lose everything you've worked for?"

I furrowed my brow. In the corner of my eye I saw Cera grin, and that just made me angrier.

"She's not going to get in any trouble unless you get her in it," Ronin said, hopping down from his platform.

"I can take care of myself," I said. "It's not my fault you wandered in here."

"I wanted to know what interested you about these woods. Now I know." He looked between Ronin and me.

I crossed my arms. "I should have left you hanging up there."

Christopher snorted. "You never should have entered these woods."

Ronin walked by me and held up his hands to the crowd. "Alright, back to work lads." The crowd, though displeased, listened to Ronin and started to drift off. I stood up and crossed my arms.

"Thanks for tying me to a chair instead of to a tree," I whispered to Ronin. He laughed out loud.

"What do you suggest we do about your friend here?"

"I say we throw him in the river and be done with it," Cera suggested. Christopher leapt to his feet, his blue eyes wide.

"Can we vote on that?" he said. He wiped the dirt from his pants.

"He doesn't mean harm; I'm afraid I led him here in a way. I can take him back out."

Stepping into our circle, Christopher folded his arms and puffed up his chest. "I'm not leaving until I talk to your friend here." He turned his nose toward Ronin. "We have business to discuss."

"Oh, do we really?" Ronin asked with a frown. "You barge into my home and dare to make demands?"

"You've been prowling on people in my home. So yes, I came to yours to ask you to stop." The parallel between

Christopher's demand and my demand when I first came here struck me and I wondered how many others had wandered into these woods to ask them to stop. Annabeth told me I was the only one.

Ronin laughed as he peeked at me. "Did you put him up to this?" I shook my head. "Well then. My answer is no. I help people who come to me for help. You don't want them to come to me, maybe you should help them yourself."

"If you don't stop, I'm leading the king's army into this cursed forest to arrest you," Christopher threatened.

Cera scowled. "Try it. You don't know who is protecting us."

"Basiliea?" Christopher guessed. Cera, to her defense, didn't let her face give her away, but Ronin's did. His back straightened slightly, his eyes widened, and he glanced at me to see if I knew.

So it was true. He'd gotten himself mixed up with a dark sorceress.

"You think Basiliea is loyal? You think she can be controlled? You have no clue what fire you've awakened." I suspected that Christopher didn't know either. I knew everything that he knew about Basiliea, and it wasn't much.

"I can wield fire just fine. Happens to be a gift of mine," Cera said.

The word 'gift' snapped my attention. If Cera was from Westfallen then she had a Gift, something I hadn't heard mention of since moving here a year ago, other than Lady Claire's warning to me against them.

Every child in Westfallen was born with a unique Gift that granted them some sort of ability such as storytelling or turning apples to peaches on Saturdays, or changing the color of cloth from blue to scarlet. My Gift was the violin; I could play perfectly without having a lesson. It was a useless thing that I never used. Others boasted more helpful Gifts. In my home village, the Gifts were used practically to help get by day to day, but here, on the border between countries where one country had Gifts and the other didn't, the Gifts were seen as unpredictable and tainted with evil.

In the north, countries were alive with magic, but here it was hidden with great caution.

I wondered if Cera's Gift was wielding fire. That would be an extravagant Gift. Back home it was considered blessed if you could wield bread.

Ronin narrowed his dark eyes at Christopher with a dislike that I hadn't yet seen in him. It was strange how Christopher and I met Ronin under basically the same conditions, but he reacted to me much better than Christopher. He befriended me; he looked like he wanted to kill Christopher. If Christopher didn't leave soon, I suspected Ronin might try.

His eyes narrowed further. "You don't know anything about us. You don't know who we are working with or what we stand for. You have no right to come here and demand anything from us."

"I know you are enemies of the king. I know you are thieves and bandits. I know you have no morals."

Ronin clenched his fists and bared his teeth. Cera placed her hand over Ronin's and jutted out her chin as she spoke up. "We may be bandits, but at least we are trying to heal this land. All your people did was break it."

"The war broke it, not us. You are further tearing it apart with chaos. You are costing me everything!" Christopher's voice raised as I stared at them. For the first time in my life, I was the calm one of the group, which felt rather odd.

Unexpectedly, Christopher pivoted toward me. A green lantern behind me cast a glow over his face, making his anger look frightening. "And you! What are you doing here? The way to save your lands is through hard work, not banditry. There is no respect in that."

"Hey, don't drag me into this. I'm not a part of that." I took a step back.

"You are either with them or against them. There is no middle."

"What the lady does is her business. As for you, I think it's time you left," Ronin said. "The woods are no longer welcome to you."

"I got through the woods with no problem on my first try." Christopher looked proud of this, but Cera laughed.

"Because we allowed you to. The woods offered to let you through, and we accepted. Scores of men have come through before you and the Woods devoured them all. If you step foot within these trees again, you won't make it out alive, but feel free to test that."

I had thought Cera had taken my presence poorly, but the worst she did was blindfold me. She didn't banish me from the Woods. I wondered what it was about Christopher that was different enough from me to make them hate him.

Christopher's lips stretched in a thin line as his eyes flickered between the three of us. Finally, he dropped his shoulders. "Fine. It's out of my hands now. Whatever fate falls on you is of your own doing." He looked at me at the last part, and I felt it was directed more at me than the others. I ducked my head.

"I'll take you back out," I mumbled. "But I'll come back tomorrow; I still need to talk to you," I said to Ronin, who nodded at me.

Cera stayed put with her arms crossed as she glared at Christopher, waiting for him to leave her home. With a sigh, I turned around and led Christopher out.

"That was bold of you," I said once we were a distance away.

"I'm still upset at you," Christopher said.

"Oh, well at least you're honest," I mumbled. "Though I don't know why." I ducked under a branch and I put my walking stick into the ground.

Behind me, Christopher stopped walking. "You must be joking with me. You can't fathom why? I'll grant you one guess."

I sighed. "You guess for me."

"Because you're conspiring with the Silver Raiders, the people who steal from our friends and want to bring back an evil sorceress."

"We don't know she's evil, we only know she can bring people back from the dead," I pointed out as I turned to keep walking.

He laughed, but it wasn't a happy laugh. "They don't banish nice witches to these woods. There's evil in her, alright."

With a long sigh I paused. "She's bringing his son back." I twisted to face him and drove my stick into the ground harder than necessary. "Okay? Ronin had a son, and he needs Basiliea to bring him back to life. That's his motive for conspiring with her. And as long as you're so concerned about my welfare, I'm not a part of this. I've been vocal to them about my dislike for their stealing, and I don't participate in the shenanigans. In fact, I came to these woods to work my way in and put a stop to their lawbreaking."

Christopher stopped. "Is that so? Have you been successful in your endeavor?"

My tight jaw gave my answer. I had such good intentions going into this, but the line between what's right and what's wrong was blurry in Ronin's mind, and the Silver Raiders had good intentions. A criminal with good intentions was a difficult person to stand against.

Christopher resumed walking as he wiped sweat from his brow. The atmosphere hung heavy around us and my skirts dampened with perspiration. Just another part of this walk that felt uncomfortable.

After a short distance, Christopher spoke again. "I'm sorry he lost his son but bringing back Basiliea is going to bring back a lot more than his child. He's not going to like the ramifications."

"His son trumps all that in his mind. He doesn't care about anything else."

"What about Cera?" Christopher asked.

"What?"

"There's something about her that's familiar to me. What's her story?"

I raised an eyebrow at him. "She's just a strong-willed, bossy girl. I don't know anything more."

A thoughtful noise came from his throat. He stayed quiet for most of the trip back, until it came time for us to part directions. He grabbed my hands and looked into my eyes. "Anika, you need to be careful with them. There is strong magic in those woods, and they don't know what they are playing with."

His warning ran through my mind on my way home as I debated if I knew what I was getting myself into. My mama always said that my sense of adventure would be the ruin of me. Perhaps she had been right all along.

CHAPTER FOURTEEN

he candles provided little light as I knit in my bed that night. My promise to make a blanket for Mr. Bennet's daughter was made a month ago, and the blanket lay half-finished. The wool curled around my finger once as I looped it around. Knitting was a new skill that I acquired, and I was determined to put it to good use.

Occasionally I stopped to nibble on my cake next to me. It wasn't as good as the ice cream at the Carlstones' home, but it was thick and rich. Elenora it made in honor of her mother's birthday, even though her mother couldn't come to visit. I had little complaints about her spending her own money on desserts, pointless as the occasion may be. As long as she wasn't using her money to buy poison to kill me with.

I pushed the plate away. That was as much of her cake as I would be eating.

A tapping came at my window causing me to curse and drop my needles. I picked one back up, pulling it from the yarn to use as a weapon. The tap came again at the window to my right. I threw my feet off my bed and peered into the darkness.

With his dark skin, he blended into the night, but after a moment my eyes adjusted, and I made out Ronin's face. With my heart settling down from the scare, I opened the window.

"What are you doing?"

"You said you needed to talk?"

"At normal hours, not the middle of the blazing night!" I whispered. I peeked behind me at the door to be sure it was closed tight. I'd created an extra lock on my door with coarse yarn that tied the two handles together. If Elenora wanted in, she'd have to saw through that first.

"Well I'm here now, so may I come inside?" Ronin asked.

"Lady Claire is going to kill me." I pushed the window open enough for Ronin to crawl through. He brought a fair deal of mud with him, which I would have to clean later so Lady Claire didn't suspect anything.

"I have to say," Ronin said as he eyed my bed. "I didn't peg you as a knitting girl."

I blushed. "That's a blanket for a village infant." I wasn't sure why I was so quick to defend the hobby. The words felt conceited now that I had said them.

"Truly?" Ronin made an impressed noise. "Quite the selfless person, aren't you?"

I moved the knitting into a basket on the floor and pushed it under the bed. "Not usually," I admitted. "But I don't have much choice now. It's either that or lose my lands."

Ronin stayed standing as he looked over my room. There wasn't much there to look at. My small bed with light blue blankets was pushed against the stone wall. I hung another blanket against that wall, so it didn't feel so cold at night. On the opposite wall sat an ancient desk with curled legs and one drawer that held my stacks of paper and ink. It didn't get used as often as it should, but it looked like it couldn't withstand much more use. It wobbled as it was, causing me to do most of my writing on my bed.

My closet door was next to the desk. It was a large closet compared to what I had back home, and I doubted I would ever possess the clothes to fill it all. I had a rug in my closet, and another in the bedroom, giving my feet a break from the hard floors. The other two walls held my door and a window. I wish I could say my window overlooked gardens or a courtyard, but it didn't—it oversaw patchy, sharp grass cluttered with stubborn weeds.

"Did anyone see you on your way in?" I pressed my ear to my door to listen for footsteps, unsure of where I would hide Ronin if I did. I couldn't be sure that hiding him was the right choice; if he was found then it would look worse than if we hadn't tried to hide anything.

"No, I minded my footsteps. Are you against decorating? Not even a bookshelf or a vanity." Ronin took off his shoes to pace around the room. Apparently, he was staying a while.

"I don't have an eye for that stuff," I said. "It would look worse if I tried to decorate."

"Ah. I see." Ronin paused as he shifted the conversation. "You know, you don't have to lose your lands if you let us help your people."

When I first met Ronin, I didn't trust him. His bright smile and trusting demeanor appeared more of an illusion than the truth. But my opinion had changed now. He was nothing more than a man grieving the loss of his son by stealing from the ones he blamed in hopes to somehow make things right. Though I hadn't figured out how Basiliea fit into everything yet, it was clear that Ronin wished no harm against me.

And while I'd set out to take down the Silver Raiders, I now found myself wishing no harm against him either.

It was a strange situation I'd found myself in, and my morality was running wild with confusion, but I wasn't as lost as to accept his offer to join the Silver Raiders.

I sat on the edge of my bed. "I've been meaning to talk to you about that. I can't. I understand that you are doing it for good reasons, but it's wrong. Christopher is right, I need to build up my land the right way."

Ronin nodded his head slowly as he repeated Christopher's name. Then he was quiet for a second. "So, I came all this way to hear you say you don't want to join the Silver Raiders?"

"Actually, that's not what I wanted to talk about."

"No?"

"Basiliea."

"Oh." Ronin sat on the bed next to me. "How did you find out?"

I folded my hands on my lap. "It was more of a guess, really. It just made sense. I do have a few questions about her; how are you bringing her back to life?"

Ronin tipped his head back. "Well, she's not truly dead. She's simply not…complete. In order to reconnect her body with her soul she needs certain sacrifices." My eyes got big at the word sacrifice, but Ronin waved his hands.

"Not like that. It's hard to explain but I'll try. Let's

see…each person has a favorite thing, something they hold dearest of all. For many, this is their child. But for others it's an object. When we love something so much, a piece of our soul is anchored to it. Those are the sacrifices that we give to Basiliea, those parts of people's soul. With enough sacrifices, she will regain her soul, and her powers with it."

"So, when you steal from the lords, you are stealing objects, not money?"

Ronin laughed. I jerked my head toward the door to remind him to stay quiet. He mouthed an apology. "Oh no, we steal money too. But we target people with favorite items. Basiliea knows this of each person, so she tells us who to steal from."

For the first time, I was getting real information from Ronin. "How close are you to bringing her back?" I asked with eyebrows lowered.

He clicked his tongue. "It's tricky to tell, but I think we're getting close. We are planning a heist in a few months to steal from the king of Vestalin; that object should help us get there."

I think I followed. They stole from the rich nobility, who Ronin detested, acquired money for the struggling villagers, and aided the mysterious Basiliea, who would in turn bring back his lost son.

I've got the Silver Raiders figured out. But not Basiliea.

"Do you know why she wants to come back? Any secret evil motives that Basiliea might have?" I studied Ronin's eyes, wondering how thoroughly he had thought this over.

"If she brings Landon back, I don't care about anything else."

With his words, a chill ran up my spine. That was what I was afraid of. My heart would have to be cold to not wish for Ronin to get his son back, but my mind would have to be dull to think this was a good idea. We had no clue what evil Basiliea would bring with her.

But she would bring evil. There was a reason they banished her half dead to those cursed Woods in the first place.

"I trust her. I don't know why, but I do. She appeared to Cera in the Woods with the offer, and Cera brought the idea to me. You might think I'm blinded, but Cera is smart. She wouldn't do this if it wasn't a good idea."

His words furthered my concern and drew my brow inward. "What's Cera getting out of this?"

"Nothing. Just helping me out. She can be a good person, you know," Ronin said.

I looked away toward my desk. The idea that Cera was mixed up in this made me trust it even less. If Basiliea's ticket back to life was through Ronin's desire to get his son back, then she would have approached Ronin directly. Cera had to be getting something out of this deal for Basiliea to seek her out.

"What's Cera's story?" I recalled Christopher's fascination with her. He was confident he had met her somewhere.

Ronin hummed. "Her story isn't for me to share, but she has seen much heartbreak."

"Anyone she'd want back from the dead?"

Ronin's head was shaking before I finished talking. "Definitely not. She'd rather them stay dead."

There must be a story there, but Ronin wasn't willing to share it with me. I would snoop around for those details later, maybe pull from Jack again. I ran over the details again in my mind. Ronin gave me a lot of information tonight.

"Basiliea gave no indication as to what she will do when she is free?" I pressed.

Ronin sighed. "None. I don't know why you don't trust her."

"Her name is *Basiliea*. That's not the name of someone who picks flowers and knits blankets."

I thought I heard a noise. Ronin must have heard it too because he froze with his head looking toward the door. I whispered how old of a house it is, but still waited in anticipation to see if the noise belonged to a person.

Still looking at the door, Ronin whispered, "she's brining back my son. I don't care about the other details."

"You should probably go now," I whispered back. He looked at me for a few moments before nodding. He pushed off the bed and pulled on his shoes. Before leaving through the window, he turned to give me one last look.

"This Christopher, is he a friend, or something more?"

I shook my head. "Hardly even a friend."

Ronin bobbed his head a few times, looking at the floor. Finally, he said, "good," then lowered himself out from the window and disappeared into the thick cloak of night.

I closed the window once he was out of sight. My fingers felt too tired to knit anymore, but I couldn't find sleep. Instead, I stayed awake thinking of all the ways this deal with Basiliea could go very, very wrong.

CHAPTER FIFTEEN

My hands worked, but my mind remained distracted. As I weaved my hair into a braid, I felt as if my head spun with a thousand questions and worries piled up together, threatening to spill out and drive me mad. I fastened the end of my hair and leaned back into my creaking chair as I sighed with the burden of my thoughts.

A tenant farmer with a family of five had suddenly produced a large quantity of apple seeds, though we were weeks between markets. I demanded to know where he'd gotten them from, but he wouldn't say. He didn't need to; the answer was clear to me. The Silver Raiders assisted him. It was with a stricken heart that I helped him plant his new crops as I wondered which noble the funds had been stolen from to purchase those seeds.

The nobles have so much while the people have so little. I remembered what it felt like to starve; the numbness inside my stomach was a feeling I couldn't forget. But we worked hard, we didn't beg, and we pulled ourselves through. My Papa would never have condoned stealing.

But to save your child, was stealing okay? Was it okay to take from those who can spare, those who will not share, if it will feed your child? Is it more wrong to let your child starve if you can help them? Are your virtues worth your child's hunger? The moral dilemma pounded at my heart, drawing my forehead into wrinkles and my hands into twiddling.

I'd never be able to focus like this. Perhaps there was something I could do to ease my worries.

I grabbed the braided green necklace and slipped toward Elenora's room.

She wasn't there, but the strong scent of her perfume lingered in the room. All I needed to do was find the rest of this broken necklace, and I'd know for certain it was Elenora who attacked me.

Her rose colored jewelry box with flowers carved into the marble's side sat on her wooden armoire. My fingers reached for the latch, but they hesitated before opening it.

Elenora had been my one friend since moving here who, even though she didn't understand me, supported me. She knew I had no money and she knew my lands were struggling. She had nothing to gain from killing me. If I die, the manor goes to my sister, so she can't hope to claim it after I'm gone.

It made no sense. And yet, someone had attempted to murder me.

I must know if it was her. So I opened the chest.

"Anika."

Elenora's voice came from behind me and I dropped the lid and whirled around to face her. Her curls were pinned to her head, her lips painted, and her smile eerily sweet. She tilted her head at me as she came forward with steps that made no sound.

My heart raced within my chest as my mind scrambled for what to say to her while simultaneously looking for an escape route in case she attacked. I'd given her the opportunity for it.

With an innocent voice she said, "You aren't dressed yet! We leave shortly. The Yorks always serve this apple pudding which I'm sure you'll enjoy." She winked. What sort of person attempts to kill someone one night, then winks at them another?

At least she'd given me the excuse I needed. My fingers closed around the broken clasp behind my back. "I thought I'd wear jewelry tonight, but I haven't any. I'm sorry, I should have asked." With luck, my usual lack of manners would work in my favor.

I waited for her to be mad, or for her eyes to narrow and her to tell me she knew why I was really here and it's time we settled this, but instead her face lit up and she clapped her hands. "I thought you'd never ask! What color will you be wearing!"

"Um," this is something I should have known, but it took me a while to think. "Red, I believe."

"Strong color. What neckline?"

Neckline? "Er, it goes to here, I think." I pointed halfway down my chest, and she burst into laughter.

"I'll help you, you poor soul."

My body tightened as she approached, but she stepped around me and blocked the jewelry box from my sight. She grabbed something quickly then snapped the lid shut again. "Come along! I'll help make tonight one you'll never forget."

Perhaps it was the fear in my mind, but her words sounded darker than ever before.

The entire time she helped me sort out my attire—every time she brought her hand to my neck to mess with the jewelry—all I could wonder was if she was capable of murder, and how long it'd be before she struck again.

It was almost a relief when Lady Claire announced it was time to go to the ball.

"Are you not coming? I thought the Yorks were old friends of yours." This was one of the few events of the season that Lady Claire planned on attending, but her silk robe and slippers implied she'd changed her mind.

"I'm quite tired already and would rather stay home. But you girls go; you can't keep the driver waiting."

That would leave me and Elenora alone for the ride. My back stiffened as Elenora kissed Lady Claire's cheeks and beckoned for me to follow. The necklace around my neck suddenly felt as if it was choking me, and I struggled to gulp. "I think I'll stay here as well."

"Lady Anika, it'd be quite rude to not show after you said that you would. You're going." Her expression showed there was no room for argument here, and my eyes skirted between the two of them. Maybe they were in on this together, both plotting my ruin. "But you're not attending," I pointed out.

She clicked her tongue. "When you're older like me you can do such things. When you're young with a fragile place in the society, you attend every invite you receive." She ushered me out the door before I could argue further.

I sat as far away from Elenora as I possibly could before

the carriage lurched into motion. The sun dipped below the trees and cast a deep gold glow across the western sky, while behind us the sky darkened as the stars prepared to glow. I silently asked them to stay away as long as possible and leave the sun hanging in the sky. The more light in this carriage, the better.

Completely unaware of my discomfort, Elenora spoke of Berkley with enthusiasm as we rode. It seemed they had confessed feelings for each other last week and she was eager to see where the relationship led. He was set to inherit a small manor where she would live as the lady of the house, and that thrilled her. She hoped for an engagement soon. All I hoped for was to make it through this year alive.

The sky transformed into night by the time we reached the York's home, but Elenora had made no move against me and I breathed deeply again. The horses whinnied and the carriage bounced to a stop. A thin man with a wide nose reached his hand to help us step down and directed us to the ballroom. I practically flew from the carriage.

This wasn't our first time here this season; the Yorks celebrated another birthday earlier in the year. I lost at cards that night, but I planned to make up for it this evening.

As soon as we entered I steered for the cards, but Christopher caught my eye through the thin crowd. His dark suit coat draped over his arm and his other hand held a golden glass which he drank from in gulps. At the sight of me he lowered his glass and raised it again, nodding his head to invite me over.

I peeked toward the card room then back to Christopher. I could win at cards later.

"What's this?" Elenora gasped behind me. I turned quickly to see what the matter could be. She held her hand to her lips with her mouth open wide. "Something can get your attention away from cards? Oh, this is a wonder."

I laughed at her mockery. "Just stopping to say hello to a friend."

She raised her eyebrows at me and made a sound with a sly smile. I pointed out Berkley to her and all thought of me vanished from her mind as she practically skipped over to him.

She didn't have the look of a killer. If I didn't know she had a broken necklace, I never would suspect her, and part of me still didn't believe it. She was too pure.

That's what made her so dangerous. I couldn't figure out what she was thinking.

"I was hoping to see you tonight; I have news." Christopher appeared behind me, startling me. He placed a hand on my waist and led me to the side of the room. The deep color of his suit brought out the depth in his eyes, which brought out the nerves in me.

"I managed to find some more information on this Basiliea character," he said with a low voice. I leaned my head in eagerly. "She had a daughter. The girl was engaged to a man, but when they killed Basiliea they killed her daughter as well. Her daughter didn't have magic, so she's properly dead."

"Alright, so when Basiliea comes back, she will likely bring her daughter back. Does she pose some threat?"

Christopher's head shook. The hairs on his arm brushed against my skin as he twisted slightly to glance at the crowd, and when he brought his head back down toward me, his curls were close enough that I could see every defined hair. With him so close, I easily forgot about Elenora and my attempted murder. I could hardly remember my own name right now. "No, the daughter seems harmless. But the lad she was engaged to died shortly after and his lands went to a Jon Micheals, who died without an heir. As fate would have it, the next man to take over died without a child as well. His name was Lord Gregory."

I gasped. "My lands?"

Christopher nodded. "If Basiliea comes back, she will no doubt raise her daughter as well...and her fiancé if they were in love."

I tried to sort through the situation in my mind. "Would he put in a claim on my land?"

"Wouldn't you?" He shrugged and his hairs brushed mine again. "What I'd like to know is, would you be daft enough to face Basiliea for the sake of your land?"

My hand rested against my head and I cursed every word that I could think of. If Ronin brought Basiliea back, I'd likely lose my lands and would be sent back home to work at the Riverfront Tavern.

I cursed again.

Christopher licked his lips. "Has Ronin said anything more about his plans?"

"A bit. I know that Cera is the one who led him to Basiliea."

At Cera's name, Christopher's eyebrows drew down. "There's something so familiar about her. I wish I had more time with her to figure it out."

"I doubt you'd forget a character like her," I grunted. "I'll let you know if she says anything about you though."

He pursed his lips together as he thought for a moment.

Then he shook his head. "Well, anyway. Just wanted to inform you."

"I really appreciate it."

"Also, I haven't told anyone that you are associated with them, if you were worried about that."

I hadn't been, but now the possibility struck me and sweat formed on my palms. "I'm not *really* with them," I reminded him.

"But you have the opportunity to turn them in, and you've chosen not to," he pointed out. He shuffled his feet back and crossed his arms. "Is this Ronin more than a friend to you?"

The irony of them both asking that question about each other amused me. I shook my head twice. "Just a friend."

"I think he fancies you," he said bluntly.

"He doesn't know me well enough for that."

Christopher gave a small laugh. "There is such a thing as instant attraction, you know."

I peeked toward the card room. I should have gone straight there. This conversation took an uncomfortable turn. "He's several years older than me."

"So? So am I." My eyebrows raised at him, and his face turned slightly red. "I didn't mean it like that. I simply meant it wouldn't be an odd thing for him to fancy you. I just want you to be careful."

"I doubt even my parents have cautioned me as often as you have," I said. And I meant it. Christopher's persistent concern for my safety showed no signs of letting up.

He threw back his head with a laugh. "That's how much I mean it." His eyes drifted across the room over my shoulder. The song changed, and I took a moment to peek to where he was looking, but there were far too many people in the room for me to guess which one he was watching.

His eyes returned to mine. "It's not too late to turn them in. It'd be the right thing to do, and it'd secure your lands. There's a big reward on their heads."

Claiming the money from the reward and keeping my lands from Basiliea's daughter and her fiancé was enticing, but I couldn't turn on Ronin. I promised Christopher that I would think about it to ease his mind, then I let him go.

I watched him greet another guest, the same girl that held his attention so thoroughly at the Thames's party. She said something and he threw his head back in a full laugh, just as he'd done a moment before with me. A small twinge of jealousy nipped at my heart, but I pushed it aside and pivoted toward the card room.

Freddy waited like a tiger, prowling outside the door. I spun back around so he wouldn't know I'd spotted him and redirected my attention toward the dessert table. A good tartlet was exactly what I needed right now.

Deep in thought, I sat in a chair by the door to the gardens enjoying my strawberry tartlet and the smell of the outdoors as I avoided Freddy.

"Still not at the cards?" Elenora fanned out her wide blue dress and leaned into the chair next to me. My instincts went to checking her hands for a blade and our surroundings for suitable witnesses should she try anything. But Elenora remained as composed as ever with her hands crossed on her lap and her eyes glazed over with the excitement of the room. I began to suspect her of having multiple personalities, and the one that she displayed now was nothing more than a proper lady of the court. I sighed—my mind weary from constantly being on alert.

"Freddy sighting," I explained to her.

She giggled, then her expression turned serious. "Berkley hasn't been at the cards in a while, I suspect for me. I hope he doesn't resent me for it." Her gaze trailed her suitor from across the room where he spoke with an older gentleman with a short beard. At the same moment he glanced to Elenora and they shared a grin.

"I doubt he will. His heart never appeared that into the poker game anyway. I suspect it was more about making friends than betting on cards."

"Hope you're right." She looked so happy as she watched him with fawning eyes and a big smile. No doubt she was in love, and I hoped Berkley stayed true to her. If she wasn't a killer, that is. I'd hate to be the one to tell him what his sweet Elenora was capable of. I peeked to her, but she remained entirely focused on Berkley and disinterested in me.

Once again, doubt pinched me. Elenora might not be my attempted killer.

It could be anyone. They could be in this room. It was impossible not to scan the faces and hope to find a clue among them: a looming glare upon me, a dagger buried in the pocket of a skirt, a persistent figure over my shoulder. But the room kept its secrets well and I earned nothing besides the knowledge that I would soon go mad.

To find relief, I searched for Christopher. He was still talking with that girl. I poked Elenora, "Who is that?"

She followed my finger. "With Christopher? That's Alissia. She's his fiancée."

"What?" My mouth hung open. He hadn't mentioned a

beautiful fiancée to me. Then again, we hadn't talked about much besides Ronin and the Silver Raiders. Still, a part of me felt deceived.

Elenora's smile disappeared. "I'm sorry, I thought everyone knew. Did you like him?"

I shook my head harder than necessary. "No, it's not like that. I just didn't know." My eyes wouldn't leave the pair of them, standing close as they talked with oversized smiles on their faces. "When's the wedding?"

"Not sure. She keeps to herself a lot, so no one really knows much. They've been engaged for a long time though."

I didn't want to appear too interested, so I tore my eyes away and stopped asking questions. Elenora's gaze remained on mine for a few moments as she tried to read my thoughts. She wouldn't find anything. I held no secret feelings for Christopher.

I did have feelings about being murdered, however. And losing my home to a sorceress's dead daughter's fiancé, so I turned my attention back to those problems. Since I wouldn't discover my attacker unless they jumped at me tonight, the other dilemma intimidated me less and I focused my thoughts there.

I spent most of the night mulling it over and came up with no good solution. Finally, I decided the best thing to do would be to bring it up with Ronin to see if he had any ideas. There was no point in bringing myself to the point of madness if someone could help me. He had told me he didn't know her plans, but maybe once I informed him of what this could mean for me, he would ask Basiliea for more information about her intentions. It would do him good to investigate her a little better; his blind trust was unnerving.

If he didn't, I was going to seek Basiliea out and demand to know for myself. The sitting around and waiting for something to happen to me would get me nowhere. I wouldn't let someone take my life. And I wouldn't lose my lands to a sorceress from the Woods.

CHAPTER SIXTEEN

"We need to talk."

Cera waited outside the camp with her knives strapped to her sides and her shirt tight enough to show her biceps. I held myself back as she hopped off her log.

"If you think about betraying Ronin, or leading anyone into these woods, we will know. If you bring guards in to collect a ransom, we will have enough time to escape. The Woods protect us from all dangers, including you, and there is no way to sneak up on us. But if you still try to stand in our way, I will hunt you down and kill you. Am I clear?" She snarled, as if I was the main threat to her people.

My mouth felt dry. I'd never encountered another girl with this much fire in her. Cera waited patiently for my answer, her eyes staring into me like daggers.

I had no desire to fight with her. "Clear." She turned to leave but I stopped her. "What's in this for you?"

"Keeping my people safe."

"I'm talking about Basiliea. What is she offering you?"

Cera offered a rare smile, but it was more feral than friendly. "You think you have this all figured out. You have no idea. This is bigger than you, and you don't belong as a part of it."

"I know that she must be offering you something. Does Ronin know?"

Her smile left her face as she spat her words at me. "That's my business." She turned sharply and headed into camp with a pace that was difficult to match, but my questions weren't done, and her rough mannerism didn't intimidate me.

"Do you know Christopher?"

A snort came from her throat. "That foul chap you led here this week?"

"Yes, did you know him before he came?" My pace quickened in attempt to catch a glimpse of her face. She kept it blank and stayed silent.

Finally, she said, "No," and walked faster.

There was hesitation there that gave a different answer. What ties did Cera have to Christopher?

Disappointed in my lack of answers, I let it go. She said nothing more on the walk until we reached the top of the trail outside the camp lines, then she put her hands on her hips and peeked over her shoulder. "I meant what I said. If you betray him, I will kill you." Then she strolled into camp.

I waited a few moments before following after her.

The intentional choice of the word *him* over *us* stuck out to me. She didn't say if you betray *us*—she said *him*. I wondered for the first time if Cera had feelings for Ronin, and that's where she got her disdain for me from. Did she see me as a barrier between her and Ronin? It was hard to imagine the tall girl with narrow eyes and thick biceps harboring romantic feelings for anyone. Still, it wasn't impossible.

"She just can't stay away! Hard to resist my charm, eh?" Ronin and Jack came out of a tent and strode toward me, both with a different expression. Ronin's face was bright with happiness while Jack looked grim; I wondered what they had been talking about just now to make Jack's forehead crease like that.

Ronin's rolled up sleeves revealed a long cut running along the forearm toward the elbow. He caught me looking at it and pulled his left sleeve back down to cover it. "Comes with the territory." He shrugged. I looked Jack over to see if he had any cuts as well, but if he did, he kept them hidden. I tried not to worry about what trouble Ronin had been getting himself into.

"Did you give one of my farmers apple seeds this week?" I asked.

Ronin held up his hands. "You say it like we are giving them weapons to revolt against you with! We are giving them food. We are strengthening your lands. You can't be mad about that."

"How much are you taking from the nobles?"

"Nothing they miss," Jack grunted behind Ronin.

"They notice. Of course they miss it. You are making the nobles cling more tightly to their money. Their generosity toward the people is stifled because of the awareness that they will be stolen from. The people will suffer from this decrease which will drive them to you. In turn, the nobles will seal their purses to preserve any money they can. You are crippling this country by creating the need for an illegal middleman."

Ronin folded his hands and laughed. "Don't you ever just say hello?"

"Hello."

Another laugh. "Very nice. And I've already come up with a solution to that problem. Come see?" He gestured to the large, golden tent that he and Jack just came from. Shame suddenly filled me for accusing him of not thinking things through. He led me toward the tent while Jack veered off to go check on Annabeth. Ronin gave him a wiggle of his eyebrows before he left, and Jack laughed.

"Alright, come on in." Ronin held up the edge of the tent for me to duck inside.

The circular golden tent was built with wooden frames and a high roof. Two tables sat in the middle parallel to each other. One held a large map, while the other was scattered with papers. A lantern was set on each table to provide enough light to see the papers.

Ronin approached the messier table and rifled through the papers. I kept my distance to respect the privacy of whatever the papers said, but every part of me wanted to go through everything. I wondered if answers about Basiliea lay in this room.

"Here." Ronin handed me a piece of paper with scribbly writing on it. I wondered if it would be too impolite to ask him to read it for me. My reading was weak, and the writing was terrible.

Struggling, I made it through a few sentences before Ronin spoke. "See?"

"I'm not sure that I do," I said, squinting at the page.

"Can you not read?"

I gave a small laugh. "I can read, but whoever wrote this can't claim to write well."

"I wrote that." Ronin snatched the paper back, but he didn't look offended. He wore his goofy grin through everything. I wondered where he got his happiness from, after life took both his wife and son away from him.

Ronin held up the paper dramatically and said, "It's a contract for the nobles. We will not steal from them if they promise to give a certain amount back to the villagers. That amount will differ for each noble. If we find they aren't providing for their people, then we will come back and steal from them again. This agreement will take us out of the equation, if everyone agrees to it."

"How will you get them to sign it? You can't walk into the manors and hand it to them." I hoped he didn't ask me to do it for him; I didn't want to tell him no.

"I suppose we can't. Our current plan is to sneak in at night and leave it for them, including directions on where to send it back. The idea of ridding their lands of the Silver Raiders should be too good to pass up."

I hoped he was right. Peace filled me at the idea of Ronin giving up his outlawed ways.

In Ronin's head, this would all work out perfectly. The nobles would sign, the villagers would be helped, he would bring back Basiliea and have his son back. They would settle into a village together and everything would be perfect. With all my heart I hoped that things worked out for him. I wanted him to be happy. I wanted him to have his son. I wanted that big smile on his face to never falter.

Ronin's heart was so big. Even in his attempt to bring back his son, he was determined to help others along the way. He could put his entire focus into getting the prized objects to restore Basiliea faster, but he didn't want to get his son back while turning a blind eye to others' needs. He was kind, and smart, and compassionate. Handsome too.

But if Ronin got his son back, Basiliea would get her daughter back, and somewhere along the way they would take back their lands. I would lose everything. Ronin achieving his dreams meant that I lost mine.

Ronin grabbed his bow and invited me back to the river where children played in the banks, testing their toes in the water and squealing with delight when it lapped up close to them and splashed their knees. A few women sat atop rocks at the water's edge, keeping a careful eye on the joyful children. The shallow water moved slowly, and the children were well above the age of learning to swim, but the women kept a watchful eye all the same.

It was here that we stopped to shoot. Ronin positioned us near the children, so our arrows flew away from them, striking against a torn plank of wood with a white circle drawn lopsided on it. I thought of joking about the uneven circle, but I had made fun of his handwriting once already today, and it did no good to poke fun a second time.

Even though the trees separated here, providing a clearing by the water, overhead the branches still reached to meet each other, forming a barrier that blocked the sun. Silver and green spheres floated around us, gathering near the arrows as if they knew extra light was needed. I almost wished they would move away, so my terrible shots would be concealed by darkness, but Ronin would know how poorly I had shot when he went to retrieve the arrows.

After several rounds we moved on from archery to throwing knives, where I was pleased to find I possessed more skill in the trade. Still not impressive, or even good enough to be considered fair, but I was decent. I didn't fear for the knife missing the target and hitting something else; the knives stayed straight and hit the board almost every time. Ronin praised me, but when he threw his knives it was clear that my skill looked childish in comparison.

"You really should join us," Ronin said as we brought the knives back from the board.

"Based on my showcase here? I'd be the laughingstock of the group." I handed the knives back to him and planted myself down on the ground with my legs crossed. The water trickled behind us, mixed with the sweet sound of children's laughter.

"We don't use weapons in our heists. We try to avoid people if possible." Swiftly, Ronin threw his knives. They struck one after another, *crack crack*, into the wooden plank. Satisfied, he fetched them back again.

I remained on the ground, leaning back on my elbows as I watched him. It was hard to deny that I had thought about living here. The freedom of the Woods. The safety. Both things that I longed for. If I'd come here without my lands to care for, I'd live here happily.

But it was more than a charming camp. It was stealing. It was anger toward the nobles. It was lies. It was a deal with Basiliea. It was a ransom offer from the king. "I just can't bring myself to be an outlaw."

Ronin was quiet for a moment. "You surprise me. You seem like the kind of girl with a free spirit, who doesn't care what anyone else thinks."

I leaned on my hands. "There is a difference between not caring what others think and not wanting to *go to jail*."

He laughed that big laugh of his, twisting his head down to grin at me. Something in my heart fluttered at his smile. I quickly turned my head away so he wouldn't see me blush.

I distracted myself by watching the children play as my heart settled. When I felt composed, I peeked back up at Ronin.

There it was again: the subtle tug at my heart. Being here, surrounded by children playing and mothers laughing, no one worrying about food or having a home, just living free in the Woods, made my heart yearn. Being here with Ronin felt like home.

Selfishly, I couldn't bring myself to stay away. My soul felt free here. The pressures of life melted away in the mystery of the forest, and the soft light of magic in the trees calmed my worrying mind. Here, among the free-spirited folk of the Woods of Silver and Light, I felt alive. That was a feeling that I wasn't eager to let go of, and I would cling to it with all my sanity.

It didn't make sense, but these Woods felt safe to me. For a little while, just for today, I allowed myself to enjoy the evening and pretend that this was my life, that I lived here in the magical woods and didn't have a stiff manor to return to at the end of the day.

CHAPTER SEVENTEEN

rip, drip, drip. The subtle rain tapped against the window, streaking the glass and pooling on the sill. It was as if the sky was mourning for me, and I felt its condolences. I felt like crying too. This was cruel and unfair. Today brought misery upon me.

Today, I was to be fitted for a new dress.

"Ow! I swear, I will take that from you." I looked down at the seamstress and pointed my finger at her pins. I had threatened her one too many times; she was no longer fazed by my accusations.

"If you don't move, it'll go faster." Annoyance dripped in her tone.

"If I don't move, the pins will pierce me." My own annoyance was evident.

"They're already poking you," Elenora cut in.

"They would pierce me *harder*." I glared at Elenora. This was all her idea. Apparently, the prince wouldn't find any of my old dresses appropriate, because somehow, he would know that I have worn them all before. No, I needed a new dress with no stains or tears or signs of wear. Heaven forbid that I wear my clothes.

"If you didn't insist on walking through mud, then we wouldn't have this problem," Elenora so kindly pointed out. This is how she planned to kill me. With dress fittings. She stood still as a marble statue as the seamstress pinned fabric around her. I vividly recalled getting my measurements taken a few months ago, but Elenora told me that sizes easily change. That was her nice way of telling me that I've been eating too many sweets at parties. My body wasn't used to eating so well; even with my rationing of food I was still eating better than I had while growing up and it was starting to show. Not that I minded, I needed all the protection I could get from mean seamstresses and jarring needles.

The Prince's ball remained several months away, so I expected Elenora to dutifully remind me not to change my measurements in the meantime.

The seamstress prodded at me again, and I cursed richly.

"Oh!" She started, dropping her needle. Elenora raised her eyebrows at me, but I wasn't sorry.

"Lady Anika, darling. That is not the language of a lady." Lady Claire chose the perfect time to enter the room. I might have suppressed my words if I knew she stood around the corner. I mumbled my apologies.

"You will thank us when you see the dress," Lady Claire said. I couldn't tell if she meant that as encouragement or a demand that I thank them later. Something about her tone suggested the latter. If this dress wasn't coming from Elenora's generosity, I wouldn't have consented. There was no reason I could find to justify spending money on a new dress when my manor was in such a state.

A hard thud came from our doorknocker. All heads turned in unison, and while I took several eager steps off my platform, Lady Claire held up her hand.

"You stay, I'll go see to it."

She just heard me curse, so I held my tongue back from doing it again. The seamstress promised me that she was almost done. She lied. It took her several minutes before she freed me from my bondage.

Released at last, I ventured out into the corridor to go see who had come to the door. We didn't get visitors often. My bare feet patted along the floor while my nose picked up a hint of something glorious cooking. Elenora and her chef would be greatly missed when this season ended.

The front room was down the corridor then to the left, but I heard Lady Claire speaking before I turned the corner.

"Don't come at this time of day again. It isn't safe."

That sentence would have stopped anyone. I don't care how pious one claimed to be; when you hear that, you stop and eavesdrop. I was no saint; I was planning to eavesdrop anyway, but that sentence piqued my curiosity.

My body pushed against the wall and I dared a peek around the corner, praying that Lady Claire was facing the door and not me. Luck blessed me. She stood with her back to me and arms up, almost as if they were crossed. I don't know if I have ever seen her arms crossed. I had to see who she was upset with. Only the shoulder and arm of the person could be seen, dressed in black. Lady Claire wasn't much taller than me, so still technically on the short side. The visitor was much taller, but already backed out of the door and down a step so their height fell below Lady

Claire's. I could see a fair amount of muscle on the shoulder hidden beneath the clothes, so either a strong female or a slender toned male.

A handsome suitor for Lady Claire?

The door shut and locked before my prying eyes could get another look.

Rapidly, I retraced my steps down the corridor then started walking back again, so I was halfway down when Lady Claire came around the bend. Her eyes widened ever so slightly at the sight of me, but she recomposed herself quickly.

"Who was that?" I hoped my tone was flat as I asked, not too curious.

"Nothing to concern yourself with," was her sneaky reply.

"Ah. A mysterious visitor?"

She wagged her finger in a very un-Lady Claire gesture. "Unless you want me bringing up *your* mysterious night-time visitor, I suggest you leave it be."

I lacked the ability to recompose myself as well as Lady Claire. She knew that Ronin had visited in the night. Embarrassment washed over me, and I longed to tell her that it was innocent in nature, but I was too stunned by her knowledge of the fact to know what to say for myself.

She nodded her head. "Very well then. Good day."

My feet held me planted in place as she walked around me. I debated running after the visitor to find out who it was, but that felt childish. I wasn't sure which shocked me more: the fact that Lady Claire knew of my midnight visitor and said nothing, or that she had a secret of her own. I hadn't forgotten how someone broke into the manor and she hadn't been upset about it.

She was turning into quite the puzzle.

One thing was for certain, my mind was filled with too many of my own secrets and worries to properly solve the mystery of Lady Claire.

I RECOUNTED THE STRANGE ENCOUNTER WITH Lady Claire to Christopher who leaned forward in his chair, clutching his drink with both hands as he ran his thumbs along the brim. His eyes were steady on the dance floor, looping around with the turns of the dance, but I knew his ears remained open to me. Every so often he would make a noise or lift his eyebrow, signaling that I still held his attention.

"And she didn't explain herself?" His head turned at last to look at me. I had one leg crossed over the other, sitting sideways in my chair that sat against the wall, so my back could lean up on the stone while I looked at Christopher.

"No, she asked that I let it go."

"I'm surprised you didn't push her about it. Not like you to drop something so easily," he commented.

My eyes ducked to my drink. I wasn't willing to share the part about my scandalous midnight visitor, however innocent in nature it had been. "It makes her seem more human somehow, like she could be capable of some big dark secret. In likelihood, it's probably nothing."

"If it was nothing, she wouldn't have hidden it. Golly Anika, how do you always get wrapped up in such big mysteries? Outlawed bandits, strange visitors..."

"I'm not *wrapped up* in anything. I could walk away from the Silver Raiders any time I'd like."

He grunted, turning his eyes back to the dancers. "Something tells me you can't."

Christopher took a swig of his drink then wiped his mouth with his wrist. "I'm losing all patience with your friend Ronin. The Beckhams, kind folks who have lived on our lands for generations, moved away this week. They've been some of our family's closest friends, but they feel they are bringing shame upon their family by living so close to the Woods, as if people associate them with those trees. Harvest season is approaching, and we won't easily find new tenants to move so close to the Woods, not as long as the Silver Raiders run wild within them."

He took another swig of his drink, obviously upset over the situation. His eyebrows hung low and he stared through his lashes at the dancers.

I felt his frustration. His lands weren't struggling in the way that mine were, but a vacant tenancy would lead to a loss of money, and from the way he spoke it sounded like more families might be leaving his lands in the future. It was a dangerous pattern for his tenants to fall into, each turning one by one from suspicion of the Woods, packing their bags and fleeing their homes. He would be ruined. Christopher would lose everything if his people left his land.

Christopher's eyes shifted and I followed the gaze to his fiancée across the room. Alissia dressed tonight in a soft gold dress that hugged her waist and fell straight to the floor. Gold bands circled her wrist and a matching necklace draped over her neck.

She was breathtakingly beautiful.

"You should probably go." I straightened myself if my

seat, not wanting Alissia to catch a glimpse of us talking and come to the wrong idea.

"You have people to beat in cards?" He looked at me with a grin, but I groaned.

"There is no card room here."

"Oh, then why—"

"I don't want anyone getting the wrong idea about us." I nodded my head toward Alissia as I stood up with my empty glass. Christopher stood up next to me and looked in the direction I nodded, scanning the people as if he didn't know who I was talking about. Alissia wasn't looking our direction, instead she was caught up in conversation with another girl that I couldn't name.

"Right then. I wouldn't want to make you uncomfortable," Christopher said.

"Or Alissia," I added. I gave him a slight curtsy before turning away. His face looked puzzled, but I couldn't figure out why. He waited a moment before crossing the room to join his fiancée, while I located a new corner and fresh glass of wine and spent the rest of the evening making small talk amongst tall gentlemen with thick accents and prim manners.

While speaking with one of these gentlemen, they narrowed their eyes and stared out the window behind me. "Do you see that?"

I peered into the dark, but saw nothing besides the fields. He grunted. "Must have been nothing. But I was sure there was someone outside watching through the window."

He discounted it easily, but it left a chill on my back that couldn't be forgotten.

• • •

ONE EYE OPENED INTO DARKNESS, THEN THE other. Lately I found myself easily awoken by noises and had such a difficult time falling back asleep. This particular night I sat up to fetch my water from the bedside table when my skin went cold.

The door was slightly ajar.

I'm certain I left it closed with the yarn locked around the handles.

The only way it could be open is if someone tried to get in. As my eyes began to adjust to the night, they spotted the frayed ends of the thick yarn.

Someone tried to cut their way in.

My heart sped up and my body woke fully as the magnitude of this discovery came upon me. The killer was back. My hands slid under my pillow to retrieve the newly sharpened dagger hidden beneath and I settled back into bed with the blade clutched close and an eye on the door.

Then came a scratching noise like wood sliding against paneling, and a click.

They were coming through the window.

If I moved now, I'd scare them away. I needed to let them get closer before I jumped from bed, but every muscle in me screamed to move. Soft sounds came as the figure brought themselves through the window. With my eyes facing the door, I couldn't know how fast they would come toward the bed.

I couldn't wait any longer. I threw back the blankets and jumped from the bed.

The figure startled and let out a curse with a voice that was definitely female, though I couldn't place it. I raised my knife, but they had no interest in fighting. If I'd waited longer before moving they would be closer, but right now they were still by the window, and it took them two seconds to get back out. Their feet hit the ground and they started running with unbelievable speed.

They wouldn't get away this time.

I ran to the window and threw myself out, rolling on the ground. By the time I got back up, they'd already mounted a horse and were riding away. With little option left, I called out for them to stop, but they didn't turn and they didn't slow.

So I stood in the dirt with my knife in my hands, no closer to finding out who wanted me dead.

"Anika, is that you? What on earth are you doing?" Elenora's window opened as she poked her head out the window. Her voice made me jump and looked between her and the rider with both shock and relief.

"Are you alright?" she asked. "And who was that?"

It took me a moment to answer as my mind felt thick with questions. Elenora wasn't the one trying to kill me. Someone else was. Someone female.

"Come back in before Lady Claire finds you out here."

"I will. I'm sorry for waking you. You can go back to sleep."

With my head still in a daze, I climbed back through the window and shut it tightly. They'd stuck a knife through to break the lock, and now I'd need a new one. Blast. Tomorrow I'd follow the footsteps and see if I could figure out who wanted me dead. Then they would pay.

CHAPTER EIGHTEEN

There were two mysteries on my hands. Who wanted me dead, and who was visiting Lady Claire. The rain came during the night and washed away the hoofprints of the horse so they couldn't be tracked, leaving me with nothing more than guesses. Cera was at the top of my list, but it still made no sense.

So I turned my focus to Lady Claire's visitor. Now suspicious, I stored every action performed by her away in my brain to mull over later. When she hummed, perhaps it was a mystery suitor making her giddy. When she jumped at a closing door, perhaps she was in some sort of trouble, and the visitor was an agent sent to remind her of her debts. When she stared at a painting too hard, maybe she had an unquenchable love for art, and the visitor had come to show her more.

My ideas were getting ludicrous.

Whatever the story, my mind had created hundreds of possibilities. Surely one of them was right. I couldn't think of any more suspicious activities that she could have gotten involved with. My mind even toyed with the idea that she was mixed up with Basiliea, and maybe that was Basiliea herself at the door. But no, what could an ancient sorceress want with Lady Claire?

Now that it was in my mind, I couldn't get the idea out. To save myself from constant stress, I decided to search for more answers.

"Have you ever lost anyone that you love?" I asked Lady Claire. She sat in the chair beside me as she read her book by the light of the sunrise. It was her love of books that first connected her with my sister, and it was that same fact that alienated her from me. Instead of a book, I held work papers in front of me, scattered with the crumbs of my crumpet. I'd wound my hair up that morning, but one pesky piece kept falling down by my ears, no matter how tightly I pinned it back up.

Lady Claire looked up from the book with her eyebrows knitted in. She dropped the book on her lap. "Did someone in your family die?"

"No no," I hadn't realized she would think that from my question. "They are all in good health."

"Good. Lady Cosette would have made such a good lady of the court had she stayed." She picked back up her book.

The slight insult in her words was not lost on me, but I moved past it. "But have you ever lost someone, who you wish you had back?"

If she was working with Basiliea, I worried that the specificness of my question would flag her, but her face gave away nothing. She thought for a moment before replying, "Both of my parents have passed, but it was their time. I've been very lucky."

Once more the book was raised to her nose as a barricade from my questions. I studied her for a few moments more before giving up. Hadn't I told myself that I wouldn't get wrapped up in whatever she was hiding? Then a week later I go marching in trying to solve the puzzle. My excitement over the mystery made me forget that there's a chance she was hiding nothing; this could be a waste of my attention.

I had enough on my mind without prying into her life.

Disappointed with the lack of results, I settled back into the couch with my papers and left Lady Claire alone.

A knock at the door interrupted us. I sprang from my seat, knocking my papers everywhere, determined to find who was at the door before Lady Claire could stop me. She spoke my name, but I raced from the room too fast to be stopped. Just as I settled to leave the matter alone, the chance at another clue got me all excited again. I flung myself around the corner and toward the door in antic-ipation.

When I pulled open the door, my disappointment read all across my face.

"Where you expecting someone? I'm sorry to disap-point you?" Christopher stood behind the door, with his arms crossed as he looked at me.

"What are you doing here?"

He laughed. "Anika, your manners need work. Berkley wanted to see Elenora and I came along for the *charming* company."

"Oh, you wanted to see Lady Claire?" I joked.

"At least she'd pretend to be excited to see me."

"I thought you might be her visitor from the other day," I confessed to him. He tilted his head back then slowly let it drop again. Behind him, Berkley was leading the horses to the small stable after unlatching the carriage.

"In that case, I'll try not to be offended."

"I haven't seen Elenora yet this morning, but I can go fetch her—" As I turned around Elenora was walking through the entryway to see us, her smile stretched wide.

Now that I knew she wasn't the one who tried to kill me, I felt silly for ever thinking so. She hadn't the physical strength to stab through my pillow or kick me across the room. She didn't have the temperament for murder, nor the motive. And she'd never be caught wearing green, she only owned rosy colors.

My suspicions of her were satisfied, and even though I'd never thought of us as terribly close, it was a weight off my heart to have our friendship back. Perhaps one day when this is over, if the idea of someone sneaking into the manor with a knife wouldn't frighten her too badly. I'd tell her of the story, and we'd have a good laugh.

I had to catch the killer first.

"Christopher! I didn't expect see you this morning!" She embraced him in an eager hug as she looked over his shoulder to search for Berkley. By how she was dressed, she might not have expected Christopher, but she certainly knew company was coming over. I looked like a dinner rag next to her.

"Lady Elenora, you look beautiful," Christopher kissed her hand politely. She placed a delicate hand on her blonde curls and beamed as she thanked him.

"There she is!" Berkley bounded up the stairs and swept Elenora up in a hug. She laughed with glee until he set her down again. Giddy, she led us into the sitting room.

Lady Claire raised an eyebrow at the group of us but didn't say anything more.

Berkley and Elenora sat close on the couch, turned in toward each other so it was obvious the conversation was meant for just the two of them, despite their loud volume. That left three options: talk to Lady Claire, talk to Christopher, or resume my work.

I crossed my legs and picked back up my papers.

"What are you doing?" Christopher sat by me on the couch and looked over my shoulder. I sighed as I lowered my papers.

"I should let you know, that is one of my least favorite qualities about a boy: someone who looks over my shoulder."

"Good thing I'm not a boy," he said. I turned and gave him a puzzled look. He grinned. "I'm a man."

I rolled my eyes, but a small smile gave me away. He laughed. "But really, out of all the qualities, that's one of your least favorites? What about eating with their mouth open or being self-centered?"

I shook my head. "Those are too obvious, of course no one likes those. But specific qualities, yes, I don't like a lurker."

"Well I wouldn't call reading over your shoulder the same thing as lurking, but noted. No lurking."

"Thank you." I fluffed out my paper and resumed reading. Christopher stayed quiet for a few moments. Lady Claire ended up abandoning the room in search of a quieter place, leaving us behind with the sound of Elenora's chipper voice mixed with the bird's morning songs drifting through the windows. The sweet smell of breakfast wafted through the air, causing my stomach to grumble. The crumpet I'd snuck from the kitchen this morning did little to satisfy me. I rubbed the edge of the paper with my thumb, distracting myself from my hunger as I navigated the complicated page.

"Dishonesty," Christopher said.

"What?"

"That's one of the things that turns me away from a girl. Dishonesty."

"Again, everyone dislikes that. No one enjoys being lied to."

"Not everyone dislikes it as much as I do."

Another knock came at the door, loud and quick. The hand backed off long enough for us to look at each other in surprise before coming down on the door again. Bang bang bang... bang bang bang bang.

"That sounds urgent." Elenora looked out the window to see if she could catch a peek of the visitor with the demanding knock. I knew she couldn't; the window wasn't at the right angle. I discarded my papers, certain that my work would take all day at this point. The four of us paraded out into the corridor to see who had come to the door. Lady Claire got there first and pulled back the handle to welcome the visitor.

An elderly man in plain, loose clothes stood in the doorway panting. He put his hand to his chest when he saw Lady Claire.

"Barrow, what are you doing here?" Lady Claire welcomed him in as a friend, but he didn't cross the threshold. His face was white and his eyes were wide. The sweat on his forehead sparkled in the sun. I was about to turn to get him some water when his voice caught me.

"There's been a murder."

We all froze, breaths in our throat. What are the odds that on the same night someone attempted to kill me, someone else would be killed? That as I was chasing the intruder, someone else was fighting for their life?

Everyone that I knew well in society was here in this room, but I still caught my breath as I waited for him to say who. Lady Claire clutched her chest and took a step back, as if this Barrow brought trouble with him.

The questions came not long after, sometimes one by one and other times all at once. Barrow finally moved in from the doorway and shook his head as he answered each question. His shoulders slumped with the grief. Poor man —he looked traumatized.

"It was last night, in the cloak of darkness that the night brings. Over at the Thames home, they snuck in like the thieves they are. Quiet as a fox, they couldn't be heard. Or so they thought, but they wandered too close to Lord Thames's room, and he came out to see. That's when he was taken. When his manservant came to check on the noise, they killed Lord Thames and ran off."

Lady Claire kept her hand tight on her chest, and Elenora ducked into Berkley. He wrapped his arms protectively around her as if he could shield her from the horrors of the story.

"But who would do this?" Christopher asked. The man looked him right in the eye as he answered.

"The driver saw. T'was the Silver Raiders."

For the second time that morning, my heart stopped. This time it took longer to restart.

"Are you certain?" I stammered, licking my lips. Christopher shot me as look as if this was somehow my fault, but I wouldn't meet his eye.

Barrow nodded. "Aye. The driver said there was no mistake; he saw their masks. The ransom will be raised on them for sure."

Lady Claire asked about his family as Christopher grabbed my elbow and pulled me to the side. He crossed his arms and looked at me with dark eyes.

"Cut them loose," he hissed at me.

"What?"

"You need to stop all contact with the Silver Raiders. You can't be associated with them now. Forget anything else, if you are found to be in their company, you will lose a lot more than your lands. You will lose your life."

I shook my head, causing that pesky piece of hair to fall loose again. "They didn't do this. They have no reason to do this."

Christopher raised his eyebrows at me. "You don't know why they do what they do."

"I do, actually. Basiliea asks them to steal objects. Favorite objects. These will bring her back somehow. Killing someone has absolutely no benefits for them."

Christopher looked stunned, assumingly confused, so I tried to explain the best that I could. "They steal a person's most prized object, I guess a piece of our soul is anchored to it. Since he's already stolen from Lord Thames, unless Ronin was stealing from someone else in the household, he has no reason to go back there."

Christopher's face remained blank, and I waited for his reply. It took longer to come than I thought it would. He licked his lips then shook his head. His eyes gazed around the room before dropping down to me again. When he responded, his voice was low. "How long have you known this?"

"Why does that—"

"How long?"

I frowned. "A few weeks. Maybe a month."

He sucked in his breath. "Did you know when I told you about Basiliea's daughter?"

Oh. "Yes." My voice was timid.

"And you didn't tell me? I shared everything I knew with you, and you didn't tell me this? You know the Silver Raider's motive, intentions," he ticked off on his fingers as he spoke, "goals, and you didn't tell me any of this?"

I held up my hands. "It's not really mine to share."

"I thought we were in this together!" He took a step back and ran his fingers through his short hair.

"Together? I don't even know what this is!" I pointed between the two of us. "But there's nothing either of us can do about the Silver Raiders."

"You didn't even give us a chance! You kept this from me. Do you know what I went through to get more information for you? Did it even cross your mind to share yours with me?"

I cast my eyes to the floor, embarrassed. After a shaky breath he stepped back toward me. "Dishonesty, remember? That's the thing I despise the most."

He had no right to be upset with me, or act like there was something between us worth protecting. Alissia was his fiancé, and that's all he needed to worry about. I didn't need him worrying over me. So I said, "Well hopefully Alissia doesn't lie then."

His brow knit together, and he opened his mouth, but Berkley spoke first.

"We should go pay our respects." Berkley pulled away from Elenora and straightened his jacket. Elenora's eyes were red, and I tried to think of all the times she had inter-acted with Lord Thames. She'd been in society much longer than I had, and therefore knew him much better. We had played cards a few times, but that was it. She was a friendlier person than me by far, so she often knew people much better than I could claim to, even people that we both met this year.

Christopher nodded to Berkley as he stepped away from me. "We should; *they* deserve our respect." I knew that last part was aimed at me, like I didn't deserve respect. I hated not getting the last word, but I found myself at a loss for what to say.

"Well," Barrow kissed Lady Claire's cheeks, "I must be off. I just wanted to bring the news to an old friend."

"Thank you, Barrow. Thank you very much."

"Of course I didn't bloody kill someone." Ronin looked offended that I even asked. My body relaxed and I dropped into a chair, relieved. I knew it wasn't him. Deep in my heart, I knew it. But I still had to be sure. I needed to hear it from his mouth, see his eyes when I asked.

Ronin was a criminal, no mistake. His disregard for the law and for the common moral code was obvious, as was his casual attitude about thievery, but he wouldn't go as far as killing. No, that was too far. Ronin wouldn't do that.

This confirmation lifted a heavy weight from my shoulders and repositioned Ronin into a place of trust. I couldn't be sure what I would have done if I learned he had killed that poor man, but I was immensely grateful I would never need to find out. Ronin wasn't a murderer, but simply a man doing everything in his power to bring back his son.

"I must admit I'm offended that you suspected me in this crime. I'm a better man than that."

I quickly explained my accusation. His eyebrows raised.

"Dressed like us you say? Well that's not good."

"No, it's not good at all. It means the reward on you will be raised, the pursuit after you strengthened, and all the while a murderer is left alone because he was smart enough to put the blame on a criminal that everyone would have suspected in the first place." With his look at the end I bowed my head. "Except for me."

"Thank you." He stroked his chin as he walked around the tent. As soon as I got away from the grieving Lady Claire and Elenora this morning, I made my way to the Woods of Silver and Light. I found the camp in the afternoon alive with activity, and asked Ronin into the tent to question him in private. Now I was glad that I did, because I didn't want my lack of faith in him to be seen so evidently by everyone else. "Makes me want to figure out who did it, but it's really none of my business."

"I think them framing you made it your business, but I don't see how you could figure it out anyway," I said. "Will you be safe, though?"

Ronin hovered by the open flap of the tent, looking out intently. He peeked back as I spoke. "Safe? Oh yes, I'm very safe in these woods. We have an excellent gatekeeper." He resumed staring out the tent. By the tone of his voice, I almost asked who this gatekeeper was, but I didn't.

"Can't be that good, they let me in," I reminded him. Ronin turned away from the entrance and grinned.

"That's because I let you in; didn't see you as a threat. But soldiers? An army? They won't reach us."

For the second time that afternoon, I felt relieved. No army could get in, but the dangers still existed when Ronin and the Silver Raiders left the Woods to go on raids. I doubted this gatekeeper could keep them safe throughout the lands, but they would not be harmed in their own home. The children here, they were safe.

At least for now. Who knew what waking Basiliea would bring?

Ronin walked over and sat in one of the wooden chairs with me while I mindlessly traced the etchings in the armrest. Though somewhat settled, there was still an uneasiness that lay inside me, bubbling up from moment to moment, reminding me that even though Ronin had no part in Lord Thames' death, someone did. Someone killed him.

And someone was trying to kill me.

That wasn't something that was easily forgotten. Ronin held my hand in a comforting gesture, sensing my worry. His voice carried warmth with it while he spoke. "The Lord Thames was a wealthy, powerful man. He must have had enemies. But if you're really worried, I will station a man beneath your window to guard you each night. Just say the word and I will make it happen."

The image of someone patrolling my house all night to protect me from danger sounded tempting, but Ronin didn't know that it was likely someone would return to my window to try to kill me, and they might kill whoever waited there. I wouldn't have someone's blood on my hands. I removed my hand from his and straightened myself. "No, I'll be just fine. Thank you."

He nodded, but he didn't look so sure.

"Well, good. Because I don't have the authority to make that call anyway."

An unexpected laugh escaped my lips. "What would you have done if I said yes?"

He looked at me as if the answer was obvious. "I would

have stood outside your window myself. I'm a heavy sleeper though, and likely wouldn't have made you any safer." I laughed again.

Thankfulness filled my heart. I didn't deserve his loyalty. This morning I set out to accuse Ronin of killing a person, when he was willing to give up his sleep for me. That might not mean much to some people, but I adored sleep, so it meant the world to me. His generosity toward me was unlike any I had ever experienced.

The idea came again that Ronin harbored feelings greater than a friendship toward me, and it felt cruel of me to continue coming here so frequently if I thought that he hoped for something more of this relationship than I was willing to give. There would need to be clarity before I proceeded.

So with a sigh I turned my body in toward Ronin to look him in the eye.

"I need you to know, no, that's not how I want to say this. Drat, I should have thought about this first." I cursed as I pursed my lips together, regretting rushing into this conversation so suddenly without planning first. My sister would have planned out every word before ever having an important conversation. I needed some of her grace in this moment.

"You see, Ronin, I love coming here because no one expects anything of me. No, that sounds selfish. I mean, I feel free here. I can't explain it, but I love these woods, darkness and everything. And I love you all," I put a little more emphasis on the word all than perhaps I should have. Ronin's dark eyes studied me as his smile lowered slightly. "The thing is, I don't want you getting the wrong idea."

I didn't know what else to say, but there seemed like a

good place to stop. He was nodding, so he must understand me; maybe nothing more needed to be said on the matter.

"Are you thinking of moving here and joining us?"

Apparently more did need to be said on the subject. "I'm not talking about that. This is more of a personal matter. See, I don't want you thinking that I'm here for romantic reasons." There, that was clear enough.

"You don't like me the way I like you." He spoke gently, as if he was stating a fact. He didn't look hurt, or even surprised. Grateful that this conversation wasn't as difficult as I thought it would be, I nodded my head.

"Maybe if you weren't wanted for more money than I own, I could like you. Or if you didn't steal from people. But things being the way they are…"

"Is this because of Christopher?"

I snorted. "You two are a little obsessed with each other, but that's a different issue. No, this isn't about anybody. It's because I didn't do all this work to get myself to where I am today to have that ruined by being associated with outlaws."

"But it's not personal." His smile was back on his face.

I squinted my eyes and spoke slowly. "Besides all the personal facts I just stated, no it's not personal."

"That's all I need to hear." He hopped up with a smile on his face, making me fear this conversation would repeat itself soon.

CHAPTER TWENTY

urder. The word fluttered on every tongue tonight, whispered across the room as if the topic were a secret when in truth it was all anyone could talk about. Every time the conversation drifted away from Lord Thames's death, someone would say something to bring it right back again, and the discussion repeated itself. The room was in a constant dance of the same conversations being replayed over and over in different groups all evening. It was all anyone could talk about.

Murder.

The dark word echoed from the walls and appeared in every corner, tempting even the most pious who stayed from the evils of gossip. Not tonight. Tonight, everyone gossiped.

At first, I felt sorry for the twins, whose birthday ball would no doubt be ruined by the scandal. They were both set on finding a suitor this season, and tonight was an ideal time to stand out. Little attention came their way, however. Tonight, the pursuit of marriage, friendship, even gambling was pushed to the side as clusters formed to speak of the strangeness that occurred two nights ago at the Thames house.

The twins, Clara and Katrina, didn't seem as bothered by the damper on their party as I guessed they would be. At first, I thought them mature in how they handled it, but as the evening went on, I guessed it was more of a love for gossip and a good story than anything. Most of the nobles in the area had turned up tonight, and this birthday ball was one of the highest attended occasions of the year.

"How can you eat at a time like this?" Elenora caught me with my cheek full and she pulled my plate away from me.

"Dinner time?" I grabbed my plate back and popped another grape into my mouth. Elenora rolled her eyes at me. Tear stains marked her cheeks that she dabbed periodically with a handkerchief. I seemed to be the only lady who didn't think to bring a handkerchief tonight. I was also the only lady with dry eyes, a fact that no doubt made me appear cold.

"Were you close with Lord Thames?" Matthew Thompson approached us and handed another handkerchief to Elenora, who wiped her face with it. He showed his cleverness tonight; I'd seen him handing out an array of handkerchiefs to dozens of ladies this evening, always follow the gesture with a kind pat on the back. Leave it to Matthew Thompson to turn a murder into a chance to impress the ladies.

I rolled my eyes as I turned my head away, not eager for the same conversation for the hundredth time. No one really knew anything anyway. The assumption stood that the Silver Raiders carried out the deed, and several times the proclamation was made by men with gusto who raised their drink in the air and declared they would march into the Woods of Silver and Light in the morning and drag the Silver Raiders out. That normally got a few more cheers from surrounding gentlemen while the ladies hushed them.

I would be worried had I not spoken to Ronin earlier today and learned that they remained safe if they stayed within the Woods' protection. They needed all the protection they could get.

My eyes scanned the room several times for Christopher. As the people shifted, I caught glimpses of him speaking to a small group of people. For a moment I worried about what he might be telling them, about me, Ronin, or the Woods, but I hoped I knew him better than that. I hoped he wouldn't turn me in so quickly.

Once I caught his eye, but he turned his face away before I could read his expression. It wasn't happy, I could tell that much. I weighed the situation out in my mind and decided that the friendship needed to be reconciled quickly. Aside from valuing his companionship more than I ought to, he knew too much to be let loose, and my secrets would be safer with him if we were in good graces.

My nose turned up at the thought of apologizing. I still thought I didn't do anything wrong, but his actions made it clear that he thought I did. An apology would need to be made.

I took a lesson from yesterday and planned out the conversation before attempting an apology.

Hey Christopher, I'm really sorry for keeping information from you, when you were so open with me. I won't do it again.

Thanks for the apology. I'm still upset, but we are friends and I won't tell anyone your secret.

That'd be great, I'll give you your space until you calm down.

Christopher was a gentleman, and in a room full of people, there was only one way this conversation could pan out. I had nothing to worry about. Filled with newfound confidence I discarded my plate and strolled over to Christopher. He saw me approach but stayed focused in his group, so I folded my hands and waited outside the ring patiently for him to step away. It took several minutes longer than it needed to, but finally he sighed and turned around.

"Yes?"

"May I speak with you?" I asked, ignoring the glances from his friends. At least Alissia wasn't among them, I didn't want to deal with a mistakenly jealous betrothed.

"Go ahead."

I shifted my eyes. "Erm, in private?"

Another sigh. With his arms crossed and his steps slow, Christopher followed me to the side of the room. It was the perfect spot, far enough away that we wouldn't be heard but close enough to people that he couldn't put on any sort of display. Not that I expected a display of any sort, but it couldn't help to be prepared.

Cosette would be proud of the thought I put toward this.

"Christopher, I'm sorry that I held information back from you, especially when you were so open with—"

"Are you serious?" He looked down at me and raised his eyebrows. I looked to the side then back at him.

"Yes? I wanted to say that I am sorry for holding back information from—" I restarted the apology but got cut off again.

Christopher's tone was sharp. "I heard you. I just don't believe it."

My mind scrambled to continue the course. "Well, I am sorry. You were honest with me and I—"

"You don't mean it." He shrugged his shoulders while I threw my arms up.

"Will you just let me finish! You obviously want an apology, and I've got a really good one prepared!"

He leaned down slightly so I could feel his breath when he forced his words out sharply. "But you don't mean it."

I huffed. No, I didn't mean it, but he wasn't supposed to know that. "Would you just listen to it? *All* of it?"

"No. I don't want a fake apology. I'd love the real one, whenever you're ready."

"You had no reason to be upset in the first place!" I challenged a little too loudly, drawing the eye of people nearby, whose questioning glances I ignored. I should have chosen a more private location to talk.

Christopher blinked rapidly. "Your apology is dreadful."

"Your attitude is dreadfuller."

"That's not—"

"I know that's not a word!" I huffed, unsure of how to get this back on track. I turned over my hands, so the palms faced the ceilings. It was an action I had seen Lady Claire do when she spoke with me, and our conversations usually ended well. With luck it would do the same here. "Listen. I don't want this to come between us. I'm sorry I held back information, and I will give you all the space you need until you are ready to resume our friendship."

Christopher, to his credit, let me finish this time. When I was done, I folded my hands together in front of my stomach and waited patiently for his reply. It was another move from Lady Claire.

His eyes narrowed ever so slightly before opening again. "I'm not going to tell anyone about you and Ronin, if that's what you're worried about."

I raised my eyebrow, as if the thought hadn't crossed my mind. "Oh? Well that's very nice of you."

"Don't pretend like that's not why you apologized." Christopher ran his hands through his hair. "Really Anika, you've got some nerve. I suppose that's what draws me to you, but it's going to get you in trouble one of these days." He took a deep breath and leaned back on his feet, appearing calmer.

I risked speech. "So how mad are you? Because, to be fair, I kept it from you for a short while, but then I told you; but I haven't told another soul anything, so you should be honored."

His eyebrows shot up. "Not even Elenora? She doesn't know?"

I peeked over to Elenora, but the room was too crowded to spot her. "No, Elenora wouldn't approve."

"*I* don't approve."

I shot him a look, but I was grateful that the worst seemed over with. "Well you won't tell Lady Claire on me —she might."

Christopher smirked. "I might tell her. See if I can trade information, your secret for information on her mystery visitor."

The idea was tempting for a moment, but I was certain my secret was bigger than hers, so it wouldn't be a fair trade. I could picture the look on her face when she found out I was involved with the Silver Raiders, and it was enough to almost make me giggle.

"Bit of a gloomy night, isn't it?" Christopher commented.

"A murder would do that." I nodded as I looked over the people. The musicians gave up playing anything lively, and instead played simple background noise to keep the evening going. It seemed people finally remembered that they were hungry, because the snack table was flocked with people. The older generation started to leave, picking up their walking canes and coats and shaking their heads as they strolled out.

The Thameses weren't here tonight, of course, nor anyone especially close to them. I couldn't image what they must be going through right now. Even though I lived far from my family, I considered myself close to them, and it would break me if one of them died.

"The Silver Raiders will be hated even more after this. It's not safe to continue seeing them."

"In honor of respecting your desire for honesty, I went there yesterday. They didn't do this, but they are safe inside the Woods from the people who think they did. No one can get to them."

Christopher nodded. "I assumed they had a protection of some sort, but outside the Woods they are vulnerable. And anyone leaving or entering the Woods is especially at risk. It's not safe for you."

My arms crossed. "I can protect myself."

Christopher laughed, which didn't seem polite. He shook his head at me. "No, you can't. You'll be killed before you can take a swing." At that image, something in his eyes went dark, and he crossed his arms to match mine.

"In fact, you can't use my lands any longer to enter the Woods."

My jaw dropped open. "You don't have the authority to banish people from your lands."

"It's to keep you safe, Anika. I'm serious. If I see you crossing my lands, I'll turn you in."

CHAPTER TWENTY-ONE

I pulled back after Lord Thames's death, declining invitations to masquerades and luncheons. With my spare time I traveled through the villages, eating dinners with local families and learning about their businesses. Each shop fascinated me in a new way, with each owner carrying out their trade in a different style, but each with the same passion.

The time I spent in the villages was so valuable to me. The difference between where they were now and where they were a year ago was obvious, and that gave me hope for the growth that would continue to take place over the next few years, but by no means were my lands healed. The hearts of the people bled into the lands, filling it with misery and grief and loss. My heart bled alongside theirs to see such pain, though I couldn't pretend to relate.

Over the next month I spent countless hours sitting in dusty rooms listening to elderly ladies tell me stories about their lost sons. Some spoke knowing their son was gone forever, others spoke as if their son was coming home any day. Yet others spoke as if their son was home and well, though I knew that wasn't the case.

The murder of their friend caused the nobles to feel hurt as well, but it wasn't the same. The sadness through the villages ran deeper. Their sorrow wove itself into the ground, and I felt certain it would be there long after they were no longer there to tell their sad tale.

Not all was bleak, however. Those untouched by the war had been stepping up with joyful hearts to help their war-stricken neighbors. Extra hours were put in for the farms which were now in need of extra labor. The fallen sons' positions were filled, and the flour mill wheel started churning again.

With each visit, a new request was made.

People can't afford shoes at this time, and while my prices lowered to accommodate, the price of cloth and leather has not. I don't have enough to last through the winter.

My horse fell sick and died, I will need another one if I'm to make it to the markets this year. The Elkridge market is where I make most of my money, you know, and it's a ways beyond the river.

My roof is leaking in three places and needs to be repaired. I don't have the money.

Money. It always came down to the money. They needed more money.

It was a bold thing to ask, as they paid rent to me.

Several times a villager eagerly suggested calling on the Silver Raiders, but I rejected it. I would ask-*do you think it would be right if they stole from me?* The answer was always no. *Right, then it wouldn't be fair to steal from someone else.* Often the villager would make another excuse here, but I wouldn't have it. My people were hard workers, not thieves.

Guilt burned inside me, growing stronger all the time, knowing that I associated with the same Silver Raiders that I asked my people to have nothing to do with. Perhaps that guilt was the reason why I hadn't visited Ronin in nearly a month.

It was as I pondered these things under the shade of a tree that Marty had the idea.

She sat up straight and snapped her fingers. "I got it! A talent showing!"

I furrowed my brows as I wiped sweat from my forehead.

She went on. "A talent showing! It's perfect. Find someone to host it, and anyone with a talent can showcase in it. There's plenty of Gifts that are unused. Then people can donate to us if they like the talent. We can make little trinkets or cakes and sell those too! It doesn't need to be just our village, other lands can participate too, so it doesn't seem like us exclusively asking for money."

The idea of broadcasting our desolate financial state made me groan, but the talent show was a good idea.

"You can advertise it as a rebuilding from the war. Bringing people together. Harmonizing the lands." Marty bounced as she spoke, circling her hands around each other as she set the scene. I wanted to say no right away, but the look on her face told me I'd better at least consider it.

"If I can't convince other lords to join us, I won't do it," I told her firmly. I wouldn't be alone in this humiliation. Her head bobbed but the spark in her eye didn't die down. After giving her the hope of the talent showing, I stood to leave. Lady Claire was firm that I be back in time for dinner tonight.

"This will be splendid," Marty said as I left. "You won't regret it."

LADY CLAIRE WAS DRESSED IN CREAM FABRIC THE color of her skin with her hair twisted into a neat bun that sat on her neck. She smiled as I asked for her advice, then tapped her chin once I'd described the idea.

"If you present it as a festival, I think it will be very well received. Of course, it's well within your rights to hold a fundraiser, but I think a festival is exactly what this town needs right now."

Her words said yes, but there was a slight twitch in the corner of her lips and a tightness in the skin around her eyes that gave me a different impression. "Do you have any reservations?"

I counted her breaths as she thought. Three times her chest rose and fell before she spoke. "Magic isn't used as freely here as you might be used to."

I laughed gently. "I've noticed. Folks seem to think it'll eat them if they use their Gifts."

Lady Claire did not share in my humor. "Not everyone here has Gifts, and while we are under King Gerard, we live much closer to kind King Rinaldo, and he's eminently against magic."

I pursed my lips. "That's not a law though, he can't outlaw magic. And he has no jurisdiction in this town."

Her eyes told me I was playing with fire. "As it is, he's left the matter alone because the magic is under control, but it's not wise to stir the magic within the people. Magic is...unpredictable and shouldn't be taken lightly. If you ask my opinion, it's best if the people leave it alone all together. Have them present talents that aren't associated with their Gifts."

"Those aren't nearly as impressive," I sighed. The uneasiness about magic was one I couldn't comprehend. Back home folks used their Gifts each day to make lives easier. People didn't starve because others had Gifts that made bread, and they shared it freely. If the villagers could use magic to make their lives better, then I couldn't understand why they hesitated.

Suddenly, I wondered if my people had any Gifts they refrained from using that could help us.

I dropped the conversation with Lady Claire because I knew I couldn't convince her that magic wasn't evil. Though, as I thought of the magic that lives in the Woods of Silver and Light, I wasn't surprised that King Rinaldo was cautious to let magic roam the land with a dark forest sitting so close to his home. But I wasn't the king, and I wasn't afraid to use any advantage that I found to help my lands survive, magical or not.

CHAPTER TWENTY-TWO

lick click…click. My head whipped up as something tapped against my window three times. My hand reached to the top edge of the desk where my dagger rested, wrapped in a cloth. A scratching noise came, bringing me to my feet and sending my chair to the floor. I held up the dagger so the intruder could see I wasn't defenseless, and prayed it was nothing but a stray animal peering through the window at night.

Gulping down my fear, I approached the glass and peered outside.

I saw nothing.

Another look, still nothing. I pushed my face against the window, so my nose scrunched into my lip as I scanned the darkness. I'd gotten a new lock for the window that couldn't easily be broken, as well as ordered bear traps that would be set up along the ground. The traps wouldn't be ready for another few days, but they'd help me sleep better. An intruder wouldn't easily get past them.

Convinced and relieved that it was nothing, I pulled

back, lowering my eyes to the ground outside my window to look for footprints. Instead of footprints, a note was folded up on the sill.

Carefully, so as to not be overheard by anyone, I unlocked the door and pushed open the window and picked up the note, taking a moment to listen for any sounds such as a departing horse or carriage. However the mysterious visitor arrived or departed, they did so quietly.

Brimming with curiosity, I closed the window and unfolded the short note to find handwriting so terrible that it rivaled my own.

Anika,

These weeks have been long without your companionship, and I'm sorry if my feelings for you drove you away. If you wish to return to the Woods, I won't take your visit as anything but innocent in nature. I miss my companion.

Your friend,

Ronin

HE WAS RIGHT; THE THOUGHT OF MY CONSTANT visits leading on his kind heart kept me from visiting this past month, but I longed to return to the Woods where my soul felt free. Each day the call to the Woods grew stronger and visions of the camp filled my dreams at night until I felt sure the Woods had a magical hold over me, beckoning me back into their fold. I possessed barely enough strength to resist their calling, keeping away for the sake of Ronin's heart and for my mind to focus on the villagers in preparation for the upcoming festival.

Perhaps a trip there would do me good, restore some

joy to my downcast heart after struggling for the past month with the affairs of the manor.

By morning I resolved to visit Ronin, and I set off early for the trip. Still banned from Christopher's lands, I needed a new route to enter the Woods, and it involved going around Christopher's lands and into his neighbor's, Earl Lundoi, a short man with a big laugh. I didn't have much opinion on the man one way or the other, but I knew I couldn't trust him to keep my secrets and would need to do my best to not get caught.

A difficult task, it seemed.

Upon seeing farmers by the road who stopped my horse to ask me if they could help, I blurted the first thing that came to mind and told them about the festival of talents that I would be hosting in two weeks, and claimed I carried word of it to Earl Lundoi. They then, after exclaiming excitement over the prospect, pointed out that the mighty earl lived on the opposite side of the lands, and I was heading the wrong way. This brought about another lie about visiting Christopher along the way and how I took the wrong path but was enjoying the route, garnering laughter about women not having a sense of direction.

I pressed my lips tight and pushed forward, not wanting to snap back at them and leave them with a story to spread.

The laughs of the men continued as I rode past. I did my best to avoid seeing anyone after that, branching off the path whenever I thought I spotted someone ahead.

Relief filled me as the start of the vast Woods loomed ahead. Without a place to tie my nervous horse, I brought her with me into the Woods, hoping her presence would be as accepted as my own. Together we wandered on the unknown trail.

I pictured Cera sitting in the tree house watching me enter the Woods, and hoped she wasn't on lookout today.

Deep into the trees I roamed, veering to the right to find my familiar path. It never came. Finally, when I thought I was lost, a voice called out. "You came."

I shifted to find Ronin; who's cloak allowed him to blend in with the trees. His ever-present smile was wide causing his eyes to be squinted with joy. I couldn't help but smile back; it was good to see him again.

"How are you?"

"Blessed," he said, "now that you are here. I've been missing you." He led me into camp and to the sparkling lake where we sat by the water's edge and talked. I'd forgotten how easy he was to talk to.

"You've been busy!" He raised his eyebrows as I filled him in on all I was doing in the villages.

"I have, but it's been amazing to see the growth in the village and how the people are coming together to help each other. I'm hoping the festival will boost spirits and maybe I can get this land back to thriving."

"I'm sure you will. The festival is a great idea; this Marty sounds like a smart person."

I rested my hands on my knees as my bare feet swirled in the water. "So you've never met her? It was Joshua who came looking for help then."

Ronin smirked. "I can't say, but I will say this: they haven't asked for help since."

So Marty and Joshua stayed true to their word and stayed away from the Woods. "Good. And how about you? Have you stolen anything recently?"

"I have been on my best behavior." Ronin held up his hand in a pledge signal. "So only a little. We are so close,

Anika. Basiliea is starting to become whole again. I'd give it three more months—only three more months until I get my son back." His eyes lit up with the excitement of seeing his son again soon. I wanted to share in his excitement, but the fear that grasped my heart was too tight to allow me to rejoice. Potentially in three months' time Basiliea could be released, and the kingdom wasn't prepared to deal with whatever evil she brought with her.

"What does it mean, when you say she's starting to become whole?" I asked tentatively.

Ronin lay on the ground beside me with his back against the rock and his eyes fixed on the trees above us. He took a few moments to answer, and when he spoke it was slow. "It's hard to say, exactly. She's here, in shimmering form, but she has no power and she can't leave the Woods."

"But you can see her, and talk to her?"

"If we enter the tent, yes." Ronin gave me a look. "You still don't trust her, do you?"

I didn't need to reply, the answer was obvious. Ronin's disregard for Basiliea's intentions didn't surprise me because she was bringing his son back and he was blinded by that, but Jack carried more sense in him. He should have stopped Ronin from getting involved with an unknown sorceress the moment Cera brought her forth; it never should have gotten this far. It shouldn't have been me voicing concerns to Ronin about Basiliea; it should've been Jack.

Jack struck me as a sensible fellow, and that knowledge brought two possibilities with it. The first, and more reassuring idea of the two, was that Jack was comfortable with Basiliea because he'd investigated her, knew her true intentions, and saw no threat. It would put my mind at ease if at least someone had thought this through before inviting her back to life, and if anyone was keeping their head about this it would've been Jack.

The second, and scarier idea, was that Jack was turning a blind eye to Basiliea because she, as with Ronin, was offering him something, and he was indebted to her.

In the end, I gave Ronin a simple 'no' and let the conversation wander elsewhere, but an idea formed in my mind.

That day I purposefully stayed longer than ever before, feigning a loss of recollection of the time, and when Ronin offered me a place to stay for the night, I accepted eagerly. Annabeth offered me clothes to sleep in, and I was placed in Ronin's hut while he made a bed for himself and slept outside the door.

Long into the night I waited, pinching myself to keep awake. Time drifted by, and I hesitated until I could be sure that sleep had captured both the camp and, most importantly, Ronin.

Then, quiet as an owl, I pulled back the sheet over the doorway and tiptoed over his sleeping body and toward the edge of camp.

No other creature stirred as I slinked through the camp and approached the tent. It glowed golden in the thicket of trees, drawing me in. I practiced my intimidating voice in my head as I lifted the flap to enter the tent.

The floor inside the golden tent was lined with the softest grass that my toes had ever felt, and the air held a smell so sweet it rivaled my cook's cakes. There was no lantern or magical ball to light the inside of the tent, but light still burned within; a yellow glow illuminated from the fabric of the tent and lit up the room.

With that light I could see designs etched into the wall of the tent, painting pictures of stories that I didn't recognize, though I felt certain they were *her* stories.

The tent was empty except for a simple, thick tree stump near the back of the tent cut almost to its roots and black with scorch.

How do I call upon a magical being? I looked back behind me and peeked out the tent where the forest remained still with night.

When I turned back, my heart lept from my chest. Standing on the tree stump was a woman with silver hair and gray eyes wearing a long silver dress that billowed at the sleeves and blossomed from the bottom, encompassing the tree stump underneath. Her pale skin glowed like the moon and her ruby lips drew back into a thin smile.

Though she was a great beauty, her appearance struck pure dread within me.

When she spoke, her voice sounded like sword blades clashing against each other.

"Welcome, Anika," Basiliea said. "I've been waiting for you."

CHAPTER TWENTY-THREE

"*I* need to speak with you." I held my chin up and I crossed my arms. The corners of Basiliea's lips turned up in amusement.

"Yes, I see that." Her voice came slow and calculated. Basiliea was taller than I expected her to be, towering over me on the tree stump. I kept back toward the entrance of the tent, both so that I had an easy escape, and so the height difference between us wasn't as noticeable.

She waited patiently for my words.

"Did Ronin tell you about me?" I asked her in a hushed tone so we weren't overhead.

She didn't keep her volume as low as mine. "No, dear child. I see all things of creatures like you in these woods."

"What do you want?"

Another slow smile. "Simple, I want life. I want to be life, I want to save life, and I want to give back life."

I furrowed my brow slightly. "And take it?"

She stayed on the stump as her gray eyes looked straight into my own. There were no wrinkles on her face, no hint of age besides the raspy tone to her voice. "I'm more curious about what you want, dear child."

I answered without thinking. "I want Ronin to be safe."

"Yes, you do care for him."

My face flushed as I continued on, "I want the people in the villages to stay safe, and I want to keep my home."

She laughed. "And you think I'm a threat to all that? You see me as a mistress of evil."

I sucked in my lip.

"I see. Well, I can promise you that your home is safe with you. I have no desire to return to that crippling manor," she informed me. I should have felt a small bit of relief at her promise, but I felt nothing.

"So what do you want?"

"You are a complicated girl, dear one. A part of two worlds but belonging to none. You desire to be a part of something, but you don't know where you want to belong. I see the battle in your heart and the confusion in your head."

"Do you see the strength in my hand? Because I'm not afraid to fight against you."

Her head tilted back as she laughed. "Yes, I see the fire inside you as well. You remind me much of myself at your age: young, passionate, and confused."

"I'm not confused; I know that you can't be trusted." My voice stayed strong as I grew comfortable in her presence. Nothing about her evoked fear within me, especially with her confined to the tree stump across the tent. I might be afraid if she could walk, but knowing that she was stuck to that one place made her seem less threatening, like an animal in a cage.

"My child, the people who you can trust would surprise

you, and I am one of them. My motives are to find a life free of these dark woods and the stipulations of others."

"So when you come back, you'll leave everyone alone?"

She took a long breath. "You think you have the world figured out, but you stand on the wrong side of the fight."

I raised an eyebrow. I knew she had more planned than quiet retirement. "A fight?"

She stepped off the stump, shooting fear into me as I shuffled back, sending a look of satisfaction to her face. "Yes, Anika. There is a fight going on that is as old as the trees and the soil they are planted in. This is a fight as old as the sky itself. The magic that stirs in these woods is ready to wake, and it will wake without my help. And when it does…" she walked as she spoke, not stopping until she stood a few paces from me. "When it wakes, I can help heal your land or destroy it, so heed my words and don't cross me. I will either be your greatest ally, or the one who sends you back home to your hated Riverfront Tavern."

My hand folded into a fist to hide the shaking, and I took a bold step toward her. "No, you heed my words. While you've been rotting away here in these woods, the world outside has been growing stronger. We defeated you once, and we will do it again."

She grinned. "Victory always tastes sweeter when it's fought for." Basiliea leaned down to me and narrowed her eyes. "Try."

With that, she vanished, leaving me to an empty tent and a fast beating heart.

I opened my mouth wide to suck in a deep breath while placing a hand over my chest in effort to soothe my heartbeat. The action brought little relief.

Basiliea was not what I expected. I pictured a rugged

creature with an uneven smile, a ruthless temper, and a bad habit of cracking their knuckles. Basiliea was far from that; instead she was beautiful and calm and unnervingly tall.

I knew more now than I did this morning, and that was enough to assure me I had done the right thing by confronting her. Whatever she told Ronin, Basiliea was looking for trouble and had to be stopped.

My first thought involved telling Christopher everything I'd learned and asking his advice, but our friendship remained broken and I didn't have the tools to fix it. My second thought went to Ronin, who I doubted I could get to listen to my argument.

The thought of Ronin reminded me that I left him outside the door sleeping, and I didn't want to risk getting caught. I cursed at the tree stump in the tent before turning to pull back the flap. It moved first, and I lept back in fear.

Ronin ducked into the tent with a deep frown on his face as he pulled himself tall and crossed his arms. His voice remained low but his tone was sharp.

"What. Are. You. Doing?"

I was in trouble.

"I needed answers," I explained to Ronin.

"I told you not to come in here."

"Did you?" I asked with a tilt of my head, unsure if that specific request was ever made. Ronin wasn't amused. He crossed the distance between us in one long stride.

"Was there any confusion on your part? Isn't that why you snuck off in the middle of the night so I wouldn't catch you? You have no business being here! I have opened up my home, my heart, and my plans to you, and you go behind my back to interfere with the one thing that will get my son back for me."

"I see that you're upset, but I'm worried she's deceiving you."

Ronin put his hands on his hips. "I don't care."

"You should! I do! You have no idea who she's planning to hurt once you bring her back. When she does, that'll be on you."

Ronin raised his voice and shook as he spoke. "She's bringing back my son! She is the only person who can give that to me."

My breath shook along with my hands while I attempted to reason with Ronin. "Both Vestalin and West-fallen just fought a war; neither of them can deal with her right now. She could destroy us if she wanted. You need to think about Basiliea and what happens to this country if she comes back, and forget about your son for a moment."

As soon as I said it, I wished I could reword my sentence, so it didn't sound so heartless at the end, but the damage was done. Ronin's voice was loud enough to wake up the whole camp when he spoke.

"Forget about my son? He is everything to me. You don't understand what it's like to be a parent; you don't understand the unbelievable love that comes with it, or the unbearable fear of your child getting hurt. I had that, I lived with that pain and fear as my child suffered. He was eight! He was only eight, but he died. You can't know how that felt. I held Landon as tears slid down his cheeks; he knew he was dying. I held him as he struggled to breathe, and as he squeezed my fingers and curled up in my lap. I held him as his body burned up and didn't stop holding him until his body turned cold."

Somewhere along the way, tears started rolling down his cheeks, and he shut his eyes as the memory replayed. His voice grew gradually quieter.

"Landon was the only thing that mattered in my life; he was everything to me. He is all that I can think about, day and night. I'm stricken with memories of him alive and plagued by the image of him dead. If I can get him back, that is my number one priority, and I'm not going to let anything stand in my way. He's my son, and I will fight for him."

I wanted to tell him he was being irrational, and that the life of his son who was already dead did not mean more than the lives of everyone in the kingdom that he was putting at risk, but I couldn't find the words. To him, his son was the world, and he wouldn't see it any other way. It was noble, how deeply he loved his son and how relentlessly he fought for him, even to the point of recklessness.

I could still fight Basiliea, but I saw now that it would never be with Ronin. He would never raise a finger against the person who was giving him back his son.

Ronin took a deep breath and straightened his shirt.

"So, if we are done here, we should get back to bed. I expect for you to never bring up Basiliea again. And, if you sneak out of my hut one more time, you will be giving up your right to the bed and you will be sleeping on the floor."

CHAPTER TWENTY-FOUR

With all that was on my mind, Elenora's birthday ball was the last place I desired to be. But here I was.

Gold and red roses lined the room, set in elegant golden vases. The intricate flowers adorned the cake and the tables, spilling toward the musicians who were dressed to match. Elenora looked beautiful in her golden gown with roses pinned in her hair. She insisted I wear red, so I complimented the color of the room.

She spent her time with Berkley while Christopher and I ignored each other all night. Just as the violin played its last note of the song, our eyes met, but he turned away sharply.

It seemed he didn't want to talk right now.

Defaulting to the dessert spread, I picked up a twist of dough and nibbled on it while the next dance started. No sooner had the flutes begun their tune than the garden doors burst open. My breath sucked in and I almost dropped my twist as I anticipated the Silver Raiders, but it was merely Berkley with a flushed Elenora behind him. He bolted to the front of the room where he shouted for attention and for the music to quiet.

"Good evening, all! I simply wanted to take a moment to declare that I am the happiest man alive!" Next to Berkley, Elenora ducked her head into her hands when he held his arms out to her. "Today, the Lady Elenora has agreed to be my bride."

The room broke into a flurry of cheers and exclamations while Berkley picked up Elenora and swung her around the room. The band jumped back into action, picking up the tempo of the music to match the liveliness of the guests.

Once the room settled, I peeked back to Christopher. He stood alone with his drink in hand and his back to the wall.

For a fourth time that evening, our eyes met and his seemed to hold a night's worth of darkness within them.

I waited to see if he would look away, but this time he didn't. What made this time different, I couldn't know, but I held his gaze for as long as he'd let me. We hadn't spoken in a month since he banned me from his lands, and though our last conversation included me apologizing to him, the air between us still felt thick.

His shoulders raised then fell with a deep breath as he pushed off the wall and moved toward me with a great deal of reluctance that I didn't fail to notice. I stepped away from the table where I stood and went to meet him along the private side wall where I'd first seen him tonight. I wouldn't let our first conversation in a month be overheard by eager parties huddled around the dessert table.

He discarded his drink along the way, sliding his hands

into his pockets before stopping in front of me. We both stood uncomfortably as we faced each other.

"I'm sorry." I wasn't certain why I was saying it, but I felt as if it needed to be said. If he didn't accept my apology this time, however, I wouldn't beg for his forgiveness.

To my relief, his words carried a hint of kindness in them. "Me too."

He nodded his head back toward the corridor and led me away from crowds of people. I thought we would stop in the corridor, but he looped around toward the gardens and held the door open for me, all without saying a word.

Above our heads, the stars stretched out across the sky without a cloud to hide their beauty. The cool air greeted me fondly and a wisp of wind curled around my arms. Christopher walked quietly toward the trellises before turning back to me.

"I know you went back into those woods."

The pleasure that the outdoors brought me quickly left as I raised my hands. "How? How do you always know when I go there? I went *one time*, and you know about it. How?"

His hands crossed. "Why do you do this, Anika? Why do you keep going there? To *him*?"

I scoffed. "*Him* has nothing to do with it. I enjoy the people; *they* don't yell at me." Not all of them, at least. Then a thought came to my mind. For him to mind that I went to visit Ronin, he had to care, at least a little. Intriguing. I watched him trace the sight of my arm as I reached up to realign several pieces of hair and his gaze lingered before falling back to my eyes. Very intriguing.

He cleared his throat. "They don't have your best interests in mind."

My interests. To be fair, my interests were simple: to save my lands from poverty, and Ronin shared in those interests. It wasn't my interests that worried me about the Silver Raiders, and I knew those weren't the interests Christopher spoke of. Ronin's desire to bring back Basiliea proved the only threat to my allegiance with them should this deal prove faulty and bring danger to me as result.

But if we spoke of interests, I couldn't be certain Christopher thought of my interests either, but rather he seemed keen on pulling me away from the things I'd expressed interest in. "And you do?"

Christopher looked almost triumphant. "As a matter of fact, yes. You should know that you weren't as careful about entering those dark woods as you might have thought; you were caught. Earl Lundoi claims to have seen you."

He caught me by surprise and by the smug look on his face he knew it. I sucked in my breath sharply, thinking of when he could have spotted me and how I could have been so careless as to miss it. When I spoke, my words came out as a stammer. "What was Earl—"

Something between a groan and a sigh came out of Christopher's mouth as the look on his face turned to exasperation. "He's not the point! Did you know he came here with his story in hand, ready to start a scandal? Luck has it that I ran into him first this evening and talked him down with a story of how I asked you to come visit me at an outskirt cabin, and you got lost along the way. I beseeched his discretion on the topic, but I can't claim to have his trust. We might find ourselves in a scandal of a different kind, but your association with those thieves isn't in question."

My face blushed, both at his cover up story and at the fact that he made one at all. That must have meant he cared.

"Elenora never would have forgiven you if you ruined this night for her," he pointed out to me, as if Elenora would be the greatest of my worries if my secret spilled tonight. Just when I thought he cared for me, he disarmed the thought with one sentence and turned it as if he was looking out for Elenora.

"Well, thank you then," I said flatly to hide the emotion swelling within.

I was surprised by the feeling in my chest, one very different from the anger and frustration that I'd felt for Christopher so far. This emotion could only be described as one much warmer. I took a step back from Christopher, hoping the distance would be all it would take to calm my heart.

"You are no longer banished from my lands."

I snorted. "That's very generous of you."

"Don't mock me. I'm doing this to protect you since you can't seem to keep away from him."

Again, I sighed, tiring of convincing each of them that there was nothing romantic between me and the other. "Your obsession with each other is beyond me but there is nothing going on between me and Ronin."

He raised an eyebrow at me as he studied my face, and I realized how close he stood to me. "Do you mean that?"

"Of course, but what does it matter?" I twisted to look back at the door to see if anyone was coming our way. Christopher and I were positioned close to the wall, partly hidden by shadows while engaging in a conversation that if overseen by anyone would be clear went beyond pleasantries.

"It matters to me."

"Why? You have…" I bit my tongue thinking of Alissia. Alissia. We shouldn't be here, out alone in the gardens when he had a betrothed inside. More than that, he shouldn't be spreading stories of me meeting him in cabins when he was betrothed to someone else. The scandal of that story suddenly hit me, and nerves curled in my chest. I didn't want to be caught in such a tale, and I didn't want to give anyone the impression that this was anything but proper.

As I searched for emotion from Christopher, I hadn't thought of what I would do once I discovered it. My desire to find it acknowledged my own feelings in the matter, but while I'd sought reciprocation from him, I'd forgotten about his pledged heart to another. Every part of me longed to stay by the trellises with Christopher. Even though our conversation usually resulted in arguments I enjoyed his company more than I ought to, and I'd selfishly hoped he enjoyed mine.

Now aware of my feelings, I realized how foolish I'd been.

"We can't do this." I began to retreat.

"What are you talking about?" He reached to catch my hand, but I slipped from his grip and hastened my steps back to the manor.

"Alissia," I called over my shoulder. "We can't do this to her."

As soon as I said it, I wished for the words back, because those seven words revealed more of my heart than I'd planned to admit, both to Christopher and to myself.

With that sentence, I revealed the part of me that cared for Christopher, and the part that hoped he cared back.

But, in the same moment that I shared my feelings, I reminded him of why I can't have them. Alissia.

Blasted. This may be the first moment I realized how much I wished something could happen, but I couldn't tarnish his name and make a fool out of Alissia.

Christopher called my name again, but I yanked open the door and bolted inside, startling someone who waited in the dimly lit corridor. I mumbled an apology as I brushed by, hiding my face so I couldn't be matched when Christopher came in after me. I thought I heard him call once more but my feet were moving too quickly to be stopped.

CHAPTER TWENTY-FIVE

he rest of the evening I devoted myself to spreading the word about the festival of talents, which was very well received. The festival might turn into a two-day event with how excited the nobles acted about it. All evening I found myself showered with eager handshakes and compliments on my thoughtfulness and devotion, which I did my best to remember so I could turn around and give them back to Marty, who rightfully deserved them.

It was almost enough to keep my mind away from Christopher.

His words played over in my head. *It matters to me.*

What did he mean by that? He cares for me?

It was inappropriate for me to linger on these thoughts, and I knew it. I tried to banish them from my mind, reminding myself that he was spoken for and it was wildly wrong to wish that he harbored secret feelings for me. More than wrong, it was disrespectful of his betrothal to

Alissia, and felt especially so on this evening, while Elenora was gushing over her betrothal to Berkley.

Engagements should be honored.

Once again, I pushed these thoughts from my mind, seeking a distraction which Elenora unknowingly provided.

She gushed about Berkley unendingly during the carriage ride home, which took place at a late enough hour to be considered morning. Elenora curled into the seat in a position that suggested drowsiness, but her eyes were alert and practically dancing as she relayed the events for me.

"I'll have to write to my parents tonight; they will be so thrilled!" She pulled her hands to her face and sighed into them, twisting so she could fall to her back on the bench where she sighed again. If I didn't know she'd gotten engaged tonight, I would suggest she was soused.

"You'll fall asleep into the ink if you attempt such a thing at this hour."

"No, I won't." She sat up with sudden seriousness that made me giggle. She giggled back, though I don't think she understood why. "I mean it, I don't think I'll ever sleep again." Another giddy chirp.

"Then you'll look like a wreck and you'll be quite irrita-ble," I ticked off on my fingers as I spoke, "and Berkley won't want you anymore." I ended with waging my finger at her which she pushed away before slumping back into the seat.

"Yes, he will, he promised he will want me *forever*."

"In that case, who needs sleep?" We giggled again. "I'm really happy for you, Elenora. He's a wonderful chap."

The driver stopped and announced we'd arrived home as he opened the door to let us spill into the foyer where Lady Claire sat up waiting, unknowingly submitting herself to all the details of the night while Elenora called the handmaid to make cocoa. I felt bad for the serving girl, who no doubt had been sleeping, but she lingered after making cocoa in such a way that I doubted she minded waking up for a bit of gossip. If Elenora didn't alert the entire staff tomorrow of her engagement, I knew this serving girl would.

In politeness, I stayed to hear Elenora's tale again, gushing at all the right parts where I knew Lady Claire wouldn't show the proper amount of enthusiasm. I guessed correctly, while Lady Claire wore a smile that hardly extended past the edge of her nose, and only twice did her teeth show. Elenora ended up turning to me again as she told her story simply because I was the one giving her a proper reaction.

Finally, she sighed and set down her cup. "I must rest," she declared with gusto.

"Good night my dear." Lady Claire was slower to stand, so Elenora skipped out of the room before she fully reached her feet.

"You should be more excited for her," I told Lady Claire while I set my cup on the small table that stood between the set of four chairs. As I did, I noticed a ring of droplets nearby, indicating another cup had rested there recently.

"I'm afraid sleep has control over my emotions; I shall make up for it in the morning," Lady Claire said slowly, yawning for effect.

I peered at the ring, then peeked at the chair next to me, where the pillow folded in such a way that suggested it had been pressed against recently. My eyebrows drew in. "Did you have company?" Lady Claire always sat in the back-corner chair nearest the fire, so she couldn't have been the one to crumple the pillow and leave the water ring on the table.

I heard her back crack when she straightened it, answering in a flat tone. "Merely a friend. Good night, Anika."

Her pace quickened as she exited the room, leaving me behind staring at the pillow to see if it would give up its secrets of who sat there last.

The hour grew late and my mind faded; I didn't have enough strength to concoct a mystery out of an unkempt pillow. I hadn't given up the idea that Lady Claire hid a secret, but tonight was not the time to solve it. To do that required sleep, a good cup of cocoa, and perhaps some twisted dough. The handmaid retreated to bed at my orders. The foyer could be cleaned in the morning; there was no need to stay up late doing a frivolous task when morning would come soon enough. Too soon. I checked the door to be sure it was locked before rounding the stairs to my room. The dark house and strange sounds did nothing but put me on edge, and I longed for the safety of my bed.

Ludicrous, I thought. *To go through the Woods of Silver and Light on my own but be frightened by my own house.*

My feet almost reached the landing when the unmistakable sound of wheels on cobblestone caused me to jump then miss my footing and fall down a stair, bashing my knee against the top step. I winced in pain while I held myself still, listening to the sounds.

Someone lurked in the dark outside.

Not giving myself time to be afraid, I fled down the stairs to catch the midnight visitor off guard. Could this be the man who'd been visiting Lady Claire? Or was this the lady set on killing me? Thoughts flew to mind of Lord

Thames's death, bringing the fear that I was trying to avoid, and it almost caused me to turn and run for the kitchens. Surely one of the cabinets was large enough to hide me.

Suppressing the fears, I drew to the window and pushed myself against the wall to peek outside while simultaneously thinking of something in the room I could use as a weapon. The cups on the table drew my eye and I snuck to the room to grab one, praying Lady Claire would forgive me if I broke one of her fine dishes.

Outside, a sophisticated carriage sat in the courtyard with horses shifting nervously while the driver shushed them. I wondered where the rider was.

A sudden knock answered that for me.

Murderers don't knock. That was my solace as I answered the door. A murderer wouldn't knock.

Wielding the teacup in my hand for good measure, I tiptoed toward the door to open it.

Christopher stood outside.

His hands twisted around each other nervously, interlacing fingers then pulling them through again. The dark suit he donned tonight now lay unbuttoned, and his hair looked like he had slept on it or ran his hands through it several times too many. I knew it wasn't the first, he left the party shortly before we did and wouldn't have had time to sleep yet. He took a sharp breath when he saw me as if he expected anyone else to open the door.

If I was worried about the appearances of us talking in the garden alone, this would be the scandal of the season.

"Christopher, what are you doing?"

"What are you doing?" He motioned toward the teacup and laughed, but his laugh sounded tense.

I lowered the teacup and returned it to the table. "I thought you were an intruder."

"And you thought *that* would save you? Your self-preservation skills are lacking, and I'm worried you're going to be killed one of these days." Another nervous shake of the hands.

His subtle mention of my business with the Silver Raiders caused me to drop my head in weariness. I had no strength left to fight. Not tonight. "What are you doing here, Christopher?"

He stepped inside the house and closed the door behind him which surely made the situation worse as we made ourselves privy to any tale the carriage driver cared to assume about what went on behind this closed door. I almost asked him to open it again, but he spoke first.

"I had to see you."

"I don't think it's appropriate. Forget about your betrothed, coming at this time of night is asking for a scandal."

He peeked behind me, causing me to look as well. If anyone else heard a noise, no one was coming to investigate. "That's why I had to come."

"Because it's an inappropriate time?" My eyebrows drew together. Perhaps it was the hour, but I couldn't figure out what he meant or why he looked as nervous as a man on death row.

"No, because you think I'm betrothed."

The word seemed to echo through the room as my breath caught in my throat. "Are... aren't you?"

"Do you think Alissia is my betrothed?"

I raised my shoulders then let them drop. "That's what I was told."

Christopher took a deep breath that moved his entire body. "Alissia isn't my betrothed; she isn't my anything."

I blinked. Christopher went on.

"It started as an innocent wish that my parents made when we were little, and that wish blossomed as friendship came naturally to us. The idea of an engagement is often assumed by people, but it has never been true, and neither she nor I want it." He took a step toward me, his nervous shudders suddenly quite still. "I am promised to nobody."

"She's not your betrothed," I breathed. He shook his head slowly.

"She's not my betrothed."

I dropped my head, ashamed with myself for all the small jabs about her I made to him that he didn't deserve. I never gave him the chance to explain himself. The feeling of guilt came first, but the feeling that came next was anything but shame. Delight. Relief. Hope.

When I looked back up, he was close enough for me to hear his breath as he looked me over with an expression I'd never seen on his face before. Awe, I placed it. Heat flooded my cheeks.

He whispered. "I thought you knew; my heart is spoken for."

Anticipation curled in my chest and threatened to bubble out of my throat. A nervous smile crossed my lips.

"She's not your betrothed," I said again, like a fool.

Christopher grinned, lowering his head down so his forehead rested against mine. "No. I'm enamored with a different girl, one with a spirit like fire and a tongue like a sword."

I made a small noise in the back of my throat. "She sounds impossible."

"She really is," he said back, keeping his head rested against mine. His hands found mine and he folded them around my fingers, pressing them to his sides. For several moments we stayed like this, still as night in each other's presence.

I felt much over the past few months while with Christopher. Confused, frustrated, distrusted, angry. Sometimes happy and many times smitten. But this was the first time I felt so calm. He sensed it too, and we stayed hidden in that fragile moment together.

His nose bent down and rubbed the tip of mine, tracing its way back up to my forehead. It paused there, and I waited to see if he would trace back down.

He didn't.

"I should go." I felt his breath on my nose as he spoke. I tried not to let the disappointment show.

"Come back in the morning?"

"I can't promise I'll wake while it's still morning, but I'll return as soon as I can."

I remembered the late hour, and almost offered him a room to stay in before realizing how freely his driver could run with that story. Between tonight and the tale Christopher told earlier to Earl Lundoi, we were setting ourselves up for quite the gossip.

I smiled as I realized that I didn't care; let the people talk.

"I'll see you then."

He held my hand until he was out the door. He left then, but the warm feeling remained along with a smile as wide as Elenora's tonight.

Christopher wasn't Alissia's. Christopher wanted to be mine.

CHAPTER TWENTY-SIX

Christopher didn't come back in the morning, which was good because I slept soundly through it. Elenora did too; I could tell when she woke up because she came straight to my room to chirp over her engagement again. I rolled over in bed and listened as she talked about wedding arrangements and where they wanted to live once married. I wasn't surprised they'd already planned all this out.

Soon enough she skipped off to alert the rest of the household, and I pulled myself from the comfort of the bed to get ready before Christopher came by.

Christopher.

Perhaps I should have stayed in bed and not woken until he was here so I wouldn't have time alone with my thoughts. But that's not how it happened. Instead my midday was spent perplexed by my own doubts until I reached the point of utter confusion.

Elenora told me Christopher and Alissia were engaged, but I had assumed something was there before that. There had been enough between them that I assumed a courtship.

More than that, Elenora wasn't the type to be mistaken about a relationship; she was quite adept at reading people. If she'd been born in Westfallen and given a Gift, I'd have guessed it to be a remarkable perception of others. Even without magical assistance, she was rarely wrong, and they had managed to fool her.

Even when I believed them to be betrothed, my eye remained on Christopher for a while, and nothing I saw indicated anything less than a betrothal. The way that he laughed with her, stood close as he talked, sought her out in a room—it was all more than a friendship.

Perhaps Christopher told the truth when he said he desired nothing from Alissia, which right now I doubted, but I was certain she couldn't say the same. That girl believed him to be hers. It'd be improper for me to accept advances from him right now.

That thought left a dull ache in my stomach and a bitter taste in my mouth at the remembrance of last night. *I wanted him to kiss me.* I was grateful that he possessed more self-control than I could claim to.

I was so foolish.

I choose my plain teal dress instead of the blush pink one and pulled my hair back in a simple knot before flying down the stairs in an attempt to leave for the village before Christopher arrived. My head still spun with the events of last night and our almost kiss, and clarity would be needed before we spoke again.

I informed Elenora that Christopher may be stopping by and, while he had my kind regards, I was otherwise occupied today. She raised a dainty brow but kept her questions to herself. Truly, I didn't deserve her friendship, especially after thinking her a killer.

The courtyard outside remained empty. Fast as my horse could take me, I rode from Wateredge Manor toward the village to distract myself with arrangements for the festival of talents in two weeks' time.

Festival preparations proved an adequate distraction.

On the south edge of Jounith Village sat a deep grove, surrounded by a vineyard on one side, an orchard on the other, and a shallow stream that curved back before looping up again to run through the orchard and past the village. The field had long served as a play space for children, and while the people had little resources or power to sow into the land, which was fertile enough to provide good crop, none seemed to mind it sitting idle for the curious children to wander. Most days, after lessons and chores were completed, the children could be found frolicking in the field playing their games or wading along the stream's edge. So long as they minded Barrows Bend, where the water fell deeper and had been known to pull a child or two in with its sudden heavier current, there was little danger.

This provided the perfect place for the festival. The main road came right into the village which fed into the field, so transportation shouldn't have limited anyone who wished to come. I offered what skills I had toward building a main stage, but I was little help besides transporting sawed beams to men who fastened them in place.

A hefty list revealed the other lands that would send villagers to participate in the festival alongside my own, so we divided the field into regions for each noble's land so donations could be easily gathered and given to the proper owners. The plans spilled into the village, where my own people would line the few roads with their stands, leaving enough room for visitors in the field.

It wasn't a perfect plan, but it would do.

The village lit up with the idea of the festival, and most of my time went to helping the villagers brainstorm what talents they had that could bring in some sort of revenue. Most told me of a famous recipe they had, either for tartlets or a cinnamon bread or fluffy dough, but I tried to talk as many as I could out of bakery and toward anything else that would set them apart. I anticipated most visitors would bring treats to sell, and I wanted my people to stand out.

"I just don't know if I have a special talent."

I heard this over and over during the day. This specific sob came from a mother who lost her husband during the war. He was an early casualty, so I wasn't around to witness her recovery but she carried herself with a strength that I guessed wasn't always there. Her two children were doing chores, one in the house and one in the yard, but both stopped to give me a timid smile when I approached.

"Well, what Gift were you born with?" I asked her as I accepted a glass of water.

She eased herself down into the chair across from me and brushed her hair back. "That's what I just said: I don't think I have any."

When my sister's husband, Rumpelstiltskin, made a deal with a sorceress to bring magic to the land, it rippled out into each person, forming itself in each person in a unique way, and as far as I knew, Cosette was the only one born in Westfallen in the past hundred years who didn't possess a Gift.

"Were you not born in Westfallen?"

"Why yes, but I don't see what…oh. Surely you don't mean…no, I can't. Not that Gift." She ducked her head as she shook it as if shooing a bug from her or an evil spirit. "No, we don't use those Gifts."

My lips pulled tight. "Why not?"

"We don't practice witchcraft around here," she said firmly. In the room next to us, I saw her daughter pause with her broom in hand, shamelessly eavesdropping. No doubt the word 'witchcraft' caught her attention.

"It's not witchcraft," I said, thinking of Basiliea. "Trust me, the Gifts are innocent."

"Magic blackens the heart. I won't have my heart blackened."

I tried to keep my face even to show her that I was listening to her and I understood her concerns, but every part of me wanted to bury my face in my hands at the disillusion. With all my might, I kept my voice even. "Magic will not hurt you. In the village I grew up in, the Gifts were used daily. We hardly even consider them magic; my Papa surly doesn't."

"Your papa sounds like a smart man," she whispered.

No, he's not. Papa is a fool who didn't believe that strong magic existed, even as he watched Mama turn apples into peaches with her hands. I always thought him to be a rational man, but now I saw him to be a narrow minded one.

"I can talk to squirrels. And bunnies too." Her daughter, no more than ten, stepped forward nervously. Her mama whipped her head around to shush her, but I offered a smile.

"That sounds like an incredible Gift. We could showcase that."

"No! I will not have my daughter's heart blacked for a show."

I sensed her mind wouldn't be changed and I didn't want to anger her any more than I already had by pushing further so I pulled the conversation away from Gifts and turned to other talents she might have or anything she could sell. In the end, she promised to make a fine batch of pumpkin muffins and we left on good terms.

The same conversation repeated itself time and time again.

Some families were wearier of the Gifts than others, and each seemed to have a different reason for abstaining from using their Gift.

Our toes will fall off one by one if we use our Gift.

Each time we use the Gift a part of us turns to stone until we are no more than a statue.

The Gift takes a year off our life each time we use it.

If we use our Gift our family will be cursed.

It was a different excuse each time and with each one I grew more curious to know the ludicrous reasons they had for forsaking their Gifts. These ideas weren't made up; someone had to spread these fables to the villagers, and I wondered who would want people to fear magic so badly.

Who was keeping the villagers from understanding their abilities?

Some families couldn't be swayed, and I didn't push them too hard. But other families were on the edge about it, and I pressed into that doubt.

"You won't be hurt by using your Gift," I explained to Dunkin as we sat on the bench outside the street of the village. Dunkin lived alone in a small loft above the cooper's workshop where the air smelled like rust and the shops faced the main square.

"I reckon you will; your ears will grow longer," he informed me.

"That's not...which way is longer, exactly?"

He thought for a moment. "You know, just, longer."

"I'm sure I don't know."

Another thought. "Well it doesn't matter; it'll happen to you if you try."

I sighed. "I would use my Gift right now to prove it to you, if you had a violin."

His eyebrows shot up. "I don't have one, but Torin has one!" He hopped up excitedly, as if the idea of seeing my ears grow longer was the most exciting thing he had heard of. I sighed, but if this would put the rumor to rest then I was happy to oblige.

Tap tap tap.

The door opened. "Got that old violin still? She's going to use her Gift!"

"Doesn't she know about the ears?"

That's the first time I've heard two people believe the same far-fetched tale.

An enthusiastic nod. "That she does! Says she don't care!"

"Come right on in. I'll go fetch it." Torin's enthusiasm matched Dunkin's, and the violin was retrieved quickly. They stood next to each other as I finished braiding my hair so they could get a good look at my ears while I played.

It's been years since I've touched a violin, but the instrument felt familiar in my hands as if it belonged there. Picking up the bow, I began to play, watching my hands move as if controlled by someone else. Both Dunkin and Torin's mouths fell open.

I didn't play long, but long enough to convince them that my ears were not, in fact, growing.

"See?"

Torin's mouth closed and his eyes narrowed. "How'd we know you didn't take lessons?"

That, I'm afraid, I couldn't prove.

"Don't matter, I'm convinced," Dunkin said, to my relief.

"Give it a moment, they may grow yet," Torin said. We waited. They didn't grow.

"What do you know, they didn't grow. Huh."

"So," I set aside the violin. "Let's talk about your Gifts."

CHAPTER TWENTY-SEVEN

The morning of the festival was filled with sweet smells and the jolly sound of laughter rolling through the village. To make room for other guests I choose to dismount my horse at one of the outlying homes, tying her up and giving her a pat before continuing the rest of the way on foot. A few carriages rode past me as I walked, as well as numerous folks on horseback. I recognized none of them.

So other villagers were coming. That alone made today feel like a victory. The small fear of no one attending kept me from sleep for a while last night and my eyes bore the proof today, but they lit up now as the village came to life. Decorations lined the streets, booths were set up by the cobblestone path, and a few villagers sat on corners playing music.

Haystacks and old crates formed rows that arched around the wooden stage in the middle of the field. A sheet was nailed to the side of the stage where visitors could sign up to perform their talent, and a booth sat next to it where donations would be received and sorted.

The village I saw today was a far cry from the village that I had first come to a year ago, and the change brought warmth into my heart. This wasn't all my doing; the people would have recovered from the war in their own way and their own time, but I took pride in the transformation before me and found hope that I was doing good and helping to change lives.

This isn't why I came; I left the Riverfront Tavern to find an adventure and explore life at court. I abandoned everything I knew back home to take on a title I didn't deserve and run a manor that I knew nothing about, hoping for some grand adventure along the way. Instead, I found a few scattered, wounded towns fighting to get their lives back together.

I never attended court. Instead I stayed for these innocent villagers who'd won over my heart and encouraged me to be a part of something bigger and do some good in the world. I'd come here a year ago looking for an adventure, and instead I built a home.

If I were a girl who cried with happiness, I might do so now.

"Ah, my lady!" Torin gave a big wave as he jogged a few steps to greet me. "I left the violin in my home, but it's all cleaned and ready for you."

"Beg pardon?"

He looked confused. "The violin—you were planning on performing during the festival, right?"

Oh. I hadn't thought of it. The idea made me squirm, but Torin went on. "Seeing as the festival was your idea and all, and you pushed us to use our Gifts, it wouldn't seem right if you didn't use yours too. Some people might think—"

"Yes, of course I will perform today. Thank you." I tried to look calm as I smiled at him, as if it was my idea to perform all along, but my stomach twisted in knots at the idea.

To distract myself from the nerves, I devoted myself to helping anyone who needed assistance this morning.

The people kept me quite busy, and it only grew as the nobles arrived. I found myself torn between the two worlds, helping both local and visiting villagers with the festival and interacting with the nobles, who all seemed quite impressed.

While grateful for their compliments, I was equally impressed. Some of the things the villagers made to sell were incredible; I had no idea they held such talent. The visiting villagers brought talents of their own, both to be shared on stage and to be sold from a booth. There were hand-carved utensils, beautiful dresses, wooden toys for children, baskets of every shape and size, fine jewelry that looked fit for a ball, seeds for gardens, written poems to give your loved one, and some of the most delicious smelling cakes I had ever seen.

The streets grew crowded before long, filled with men and women and children trading copper coins for little trinkets. I drifted to the stage where I sat on a barrel to rest my feet. Elenora and Berkley sat a few rows ahead of me, but they seemed engrossed in a conversation, so I held myself back.

Seeing Berkley reminded me of Christopher, and I wondered if he came today. The past two weeks I'd kept my distance from him, determined to sort out my feelings about the situation before seeing him again. He must have known I was working through something because in those two weeks he didn't stop by to see me once. Either he respected my space or he changed his mind.

Please don't let it be the latter.

The closeness between him and Alissia kept my heart from accepting the feelings he claimed for me, and my conflicted mind debated if it was right to care for him in such a way when another woman obviously thought him to be hers. He said there was nothing, but I wouldn't risk my heart on someone who belonged to someone else.

I'm afraid I've never known how to fully share my heart with another, but something about it caused my boots to tremble and my hands to sweat. The fear. The anticipation. The longing. It all swelled inside until there was little room for anything else. Should it scare me this much? Should I want it this much? Should it be all I'm able to think about until I'm facing the edge of madness and my body yearns with desire?

The only thing to do to keep from losing my mind was have a proper conversation with Christopher about this.

In order to sort things out I would need to stop putting off speaking with him, but if he wasn't here then I wouldn't be able to do that today, so I forced myself to push him from my mind and focus on the stage.

On the platform stood a boy with his hand over the ground in front of the stage and his eyes closed. A few seconds later the crowd gasped, drawing me to my feet.

There, peeking out of the soil, was a small tree.

As he continued to hold his hands out, the tree grew taller until it was to the top of the stage, then to the boy's knees, then his waist. Bright green leaves burst from the branches before a second color mixed in with them. The boy kept his hand out until the tree was as tall as he was, which was quite a height from the stage.

The audience burst into cheers, bringing the attention of the people behind us. I stared at the tree.

The tree, which resembled the shape of a mushroom, stayed in place after the boy lowered his hands. Some of the acts performed on the stage were merely talents, but this one had to be a Gift. From what I knew of the Gifts, this tree wouldn't disappear after the act was finished. He had made a tree.

Not just any tree.

He made an orange tree.

The tree was soon flooded with people who wanted to try an orange. Most of us, if not all, had never tasted an orange before. Westfallen wasn't built to support orange trees, and the import was only shared with royalty. But this boy, he could make them with his hands.

I drew closer along with the crowd, and while most wanted a look at the tree, I was aiming for the boy. Sure enough, it was little Tommy. Tommy had four or five older siblings who all worked at either their blacksmith shop or some neighboring farms. I spotted his mother standing nearby, looking nervous as she watched her son.

She had been against the Gifts, I remember. I wonder what changed her mind.

"That was incredible," I said to her as I drew close. She kept her arms wrapped tight around her chest.

"I just hope we don't pay for this later."

"I guarantee you; nothing bad will befall him. In the village I grew up in, some people used their Gifts daily and nothing ever happened because of it." I knew I told her this before, but I was surprised how many people didn't believe my words.

She gave me a tight smile. "I hope you're right."

Gently, I placed a hand on her arm. "Lily, his Gift alone can help save this village. The oranges can feed families and we can trade what's left to other villages."

"The tree won't survive for long, orange trees aren't meant to be grown here."

I looked at the tree and the people who were eating the fruit. They all seemed very pleased with its taste, enough to convince the boy to grow a second one. "But the fruit is fine to eat?"

"As far as I know, but the tree will die easily."

I shrugged. "So, we harvest the fruit right away. It'll be tedious work to continue making trees, but the revenue this will bring to your family will be enough that you live comfortably."

She turned her entire body to me and I saw tears in her eyes. "Do you really think so?"

I nodded. "I know it." A tear slid down her cheek and she thanked me. Tommy rejoined his mother and they walked off together, but I stayed behind to watch the other acts. I needed to know what other Gifts my people had that could be used for this village.

Again, I wondered who had turned them against their Gifts. Who made them fear magic so much that they wouldn't use it to save themselves? Likely I wouldn't ever know, and that was okay.

All I needed to know is what it would take to get them to embrace their Gifts. Magic could heal this land.

CHAPTER TWENTY-EIGHT

I was so caught up watching the performances that I almost missed when it was my turn. Luckily, I had Torin, who came running up to me with the violin in hand, dodging people to keep the instrument safe.

"Here it is! You're next, right?" He tenderly laid the violin down beside me.

"Thank you, Torin. Truly."

"Anything for m'lady. You can keep the violin; I never use it."

"I wouldn't want to take it from you," I said. The violin, now polished, looked more beautiful than I remembered.

"Nonsense." He tipped his head at me. "It would be an honor if you take it. You've already done so much for me and the village, and I reckon no one has done something for you."

His kindness touched me, and tears threatened to come again but I choked them back and thanked him again.

Shortly after that it was my turn to take the stage. My nerves didn't spike like I thought they would; I convinced myself that with such a large gathering and so many activities going on the attention on me would be limited. Still, I kept my head down and sat on the chair provided as I held up the violin. The position required for holding a violin made it hard to lift my head up anyway, so I closed my eyes until the song was over.

The music flowed effortlessly: an enchanting tune I had never heard before. Never being one for music, even I couldn't deny that this was a beautiful piece. The notes were dark and smooth, and I could picture the music playing on a pirate's long journey into some dark danger. The song grew livelier by the end, and the pace quickened until I thought my hand wouldn't move any faster. I pictured this being the part where the pirate finds the treasure but then must fight his nemesis for it. Then, just as the pirate tastes victory, the music ended.

I lowered the bow and raised my head to the applause that waited. As if by magic, my eyes looked straight at Christopher, and my breath caught in my throat.

I hadn't known he was here.

Everything else vanished except him.

He found a seat near the front where I could clearly see how his mouth hung slightly open. His dark hair was pushed slightly to the side today, but a few stubborn pieces curled back to the front. His eyes didn't blink as he stared at me, and I thought I saw something glimmer in them. He kept those eyes on me and something within my chest stirred.

Thoughts of Alissia rushed to my head but looking at Christopher made me want to ignore them. I wanted to forget about her, disregard her feelings for Christopher and pursue him for myself.

This *is* why I didn't trust myself to make my decision around Christopher. I couldn't trust the effect he had on me.

I doubted a second had passed and I prayed no one saw my internal struggle as I quickly exited the stage. I could feel Christopher's eyes on me. I peeked back to him where he abandoned his seat and followed after me. Quickly, I ordered my heart to be calm when I faced him.

Keeping the instrument in hand, I moved back from the stage and circled around the crowd of people, smiling politely at the few who stopped to offer praise. Christopher weaved his way through the mass, making his target clear, and I knew it would be incredibly rude to evade him. Instead, I pulled myself away from the crowd and patiently waited for him to reach me, reciting what I would say to him once he did.

He said nothing.

He stood in front of me for a long while, looking down at me and occasionally shaking his head. Finally, after what felt like forever, he raised his shoulders and let them drop. "Why didn't you let me come to you?"

"I needed time."

"To decide if you're willing to let me court you?"

My eyelids fluttered at those words. "No, to decide if you want to court me."

"I don't follow." He crossed his arms.

"Alissia."

A curious look. "Didn't we talk about that?"

I sighed, looking up. The thick clouds from yesterday found their way back into the sky, and I feared rain soon. "You talked about it, but I'm not convinced there isn't something there. Even if you don't like her, she has feelings for you, and I'm wary to come between something that's been there for years."

He laughed, and I furrowed my brow, causing him to hold up his hands. "I'm not laughing at you, it's just, I didn't think the Lady Anika was so concerned with other's feelings."

"Because I'm a little firm sometimes, doesn't mean I'm heartless."

"I know, it's just nice to see." He took my free hand in both of his, wrapping them around until my hand couldn't be seen. "Anika, there is nothing going on between me and Alissia."

"You say that, but—"

"She's betrothed."

That quieted me. He chuckled at the expression on my face, which I could only guess was something between stunned and embarrassed.

"She's betrothed...to my older brother," he went on. "They are keeping things quiet for nows—he's a private person—but it is official. They'll announce it as soon as he returns from his trip. I can assure you, there is nothing between us besides a brother/sister bond."

It took me a second to gain control of my words. How foolish I'd been, carrying the stress around for two weeks without asking him about it first. Slightly embarrassed, I lowered my head. "I didn't know."

He laughed again. "I'm aware of that. So that's why you've been painfully distant? Because you didn't want to hurt her?"

"And I wasn't certain if you were sure about me."

His smile melted my heart. "I can assure you I am very

certain about my feelings for you. I would kiss you right now to prove it."

My heart fluttered so hard I thought it would escape from my chest. Yes, I did want him to prove it. But I was grateful he didn't, unless we wanted our first kiss to be in a crowd full of strangers while a violin restricted one of my hands. Still, it didn't stop him from leaning a little closer to me and giving me a warm smile. The freckle on his chin moved with his grin, and little wrinkles creased the skin by his almond shaped eyes.

"So," he said. "If I come over tomorrow, will you let me see you this time?"

"I suppose so."

The festival had gone exceptionally well up to that point, but the second half was my favorite. I stored the violin in Christopher's carriage and spent the rest of the day walking through the village with him. He helped me clean up after the festival and took time to introduce himself to the villagers.

I realized if we married, he would become the Lord of Wateredge Manor and these people would become his people. I wondered if he realized that too, and that's why he gave them extra attention.

In the end I decided I was being silly. Marriage wasn't on his mind yet, and it shouldn't have been on mine. Just like that the thought was gone from my mind and my focus returned to the people. The counter would have a total tomorrow on how much each village raised, but for tonight there was nothing left we could do. Christopher gave me a ride to my horse where I paid the family who cared for him.

"I'll come visit tomorrow," Christopher said with one hand on my reins as I moved to mount.

"I look forward to it."

I hesitated for a moment, and that was all Christopher needed. He stepped into me, dropping the reins to place his hands on my jaw where his thumbs stroked my cheeks. His movements spoke confidence, and I wished I could say the same, but my body shivered with excitement.

His face bent down and his lips leaned in. He stayed still for a moment; his nose grazed against mine and his lips were posed right out of reach, where I felt his breath on my upper lip. It was enough that if I leaned in, just a little, we would touch.

I ached to feel his kiss, surprised at how much I wanted it.

His hands slid from my neck and into my hair. Then he closed the gap, and I felt the warmth of his kiss.

My hands reached up to the crook of his arm where I pulled him into me. His lips parted slightly then closed again, still gentle on my own.

I didn't think I was breathing. I *knew* I was flying.

Too soon he pulled back and his eyes fluttered open. "I've wanted to do that for so long."

"It was nice," I said. *It was nice?* I could come up with something sweeter than that, but my head remained dizzy from the kiss and my thoughts were muggy. I feared that was the best response I could give him tonight, that and the sheepish smile on my face.

He accepted my answer with a content sigh and a fond farewell. The sky showed hints of darkness and if I didn't leave now, I wouldn't be able to see on my way home.

It was lucky my horse knew the way so well, because my mind was too distracted to focus. All during the ride home I replayed that kiss in my head, certain it was the most perfect kiss ever given.

"Now don't you go telling Lady Claire on me." I patted my horse on the neck as we approached the house. The sky was almost completely dark by this point, and only one faint light could be seen coming from Elenora's room. "She'll think me properly ruined if she knew."

I stayed off the cobblestone path as I led the horse into the stables, taking extra care to clean her and put her away so I could be sure the house was asleep before I went in. I'd rather not talk to anyone tonight, certain that my face would give away my secret.

Once content, I sneaked out of the stables and back up to the house, where I slinked toward the side door that promised a shorter trip up to my room. This route brought me back past Lady Claire's room, where I ducked under the window. I had just opened the door when a noise startled me, and I jumped inside the manor, pulling the door mostly closed to leave a small gap where I could look to see where the noise came from.

Lady Claire's window was opening, and a figure was crawling out.

Fear gripped me until I heard Lady Claire's voice. "Mind yourself as you return, chances are you aren't the only one traveling at night."

Her secret visitor. Not my killer. I should have placed the bear traps beneath her window instead of my own.

I closed the door further until nothing but a tiny crack remained for me to peer through. The tall slender figure belonged to a girl, if I wasn't mistaken, who wore a dark cloak that she reached into now, fishing around until she pulled something out and fastened it around her head.

A wolf's mask. She was a Silver Raider.

I bit my lip to keep from gasping. No sooner had she fastened the mask then she dashed off into the darkness taking my chance of recognizing her away. I peered after her and waited until I heard Lady Claire's window shut to accept that I would learn no more tonight.

I was about to shut the door completely when another shape moved along the wall.

Once again, fear took hold in me. This figure was certainly female, but the Silver Raiders had taught me that I should be no less afraid of women than I am of men. The girl moved along the window, creeping toward Lady Claire's room.

If she took two more steps, she would be dangerously close to me.

I gulped down my fear, determined to know who was creeping outside the manor. I waited.

One more step. Almost there.

Another step. I flung the door open and dove at her, knocking her to the floor then pulling her back. She cried out but I flung my hand to her face to cover her mouth.

"Keep quiet, or else I'll clobber you," I hissed, attempting to pull her back inside the door so Lady Claire didn't hear us.

"Anika?" she mumbled in a voice I recognized.

"Elenora? Bejabbers! What are you doing out here?"

"Get inside!" Now it was she who pushed me toward the door. I cursed again but obediently went inside, closing the door firmly behind me.

"My room, now."

We hurried up the steps and into my room, where we both held our breath, waiting to see if we would be followed. When a while passed and no noise came, we relaxed.

"Care to explain?" I took off my overcoat and hung it over my desk chair then sat down to start unbuckling the boots.

"I could ask you the same thing? What were you thinking, tackling me like that?"

"Are you hurt?" I felt guilty for not asking her that as soon as we got inside, but she shook her head.

"No, you didn't hurt me. And if you must know, I was spying on Lady Claire."

I laughed as I yanked off one of my boots and threw it against the closet door. "That makes two of us then." Elenora was not the type of person that I expected to find late at night spying on an old lady, but relief filled me that I was not sharing in the mystery alone and I desperately wanted to know what information she had about Lady Claire.

So she wasn't a killer, but she was more than I thought her to be.

"Did you get a good look at the visitor?" Elenora sat down on my bed and rubbed her feet.

"No, did you?"

"Not this time."

My head perked up. "This time? How many times have you waited, prowling like a lion outside Lady Claire's window?"

"Honestly Anika, you make it sound scandalous. I've been spying on her for a while now; she's up to something." Her lips turned up with excitement while her eyes brightened with the adventure of it all. All this time I'd been afraid I was making up something where there was nothing, but this confirmed that Lady Claire hid a secret.

"I *knew* she was! Do you know anything specifically?"

She crossed her legs and grinned. "I know this visitor comes every two weeks exactly, but I think she's come other times too. I can't tell the nature of her visits, however. Sometimes she leaves Lady Claire in a bad mood, and other times she's practically giddy. It's very confusing." I felt slightly embarrassed to report that I knew nothing to contribute to solving this mystery, not keen on being outwitted by Elenora who didn't seem bothered that I knew nothing useful. "This is splendid, now we can spy together! I've tried following her before, but she's fast, much faster than I could hope to be, so it never gets me anywhere. Perhaps you could run faster."

"She's probably just headed back to the Woods; we could wait there to see who shows up."

Elenora's brow furrowed. "The woods? Which ones? Elthir Forest?"

Ah, so I did know something useful. Though, as soon as I said it, I debated how much I wanted to confess about the Woods and my involvement with them. "She wore a Silver Raider's mask, that's all I know."

Elenora gasped. "Do you think Lady Claire is mixed up with the outlaws?"

The image of Lady Claire wearing a Silver Raiders mask made me laugh. "I'm certain she isn't, at least not that way. But one of them is connected to her somehow, and in a manner that is suspicious enough to take place in the dark of night."

"And enough to use the window as a door," Elenora pointed out.

I leaned back into the chair. "I doubt we will figure this out tonight."

"No, I suppose not. Still, it's intriguing. Lady Claire and some scandal, who would have thought? She always says if someone were to be involved in a scandal, it'd be you." Her eyebrows wiggled, causing me to chuckle.

Little did she know what I was involved in.

CHAPTER TWENTY-NINE

"I forgot to tell you; I have more information," I said. Christopher and I sat in what could hardly be called a garden, pressed close to the manor to hide from the warm afternoon sun. Christopher and Berkley had arrived at almost the same time that morning and both looked surprised to see each other but had a good laugh. We left Elenora and Berkley in the parlor planning their wedding affairs as we escaped outside to explore this new relationship between us.

My hand rested in his, and his fingers traced each one of mine. Each movement sent a new sensation shivering up my spine with the awakening of feelings I hadn't felt in a long time. Even the sound of his breathing was intoxicating to me.

"What information?" he asked. My brows furrowed. I was so lost in him that I'd almost forgotten I had asked him a question. Meanwhile, his attention was focused on my hand as if nothing else mattered in the world.

I blinked to remember what I was going to tell him. "The Silver Raiders have a contract."

"Oh?" That got his attention, and his eyes pulled up to find mine.

"They plan to give it to each of the nobles as soon as Ronin gets his son back. It's a deal between them declaring the Silver Raiders won't plunder ever again, as long as the nobles are more generous with their people."

Christopher tilted his head. "It's a fair idea."

He must be in a good mood to call anything that Ronin came up with 'fair.'

"With any luck, will this be over in a few months?" he asked.

In truth, I had little idea when this would all be over, but I hoped so. "In the meantime," I shifted toward him. "Prince Bastian's annual ball takes place in a few days, and I don't have an escort."

His eyebrow raised. "You acquired an invitation?"

With the slew of things on my mind lately—Lady Claire's mysterious visitor, the nighttime attacks in my bedroom, my relationship with the Silver Raiders—I'd forgotten the odd invitation anonymously delivered for me.

Still unsure what to make of it, I simply nodded.

"Splendid. I've been sent my own, and thought I'd be attending alone, but I would much rather escort you." He thought for a second. "It will be our first official outing together, are you ready for that?"

"If you're certain you can handle me."

That made him laugh. "Honestly? I'm not sure that I can. But I know I want to try."

He leaned forward and cupped his hand under my chin,

lifting my lips to his own. He kissed me softly, then pulled back. "I think I'm going to enjoy trying."

His eyes looked into mine with so much warmth that my heart burned within me. "You aren't going to tell me to ease back on gambling, or tone down the swearing?" I was nervous for his answer, fully aware that those traits were not ones of a proper lady, and he likely never pictured them in his future wife. To his credit, Christopher leaned back and looked at me like I was crazy.

"And dim your fire? Never. That fire is part of your charm, and I'm growing quite fond of it." He kissed me again, though my smile was too wide to properly kiss back.

I'd never been so well kissed in all my life, and after he and Berkley left, the smile remained on my face along with the memory of his lips. In the upstairs hallway, I ran into Elenora who stood with her arms crossed and a scandalous look brewing in her eye.

"Beg pardon, I didn't see you there," I said as I moved by her.

She planted herself in front of me and continued inspecting my face with narrow eyes and a small smile.

"Is there something you need?"

She made a noise in the back of her throat, then pointed at me. "You kissed him!"

I gasped. Unsure of what response to give, I stood dumbfounded as she burst into a wide smile. Our relationship was new, and I wasn't ready to share it yet, but I also didn't want to lie to Elenora, especially after we bonded last night.

She didn't need my confirmation, so I gave in. "How did you do that?"

She shrugged. "It's a talent. But the real question is, when did this happen?"

I sidestepped her. "I'd rather keep the details to myself." I peeked back. "But it's new."

She clapped giddily. "Oh good, but what about Alissia?"

I whirled around and put my fists on my waist. I had forgotten that Elenora's mistaken information had set back my relationship with Christopher. "You told me they were betrothed! She's betrothed to his *brother*."

Her eyebrows raised and hand flew to her mouth. "How did I not know that? I'm privy to all the best gossip. Hmm. Sorry I informed you incorrectly."

I wanted to tell her the damage it caused between the two of us, but she was innocent in her assumption, and I didn't have the heart to take it out on her. In the end I waved it off. "No harm done, but please don't announce this new relationship to anyone. I don't want to make a big deal out of it quite yet."

She crossed her fingers over her chest. "I swear, it stays with me. And by that, I mean me and Berkley."

I could live with that.

I wanted to see how the villagers were doing this morning and speak to some of them about their Gifts. Last night, many abilities were revealed that would benefit the entire town and I needed to be sure no one was continuing to spread lies about the Gifts to frighten the people out of them.

Also, I wanted to know what an orange tasted like.

I left Elenora in the hallway and fetched my horse. "Ready for another ride, girl?" I patted the creature affectionately. "You're going to be as fit as the King's stallion with how much exercise you're getting." She whinnied in reply as if this idea pleased her. The saddle buckled into place and my satchel hung from the front. I stepped atop the edge of the trough to climb aboard the horse, then nudged her into motion.

We rode from the manor and onto the trail that led to the village. Rain came last night, and I steered my horse toward the main road to avoid the muddied paths of the shortcut. This route would take longer but it was safer under the current conditions.

I slipped into Baron Dorion's lands for part of the ride—only a sliver of his lands touched mine—but the path veered north to avoid the thick patch of trees on my land.

As I crossed into his territory, a new sound bit the air, though it took me a moment to place it. At first I thought it was a bird call, but the sound came again louder, and I labeled it as shouting. I pulled my horse to a stop to listen.

The noises were unidentifiable, the words drowned out by screams. Whatever the commotions entailed, it wasn't jovial. The screams I heard were far from cheerful and closer to terrified.

I kicked my horse into speed, unsure of what I would find or how I planned to help. Images of murderers and thugs and thieves crossed my mind and I prayed it was something less terrifying.

I was wrong; it was thieves. It was *my* thieves.

A carriage pulled to the side of the road, tilted with two wheels resting in the ditch. It wasn't clear if it was steered there purposefully or if the driver lost control, but I hoped it was the first. Two horses at the front stomped at the ground and shook their manes with fear.

The door to the carriage was open, and while a lady could be heard screaming inside, another was standing outside the door with something clutched in her hand. I looked closer to identify it. A knife, no bigger than her hand, held backward in her grip.

A third passenger, this time a man, stood outside the carriage with another knife, fighting the thieves. I assumed him to be the driver based on how he dressed in nothing nicer than a simple overcoat.

He may just be a driver, but he fought like a soldier.

Three Silver Raiders fought against the driver and riders, two against the man and a third by the carriage pushing the girl out of the way. She swung at the Silver Raider, who ducked to avoid the knife. The colorful cursing that followed revealed her to be a female.

Annoyingly, the girl inside the carriage continued to offer nothing more than sharp screams that pierced the air.

I hesitated, unsure of which side to assist, or if I should assist at all. Every person, save perhaps the screaming girl, carried a knife, and I wielded nothing more than a few apples in my satchel. I could test my aim and throw them, but I wouldn't know who to throw them at. Instead I trotted closer and yelled for them to stop.

No one obeyed.

The driver cocked his head toward me and yelled to stay away so I didn't get hurt. Then he followed up with an order to run for help. It wasn't clear where I was supposed to run to, but I knew I couldn't fetch anyone in time to do anything. This fight wouldn't last long.

My only goal was to get everyone out of this fight alive.

The Silver Raider by the carriage flung the girl to the ground, whose hair fell out from its updo and spilled over her face. In the time it took for her to recover, the Silver Raider made it in and out of the carriage, reappearing with something in hand. The other girl continued to scream.

The Silver Raider hopped down and kicked the girl who was trying to stand up. She curled into herself on the cobblestones and whined. Her knife had fallen by her feet, but the Silver Raider claimed it before she could retrieve it.

In the time it took them to do that, the driver fought the two other Silver Raiders. As I watched him fight, I grew confident in his status as a retired soldier. He moved with clarity that suggested training.

He swung his blade at the Silver Raiders, causing them to jump back. One lunged forward as soon as the knife was clear and tackled the driver who kicked with such force that he sent the jumper flying. The second dove for him, but the driver was quick with his blade and slashed at the Silver Raider, who anticipated a move and pulled to the side, but not before the blade caught his arm and drew blood.

The driver doubled down with a swift punch to the face that sent the Silver Raider collapsing to the ground.

I held my breath as he removed his mask. It was Ronin. His face pulled tight with pain and he clutched his arm where his sleeve was torn, revealing blood underneath. I swooned on my horse.

As the two noble ladies seemingly posed no threat, the other two Silver Raiders stood by and watched the driver to see his next move. In response, he threw the knife at one of the Silver Raiders, who deflected it with their own blade. Unfazed, the driver reached into his coat and pulled out another knife.

Ronin lay on the ground behind him, but slowly started to stand up with intent to surprise the driver from behind. Ronin didn't see the second knife.

I saw something flash in the driver's eye, and I knew that he was aware Ronin was on the move. He planned to turn around at the last second and overtake him, while Ronin thought he could move undetected. Ronin still had a blade, but he would be caught off guard both by the driver's awareness and by his second knife.

Just as Ronin stood and looked ready to lunge, I screamed, "Ronin, he has a knife!"

My scream took the driver by surprise, and I saw him look up at me with shock. That moment was all that the other Silver Raiders needed to run at him, so he was ambushed from three sides.

"No!" I pushed my horse forward. "Don't kill him!" I shouted over the chaos. Before striking, Ronin peeked at me and his eyes softened. He pulled the blade back and wrapped his arms around the man, pining his arms to his side.

"The knife, Cera!" he grunted.

One of the other Silver Raiders, who must be Cera, twisted the man's wrist until the knife dropped. Together they shoved him back to the carriage.

"I got what we need." Cera held up a small purse.

"Please let him go," I said. The driver looked ready to continue the fight, and I feared none would stop until the opponent lay bleeding to death. The girl in the carriage had quieted, and the second was on her knees, watching us. The confusion and fear that her eyes held earlier had faded.

The three Silver Raiders remained focused on the driver, waiting to see what he would do.

"I'm not afraid to kill you," Cera told him. He debated his next move. I guessed he didn't have a third blade hidden in his coat or he would have shown it by now.

From where the Silver Raiders stood, they had their back to the carriage, but I could see everything. I saw the girl slowly reach out to the ground and pick something up.

The driver's second blade. It fell within her reach.

The girl, who I didn't recognize, stood and flung the blade with surprising speed. I shouted, but they didn't have time to react. Each turned in time to see the blade come toward the middle one.

I didn't know if the driver had given the girl lessons, but she threw with remarkable accuracy. As the knife struck, the driver ran to the girl and ushered her back inside the carriage. She clutched his face before agreeing, and kissed him quickly.

They were together; no doubt the retired soldier had taught his lady how to protect herself.

Cera looked ready to retaliate but Ronin told her to let them go as he crouched over the fallen girl. She wriggled on the ground, but I couldn't see more than her legs. The carriage sped away and I dismounted my horse to run to Ronin.

"You!" Cera yanked off her mask and threw it at me. "We had this until you showed up!"

"I helped you, and I did so without hiding behind a mask. Do you know what I just risked for you? If they recognized me, I could lose everything!" I stomped toward her, furious that she couldn't say thank you. If I hadn't yelled when I did, the driver would have put a knife through Ronin's chest.

She stepped toward me and pushed me backwards. "We didn't ask for your help! We don't need you!"

I shoved her back. "I'm not here for you."

"Hey!" Ronin yelled at us. We both looked down, and I instantly wished I hadn't.

The angle of where the girl stood when the blade was thrown in comparison to Ronin blocked me from seeing where the knife struck her, but now I had a clear shot. The knife stuck out from the dip in her neck between her shoulders.

My hands flew to my mouth while Cera dove to the ground next to the girl. Ronin eased her mask off, trailing blood across her face as he did.

"Bree, it's going to be okay," Cera said as she stroked her hand. The girl continued to wriggle on the floor and I knew that Cera was lying. I boasted no medical experience, but I knew this injury would kill her. She couldn't breathe.

Dark red pooled around her neck and stained Cera and Ronin's hands. Ronin's arm looked nasty as well, but he ignored the wound.

The girl choked, and I wanted to look away, but my eyes stuck to her face. This girl couldn't be more than fourteen. Her thin blonde hair lay around her, the bottom tips drenched in blood. She had full cheeks met by blue eyes, which dripped slow tears.

She continued to struggle, grasping Cera's hand with both of hers and trying to pull herself up. She didn't have the strength and her head fell back to the ground with a thud. She tried this once more before giving up. Ronin stroked her head while Cera held her hands and they both spoke calm words to her, encouraging her through her death.

Cera's hands remained entangled with the girls while she passed. Once it was clear she was gone, Ronin sucked in his breath.

"We never should have brought her." Tears flooded his cheeks.

"She begged, and we thought this would be simple."

"Her mother is never going to forgive us."

Cera pulled the knife from the girl's throat in silence while Ronin looked up to me for the first time. I didn't know what to say. He stood slowly, the pain in his arm catching up to him as he clutched it. I circled around the girl to reach him and allowed him to collapse into me. He buried his head into my neck and cried tears down my shoulder.

Instantly, I pushed all my own sorrow away as I held him and waited for him to be okay again. As he hugged me, Cera cut a long strip out of her shirt and tied it around the girl's neck, slowing the bleeding and making her look less gruesome.

"We should go." She was obviously irked, and I knew my presence made it worse. "We need to get this girl home so her mother can say goodbye before her body goes cold."

"Do you want me to come?" I asked.

Cera flashed me a look of pure anger. "No, you stay away from us."

Ronin pulled back from me and gave me a sad smile. "Come visit soon; I need you."

I nodded. He blinked and another tear slid down his cheek. With a shaky breath he joined Cera, where they picked up the girl and began the walk back to find their horses.

A small trail of blood trickled behind them and settled in the soil as a final reminder of the spirit lost today.

CHAPTER THIRTY

"Is everything alright tonight?" Christopher rested his hand over mine in the back of his carriage. My mouth forced a smile so he wouldn't see the pain in my eyes. Images of the girl's death had haunted me for the past several days, and I longed to be free of the horrific vision. I saw red every time I closed my eyes and felt the pain of her death in my chest.

I didn't even know her. The thought of her mother's sorrow gripped me, choking me and leaving me desperate for air.

Over and over I replayed the situation, wondering if I could have done something differently. I could have helped. I could have gotten off my horse and tried to stop them. Instead, the fear of being associated with the Silver Raiders kept me at a safe distance, and a girl had died as a result.

It wasn't my fault, and I tried to sooth myself with this thought, but it didn't lessen the pain. I had never seen someone die before.

The situation caused me to reevaluate my relationship

with the Silver Raiders as I pondered how many times Ronin has asked me to join them and how easily that could have been me who died.

The Silver Raiders were loved by the townsfolk, but they were hated by the nobles, and having a relationship with them brought danger upon myself. I'd always disregarded that danger because of the freedom I felt among them, but that freedom wasn't worth my life.

Ronin wasn't worth my life.

Christopher sensed my grief, but I didn't want to burden him with it tonight. In a way, I wanted to spare myself from his knowing look as I told him how I realized the danger of the Silver Raiders. He'd known this all along, and he'd warned me about it repeatedly.

We rode toward the palace where Prince Bastian waited to supply his guests with a night promised to be full of joy and celebration. I didn't know what the ball was celebrating, per say, but I knew celebration was expected.

Celebration seemed impossible for me right now, but I didn't want to steal it from Christopher. I would tell him tomorrow, if I saw him then.

He looked handsome tonight dressed in cream sleeves and a blue vest with golden lining and a ruffled collar. His family ring circled his finger, and I felt the band move over my hand as he rubbed it.

I wished to know if Elenora gave him a clue on what to wear, because he matched my dress perfectly. My gown had a cream underskirt with a blue layered overtop, and gold designs stitched into the fabric. Elenora would know the name of the cut, or the style of fabric, but my knowledge of such things was limited. What I did know was that this was a gorgeous gown.

Its beauty was soon masked by the splendor of the Vestalin Castle.

The castle looked like something pulled from a children's storybook, and I doubted another castle could rival its beauty. It lit up the sky, putting the lingering sunlight to shame. The stonework was built into the edge of a hill, earning its name Hidden Hill Castle, which overtime changed to merely Hid'Nill Castle. The tall structure held several courtyards, ones starting at the bottom and others halfway up the hill, each bursting with trees that hinted at the coming autumn. Those trees must have witnessed much over the past several hundred years as they stood watch over the magnificent castle, and I wondered what tales they would tell if they could talk.

We rode up to the large gate where we handed our invitations to the solemn footmen. He took them while a second man opened the door so we could see the castle in all its glory.

"Have you ever been here?" I whispered to Christopher.

"Yes, but it steals my breath every time." Then he glanced down at me. "The view's never been this beautiful before."

I blushed and accepted his arm as we walked into the courtyard. Other nobles flocked around us and we soon found ourselves engulfed in a sea of vibrant colors and rich laughter. Movements pulled us toward the grand doors looming ahead, shining gold in the torchlight and guarded by seven officials on each side.

We entered the enlarged foyer where the ceiling stretched up past the first floor. A wide stairway curled around both sides where it met again on the first floor with golden doors propped open for the other guests to move through. Past the threshold came the sound of music and voices, indicating that's where they were holding the ball.

Christopher guided me up the stairs and across the landing to the doors. I looked around for Elenora but didn't see her yet. I hoped to spot her later, but by the size of the crowd I couldn't be certain we would find each other. I was sure I would lose Christopher if he wasn't pinned to my arm.

The main attraction lay inside the doors where a band sat on one side, performers on the other, dancers in the middle of the floor, and a clear air of power hung in the room. A large chandelier draped from the ceiling, illuminating the space. Gold designs spread along the stone flooring, and pillars lined the walls.

The front of the room is what took my breath away. Several steps led up to four thrones, which held the king, queen, and prince. The distance made it hard to see details, but the crowns on their head made their title clear.

This week held two firsts for me: first time in front of nobility and first time watching someone die.

A line wrapped along the wall, leading up to the thrones. "We are introduced to their Majesties first, then we can dance," Christopher said to me.

I let out a low whistle as I looked at the length of the line. "This will take a long time," I guessed.

I was wrong, the introduction was no more than a footman calling the guest's name, who offered a quick bow then moved off to the side. If the guest brought gifts, a second footman received them and disappeared for a moment before returning empty-handed.

We watched the dancers while we waited in line. Before

too long we stood close enough that when the people shifted, I caught my first look of the king's face.

His bald head gleamed in the chandelier light, and his full beard crumpled under his chin and lay down to his chest. His narrow lips grinned, but it was his wide eyes that carried his smile. Beside him sat his beautiful queen with a tanned complexion and almond eyes. She carried a bit of weight to her, but it made her look cheerful and full of life.

Prince Bastian resembled his mother almost perfectly, and it was clear from the way his father looked at him that the king adored his son.

The crowd shifted again, and I noticed a figure sitting on the fourth throne who wasn't there before. From what I knew of the royal family, I guessed this to be their second son Adrien. This son resembled his father but touches of his mother came out in his dark eyes and thin nose.

All together they looked like a happy family.

Soon enough we stood next in line to meet King Rinaldo. Christopher told the footman our name and he waited until we walked before the king to call. I prayed my curtsy didn't embarrass me as I lowered my head and held my skirts.

"The name again?" King Rinaldo called to the footman, who gave him a second look. I didn't hear the king ask for anyone else's name twice.

"Sir Christopher of Dunderin and Lady Anika of Wateredge."

King Rinaldo leaned toward his wife and nodded once. Her eyebrow raised as she turned back to look at us.

Her gaze fell directly to me.

Unsure of what to do, I repeated my curtsy, and saw

Christopher bow again beside me. When we rose, he reached for my arm, but King Rinaldo stood up and we froze in our place.

He looked behind his throne where two guards stepped out. I sucked in my breath. This didn't happen with any of the other guests. I peeked to Christopher to see his reaction and found him as uncomfortable as I felt. I wasn't sure if knowing he shared my nerves should have eased my worries or escalated them, but they only grew.

"Come with us please." One of the guards motioned to the side where a thin door waited and I gulped.

Obediently, we walked toward the door where additional gruff guards met us. I peeked behind us to see the king, but he had returned to his position of smiling at the next guest. His two sons watched after us.

Through the door and down a corridor we followed the guards to a small, dimly lit room.

"We only need the lady." One of the guards placed a hand on Christopher's arm when he tried to follow me through the doorway. My chest tightened and I looked back to him with wide eyes.

"I'm her escort for the evening, and I don't feel right abandoning her."

I wasn't sure if it was his request or the fear in my eyes but after a long hesitation the guard nodded. A small piece of comfort found me in that I wouldn't be facing this alone, whatever this was.

Three officials waited inside the room, two standing by a desk and a third rising from his chair at our arrival.

He nodded to the guards. "Thank you." Then he turned to me. "You are the lady Anika of Wateredge Manor?"

I pulled my shoulders back to feign confidence. My

throat felt unbearably dry and I didn't trust it to speak, so instead I nodded.

He rounded the desk and stood in front of me. "I am General Walter, commander of the Vestalin army." My throat tightened.

"I've called you here because we have reason to believe you are involved with the Silver Raiders."

CHAPTER THIRTY-ONE

"I'll take your silence as confirmation?"

Christopher stepped forward to save me, though I didn't see the point. "Where did you hear this?"

The driver from the carriage fight must have recognized me and reported me to the crown. That, or the girl who threw the knife.

"We've had two witnesses come forward claiming to have seen her with them."

"She's been assisting me; I had hoped to keep her involvement private, for her reputation."

Both General Walter and I looked confused, though I hoped I hid my confusion better. The General crossed his thick arms and lumbered toward Christopher. "And you are?"

"If I may," one of the officials behind General Walter broke rank to step forward. "That is the man who has been giving us valuable information concerning the Silver Raiders."

It felt as if the floor dropped from beneath me. I looked

at Christopher, but he avoided my gaze, keeping his eyes steady on General Walter. I knew I needed to look as if I knew this all along, but my feeling of betrayal was difficult to mask.

General Walter looked between his men and Christopher with piqued interest. "I've heard of this; is that truly you?"

To them, who weren't used to Christopher's voice, his reply sounded normal, but I could tell his tone lacked strength. "I am."

"Whistles and Willowfurs!" His face erupted into a smile almost hidden under his thick black mustache. "Jolly good to meet you, sir! And the Lady Anika assists you?"

Christopher coughed into his fist. I could tell he was nervous, and I hoped it was because he felt my anger. "She is the one who gets the information for me; I merely relay it back to you."

All the men in the room looked impressed, except for Christopher who now looked sick. I had strong words for him, but I bit my tongue.

"That must be truly dangerous for you, my lady. The crown thanks you for your work." General Walter tipped his head at me. While I felt grateful that he didn't look ready to run me through with a sword anymore, I felt quite ready to run Christopher through instead.

"How do you get this information?" The guard behind him spoke again. General Walter shot him a look, but he mustn't have been truly upset at him repeatedly breaking rank because he turned back to me with eager eyes awaiting my answer.

For the first time, I spoke. "They trust me."

"I'm surprised you get in those woods! Every man

we've sent in has been killed, some by beasts and others driven so mad they do it themselves. Some don't make it more than a few steps before a magnificent creature eats them whole!"

My eyes widened. I'd traveled into those woods repeatedly and while strange noises surrounded me, I'd never seen a dangerous creature. Ronin spoke of a gatekeeper that let me in, and I silently thanked him for sparing me from a creature or madness.

"Yes, the Woods like her," Christopher mumbled.

General Walter put his hands where his belt was pulled tight and gave a little laugh. "Good thing for us! Alright, be off with you." He laughed again.

That was it? That wasn't so bad. It was nothing compared to the conversation Christopher and I were about to have. With a small bow we thanked General Walter and exited the room quickly before he could change his mind and ask further questions.

As soon as the door shut, Christopher grabbed ahold of my hand, but I yanked it from his grasp. "Anika—"

"Not here."

"There's too many people everywhere else."

I stomped ahead of him. "Not in the carriage. I think I'd quite like to return home, if you don't mind."

I gave him little opportunity to stop me, and ignored all looks tossed our way as I stormed back the way we'd come. With determination I trudged through the crowds to the courtyard where I called for our carriage.

"Is everything alright, my lady?" the footman asked.

"I suddenly feel quite ill," I informed him truthfully. The man nodded and ran off to find our carriage while I tapped my foot.

"Please, don't let this ruin our evening."

"How could it not?" My voiced raised and I whipped my head back to shoot him a fiery look.

"Because you don't know why I did it."

"Did it? The way they said it sounded like this is an ongoing arrangement. How could you! All your talk about honesty, was that just for me to be honest with you? Am I not to be given the same courtesy?"

I thought of Bree who died a few days ago and wondered if I had more to do with that than I thought. I freely shared everything I knew with Christopher, who in turn freely shared it with an army intent on taking down the Silver Raiders. He made me a traitor to Ronin and a spy for Vestalin and gave me no say in the matter.

Christopher stepped close to me. "I'm doing this for you! To protect you! Everything I've done—"

"Is for you! You are doing this all for you; don't pretend that you did any of this for me. You couldn't wait to get more information out of me about Ronin, and I bet it didn't take long for you to run to the king with your precious information and get a reward for it."

"You think I'm doing this for me? I'd rather stay out of the whole thing, but you seem intent—"

"Then stay out of it!"

His hands ran through his hair. "Good lord girl, you never let me get a word in edgewise! Will you just listen to me?" He reached for my hands but didn't fight to reclaim them after I wrenched free. I backed out of reach and planted my feet firmly, ready to hear him out. We were attracting the attention of several footmen, but none came close enough to hear our words, even with our shouting.

I still wasn't convinced I shouldn't run him through

with a sword. His betrayal pierced my heart like the knife that killed Bree.

"You don't know what torment this has been for me. I'm terrified that something is going to happen to you because of him. At night I'm haunted by images of you being killed upon entering or leaving the Woods without having a chance to say that you aren't a Silver Raider. I'm terrified that their lifestyle is going to appeal to you and you will join them, and that'll lead to your death. I'm terrified that Basiliea will see you as a threat and come after you yourself. Don't you see? They aren't safe. The nobles are ready to fight them, and when the fight comes, I don't want you anywhere near it."

I quieted my anger. While I've been plagued by images of Bree's death, he's been haunted by the idea of mine.

I stayed quiet while our carriage rounded the bend. "Early night?" Christopher's driver spoke. His jacket held hints of crumbs from the dinner we must have interrupted.

"Early indeed," Christopher mumbled.

The footman held the door open and Christopher offered his arm for me to step up into the carriage. I ignored it.

The familiar sound of clicking on cobblestones came as the horses pulled away from the beauty of Hid'Nill Castle. I remained silent as we bobbed in our seats, staring out into the night.

Christopher didn't speak, which was wise. It was good to see he had a little bit of sense left.

A tear slid down my cheek, which Christopher saw and he immediately moved himself next to me to hold my hand.

"She died," I whispered.

"Who?"

I choked on my words. "That's the thing, I hardly knew her. Her name was Bree, and she was a Silver Raider. I ran into them on the road in the middle of an attack and I tried to do something, but she landed on the wrong end of a knife. I watched her die; she was no more than fourteen."

Christopher sucked in his breath and stroked my hand while he searched for the right words. "That must have been traumatic for you."

I sniffled. "I feel so foolish for letting it derail me, but I can't stop thinking about it." I couldn't help but see tears as weakness, it's how I've always felt. Turns out all it took was the death of a stranger to unleash them, and they pushed roughly while I struggled to hold them in.

"I would be concerned if you didn't feel saddened by such a thing."

He didn't say what I assumed he desired to, about how this is what happens to those mixed up with the Silver Raiders. While I felt grateful that he held his tongue now, it wasn't enough to allow my heart to forgive him.

"It was wrong of you to go behind my back to Vestalin." I searched his face for any sign of regret, but the darkness shielded him from me.

His voice came softly. "I know. But Anika, if there's any chance that my actions led to your safety, then I can't be sorry. Let us not forget, it was me who saved you tonight."

CHAPTER THIRTY-TWO

I gathered food for Ronin in my basket. I knew it wouldn't be much, but he didn't have a proper kitchen in the Woods, so I hoped these sweets would bring a little joy to what would no doubt be a grief-stricken camp.

Cera would be irked by my presence, but out of respect I'd stayed away for a week after Bree's death, and now I needed to see if Ronin was okay. Besides, I didn't care what Cera thought.

I rode hard through Christopher's lands to minimize being spotted. Our relationship remained uncertain; the last time we spoke I asked for space. I appreciated his concern for my well-being, but his blatant deceit was difficult to swallow.

Part of me felt responsible to tell Ronin about what Christopher did. He deserved to know what information the Vestalin army collected, but I feared his reaction to the news and the possibility that he would hold me accountable for Christopher's actions.

As I entered the Woods of Silver and Light, the story General Walter told of his men dying within mere steps of entering slowed my movements. My eyes stayed sharp as I treaded cautiously through the vast darkness, veering toward the hovering lights whenever I saw one. I didn't know how much I trusted this mystery gatekeeper that Ronin spoke of.

The Woods had a mind of their own, and for some reason they'd opened their barriers to accept the Silver Raiders into their midst, and I wondered what made them accept me too. Maybe they saw into my heart and thought it belonged with the Silver Raiders, and they led me to them. Though, they also spared Christopher when he entered, and I knew his heart didn't belong here.

Perhaps Basiliea was the gatekeeper Ronin told me of, and she personally cleared the way for me, but that idea terrified me.

I'd failed to gather any further information regarding Basiliea, but at least the Vestalin army was aware that she planned to return to their world.

Oh. That's a new thought. Perhaps I could be grateful for Christopher's actions after all. I never would've turned in Ronin but knowing that an army stood preparing for Basiliea helped ease my fears. I wasn't ready to forgive Christopher yet, but my thoughts softened toward him. He posed a lesser threat than Basiliea.

Despite Ronin's blind trust, my opinion of Basiliea remained unchanged. I felt certain that, if brought back, she would bring turmoil to the land. I hoped she'd keep Ronin out of the fight when it came to that, or preferably Ronin would take a stand against her, though he'd given me no indication that he'd ever stand against Basiliea.

I neared the camp and donned my best face of sorrow which wasn't difficult to conjure. No doubt I was walking into a devastated camp and I wanted to be respectful of their mourning.

Young children skipped near the wide trees that marked the border of the camp. These trees grew thicker than the others and closer together, almost forming a barricade, with dark ivy weaving along the bark. The children spotted me, and many called out my name with glee. It was a warmer welcome than the one Cera usually offered me. They sprinted toward me to give my legs a hug and to peer inside my basket. I handed out a few small loaves of sweet bread for them to split, and once they'd received their gifts, they were happy to escort me to Ronin.

The camp appeared normal: a few men heading out for their day of working fields, women caring for children who ran through the trees and tents, a few more sitting in the treehouses watching the people below or hanging laundry, and one maiden singing a sweet song.

If I didn't know better, I'd think they didn't know one of their own died last week.

Nibbling on the bread, the cheerful children led me to the lake where Ronin stood beside the still water's edge with his bow in hand, aiming toward the targets against the distant trees. Next to him stood a small boy who I hadn't seen before. His dark complexion matched Ronin's, and as he turned to look up I spotted the same big smile. Ronin's smile looked wider today than I'd ever seen it before, which was quite the feat. He showed the boy where to grip the string and handed him a few arrows to shoot. The child aimed too low, driving the arrows into the dirt, but patient Ronin laughed and showed him again.

The children ran off again with laughter on their tongue. This camp wasn't in mourning.

When Ronin looked up, he spotted me hesitating twenty paces away. I gave a small wave, confused at the sight before me. Where were the crying children who'd lost their friend? Where were the grieving mothers, comforting the one who lost her child and holding their own children close? This wasn't the scene I'd pictured.

Ronin bounded up to pick me up in his arms and spin me around twice. I couldn't help but grin as I clutched my basket in my hand. Not only did Ronin not appear to be in mourning, he looked like a giddy village boy back from his first hunting trip, alive and filled with wonder.

"These are for you," I tried to hand him the basket once he set me down, but he jittered with excitement and hurled himself back toward the child by the water's edge.

"Come meet someone!" He reached for the boy's hand and led him back to where I stayed. The child dressed in a white shirt with a black belt and rolled up trousers that looked several sizes too large for him. He clung to Ronin as he stood before me, and Ronin wrapped an arm around him.

Something in the boy's eyes was so...familiar.

The way that Ronin held the boy protectively, the way that the boy looked back up at him, the little dimple in his chin—I knew who this was before Ronin said it. A thousand questions flew through my mind as I stared at the innocent boy before me.

"Anika," Ronin beamed down at the child, "I'd like you to meet my son, Landon."

I dropped the basket.

"Hello," the timid voice of the child came. I stared back.

He slipped from his father's grasp to retrieve my basket and hold it up for me.

I stammered. "Th-thank you." Then I looked at Ronin. My eyes were wide. He seemed to be enjoying this moment and let out a hearty laugh.

"How?"

"The nice lady brought him back to me," Ronin explained in a slightly childish voice.

The nice lady. Basiliea. Yes, I'd assumed she had something to do with this; what I didn't know was how, precisely, when she didn't have her powers back yet.

Ronin wasn't answering my question, but he peeked down at his son and his eyes warned me to hold my tongue. I nodded while continuing to stare at the boy.

Ronin actually did it; he brought his son back from the dead. That explained why he wasn't in a state of grieving, but no doubt his celebration at the return of his son felt like mockery to the woman whose daughter died.

A new thought crossed my mind, and as soon as it did, I knew it to be true.

That's why the town wasn't mourning, there was no one to mourn over. Basiliea had brought back Bree. I wondered if the mother even knew that her daughter died before Basiliea put life back inside her.

No, I'm sure she did. I'm sure she let her mother grieve to the point of death before showing up like a hero to grant her back her daughter.

It was a smart move for Basiliea to keep the Silver Raiders indebted to her. What parent would stand against a creature who gave them back their dead child? She was building her loyalty list by bringing back loved ones, in hopes that they kept their eye on their child and away from her evil schemes.

I had her all figured out.

So lost in my own thoughts, I almost missed Ronin's words. "Do you want to keep practicing, Landon? Anika and I will watch you."

His son nodded eagerly and skipped off with his bow.

As soon as Landon was out of earshot, I said, "Ronin, how did she do this? I thought she wasn't strong enough yet."

"Come on, you're going to love my son." He ignored the question as he walked after Landon. Uncertainly, I sighed and followed him.

We sat down on the rocks while his son practiced. Ronin didn't act interested in speaking as all his focus remained on his son.

I allowed the silence for a while until I thought the questions would burst from within me. "Is she back?"

He turned his head subtly but didn't look at me. "No." A wave of relief surged through me, but Ronin wasn't finished speaking. "She's not back, but she is close, close enough to be able to give me my son."

"And Bree?" I guessed.

"And Bree."

Thunk. Landon's arrow hit close to the center and he spun back to see if his father saw. Ronin did, and he clapped loudly in praise, sending a look of pure joy over his son's face.

The moment felt so raw that I suddenly felt selfish for not giving Ronin a better reaction to his son. This is what he had fought for over the past few years; this is what he wanted. He had his son back in his arms, and I didn't even say congratulations.

I pulled back my fears to present him with joy. "I'm really happy for you, Ronin. I mean it. This is incredible." I gestured to his happy son.

He smiled, this time at me. "Thanks, Anika. I can hardly believe it myself." He leaned back on his hands with one knee up and the other resting over the rock's edge. "Landon fits right in with the camp; everyone loves him."

"Will you stay? I assumed once Landon returned, you'd retire to a quiet village and take up work at a flour mill or copper shop."

"A flour mill, really?" He seemed interested in the thought.

"Well, yes, they're by a river and you could have a nice little house by the coast, private enough but still close to town," I rambled. "Someplace where you can see the sun."

"The Woods have accepted Landon."

My eyebrows drew down. I tried to remember if my assumption that the Silver Raiders would leave the Woods of Silver and Light came from something Ronin said or my imagination. Either way, Ronin's idea or mine, it didn't sound like that was his plan now.

"You plan to live here forever?"

He shrugged.

I sat up straight. "Ronin, you can leave now. You can take Landon and start a new quiet life filled with honest work. If you stay here, you'll raise him as an outlaw."

His lips pursed and he breathed out roughly through his nose. "My son will be safe here."

"You can't see the sun here! This isn't a place for children."

"There was a time I thought this was a place for you, but even though you don't want to live here, it doesn't mean it's not perfect for us." He picked up a rock and skipped it across the lake rather harshly. It only jumped once before plummeting under the water.

I tried to picture Ronin raising his son here, and the scary part was it was easy to imagine. I could see Ronin out by this lake teaching his son to be a better shot than he was. I could see Jack teaching him swordplay. I could see Ronin and Landon and the whole rest of the group living in the trees until the Woods overtook them.

I could see that all so easily. What I couldn't see was a way to convince Ronin that this wasn't a smart idea. The Woods had accepted them for now, but these trees wielded a mind of their own and they wouldn't share their home forever.

"Are you going to send the contracts out to the nobles?" I asked, almost afraid of his answer.

His silence told me what I feared.

"You have no intention of abolishing the Silver Raiders."

Again, silence.

I shook my head, irritated at him. He had a chance to stop this. No one knew who the Silver Raiders were; they could leave the Woods and take up an honest life elsewhere with no repercussions. Now with his prized son back, Ronin could leave this behind him, but he chose to cling to the life of banditry even when he watched Bree die last week.

How could he choose this life?

I didn't think I could be a part of this anymore. If Christopher hadn't saved me from General Walter, I would have likely lost my life for treason at the Prince's ball a few days ago. I couldn't justify being a part of this world when they had no plans of leaving this life behind.

I stood up, prepared to tell Ronin as such, but he stood up at the same time.

"Come with me." He held out his hand. "I want to show you something."

CHAPTER THIRTY-THREE

Fifteen Silver Raiders and I sat in a bumpy wagon next to large sheepskin bags carrying unknown packages as we left the Woods and moved toward the villages. Landon wrapped his arm around his father and rested his head on his side with a smile identical to Ronin's.

I tried to take my eyes off him, but it was so difficult. A week ago that boy was dead.

We followed a westward stream as it widened where cottages appeared in the shade of tall trees. Cera let out a loud whoop which was immediately copied by several other Silver Raiders. I sucked in my breath, anticipating villagers to start fleeing, but instead children came running from the homes toward the wagon.

Ronin's laugh was loud, and his son's smile was eager.

Curious, I watched to see what the children would do. Adults appeared next, looking equally excited to see us.

"They're back!" some called.

"Come quickly! They're here!"

The bags we brought were opened, and the contents shared with the people. Two of the bags produced food which was handed to the children. The third bag had money which Jack passed out to the adults.

One by one the Silver Raiders hopped out of the wagon to visit with the villagers until I alone remained, watching the scene unfold.

"You've saved our home," I heard one man say with tears in his eyes. "Thank you."

"Without you, my children would surly starve," another said.

"I don't know what we'd do without you." I noted the difference between the first remark and the other two. The first thanked Ronin for what he had already done, but the others spoke as if they relied on the Silver Raiders to get by.

This story repeated itself over and over. We moved from place to place, staying for a short while to visit before moving on. Each town we visited rushed to greet us and collect their share.

While the others beamed, I fretted over the possibility of being recognized among the Silver Raiders. It seemed as though each small village emptied to come see us at every stop.

I realized I was wrong; Ronin couldn't claim a new life in a village without being recognized. If he wanted to find a place where he wasn't known, he would need to travel far, though I doubted any of these villagers would be eager to turn him in if he came to live among them.

Mixed feelings swirled within me as I saw the overwhelming gratitude given to the Silver Raiders for a portion of their loot. In my months of knowing them, I had never seen them treated as anything but something to fear or hate.

Never before had I seen them so loved.

When the bags reached halfway empty, we turned around and arched back. "We will have to skip Woolsey, but we will hit them first next time." Jack calculated. He was right, the bags fell empty right before the last small town and they steered around it quietly, telling the few they saw that they would return.

Back inside the Woods, Landon fell asleep on his father's back. He carried him through the trees and to his hut where I waited outside while he laid him in his bed. When he finished, he came outside and lowered himself to the ground beside me.

"*That* is why we do what we do."

"It was incredible to see how much the people love you." Now away from the fanfare, I'd had time to collect my thoughts and I chose my next words carefully. "But you will bankrupt the nobles and teach the villagers they don't need to rely on hard work."

"You'd rather I let them starve?" He asked me in a quiet tone. I put my hand against my forehead.

"I don't want them to starve. I know what it feels like to starve, and I know what it looks like to do hard work. I know that war bit this land in a way that I don't understand, but eventually the villagers need to pick themselves up and work on their own. You can't save them forever. I thought you knew this wasn't economically smart."

Ronin twisted grass between his fingers until it bent sideways. "I can't turn my back on these people, not when I can give them a better life."

"What would you have done if there were soldiers

waiting for you in those towns? Because one day, that's going to happen."

Ronin shrugged. "Fight."

My mouth gaped open. There were fifteen Silver Raiders today, including his son, and he thought they could take on soldiers. I couldn't fathom putting his son in risk like that, especially after he went through so much to get him back.

I also couldn't imagine killing someone, but Ronin didn't seem concerned with it.

"You can end this now, send out the contracts, remove yourself from Basiliea, and keep your son safe. You really want soldiers coming after your son?"

"It's because of people like them that my son died in the first place! It's because of them that Bree died! Those villagers out there are defenseless and weak, and they rely on me to survive. I won't abandon them."

"You son depends on you."

"I know how to take care of my son. I don't need you to tell me." He spoke sharply, and I let his words hang in the air as I waited his anger out.

Ronin sighed, lowering his voice. "They are neglecting their people, and I can't let them get away with it."

His words frightened me. "This is no longer about getting your son back. This is about revenge."

"This is about justice."

I couldn't argue with him, not when he so stubbornly believed himself to be right. "I need to go." I stood to leave.

"It's late," Ronin caught my hand. "Stay here."

I pulled free from him. "I can't; I don't belong here."

CHAPTER THIRTY-FOUR

I almost killed Elenora when she woke me up.

"Shh!" she hissed at me. "The visitor is back!"

"Who?"

She groaned and pulled me from the bed to the floor. "Come on! Lady Claire's mysterious visitor is back!"

If being dragged from the bed to the floor hadn't woken me up, that would have. I grabbed my slippers and snuck out of the room behind Elenora. She reached for my hand and squeezed it, which must have been a sign to stop because a moment later I ran into her.

She turned around a gave me what I could only guess to be a glare, but the darkness hid the expression from me. I mouthed sorry, but she likely didn't see it. I did see her arm exaggerate a motion toward downstairs though, and it took me a few moments to guess what she meant.

The visitor wasn't in Lady Claire's bedchambers; she was in the foyer.

We slinked forward to the top of the stairs, both

pressed against the wall so if anyone cast a light up the wide staircase, the corner would provide enough shadow to keep us hidden. Downstairs, a tiny hint of light came through the windows accompanied by soft voices.

This wouldn't be close enough to hear what they were saying. I took a few steps forward, and Elenora's hand flew to my arm.

"I need to know," I whispered to her.

"I'm coming too."

Though she couldn't see it, I smiled, grateful to have a companion in this small adventure. Between my bickering with Christopher and Ronin, it was nice to have someone I could call a friend with no complications involved.

Down the steps we slithered until the words grew clearer.

"I'd rather not." Lady Claire's unmistakable voice.

"You don't have to do it." That voice sounded familiar, but I couldn't place it.

"Still, is there another way?"

"I know you're not keen on it, but if the Vestalin general won't do something then we must. I should have tried harder to kill her before, but now Ronin's grown too attached and I don't want to hurt him like that."

For two separate reasons, my face paled. The first, from that sentence I assumed that the driver had not turned me in as I thought. Instead, Lady Claire did the deed. How she knew my involvement with the Silver Raiders was beyond me, but instead of bringing the matter to me, she went to the general. That betrayal outweighed Christopher's by far.

The second reason that caused me to feel weak came from the recognition of the stranger's voice who'd been lurking in my home.

Cera.

Anger burned within me. I knew I hated her.

"How much could she really know?" Lady Claire asked.

Cera scoffed. "She's not that bright, and her affection for Ronin should protect us, as his is protecting her now. But it's her suitor I'm more worried about."

"Christopher? He's a nice lad."

"You don't know him. He's taken trips of his own to speak with the general."

A pause. I wondered what was going through Elenora's mind right now. Suddenly I wished I'd left her at the top of the stairs.

"Can they stop Basiliea?"

"I'd rather not take that chance. If anyone else knows what Lord Thames knew, we could have a problem. I say we take care of it now." Cera sounded adamant. I wanted to jump out and tackle her just to see the look on her face when I emerged from the shadows to deck her.

"Why can't she do it?"

"Because she doesn't have strength beyond those woods yet."

Lady Claire sighed. "Fine, do what you must."

"Thank you. Consider it done." A clicking noise came and panic coursed through me. If they walked toward the door, there was a good chance they'd spot us. I turned to usher Elenora back up the stairs, but she was faster than me and already halfway to the landing. My feet skipped several steps as I flew after her with as much grace and stealth as my nervous legs could muster. At the top we both paused to be certain we weren't heard, and waited until the solid latch of the front door closed and Lady

Claire retreated to her chambers to tiptoe down the hall and back to my room.

Elenora lit a candle and looked at me with wide eyes. "What. Is. Going. On?"

In response, I flew to the closet and pulled out some riding pants and boots, undressing from my nightgown and pulling on the riding clothes. "I can't explain now; she's going after Christopher! I need to make sure he's safe."

"Anika, whoever that was, she killed Lord Thames, and it doesn't sound like she likes you. If she finds you, she might kill you."

"If she finds Christopher, she will kill him, and he doesn't know she's coming. I need to get there first."

Elenora trembled as she watched me. My own body felt like it was shaking, but I had to move quickly.

"There's a lot to explain, and I promise to tell you everything, but right now I need to get to Christopher before she does." I pulled on a jacket and gave Elenora a quick hug. "If I don't come back by evening tomorrow, report what you heard to the crown."

"Anika, I don't like this," her voice shivered.

I sighed. "Me neither. I need to go."

I couldn't wait any longer. If Cera rode here, she would beat me to Christopher's house. My only hope was that my horse was faster, and that I knew the way better. I couldn't be sure she knew exactly where Christopher lived, and I had the advantage in that she didn't know I was coming.

She had the advantage in that she already left.

From the conversation, it sounded like she might head straight to Christopher's house. There was a chance she would plan out the murder beforehand and do the deed a different night, but I didn't want to take that risk.

I opened my window and climbed out. Elenora followed me.

"What are you doing?" I stared at her as she maneuvered her small feet over the ledge.

She grunted as she worked. "Making sure...you arrive alive. I won't be able to sleep tonight anyway, and she's less likely to attack if we're together." She landed on the ground and took a deep sigh.

Gratitude curled in my chest and tears filled my eyes.

"Thank you, Elenora, I know I don't deserve it but—"

"Yes, I'm the greatest friend ever, I know. Come on, you said we need to leave now."

We didn't saddle up the horses, and I worried about Elenora holding on, but she managed with minimal commentary. We pushed our horses to their fastest speed as we raced through the night to Lord Hughes' home. I knew the path fairly well, but the darkness and the fear inside me made me second-guess the way.

"We're lost, surly she beat us there already." I felt close to tears. I attempted a short cut path and now it'd gotten us lost.

"Nonsense, we are almost there."

"How do you know?" I spoke through the lump in my throat.

"I've spent every summer in these parts since I was little. I know. Now come on." Elenora moved to the front and led me the rest of the way. To my satisfaction, I was headed the right direction after all and we were within minutes of his home.

We rode our horses directly to the main door where we jumped off and pounded our fists on the wood. I hadn't thought this part through, of what we would say, but I hoped Christopher answered.

We knocked again, louder this time. Both of us scanned the darkness with jittery eyes.

After a third knock, the door opened, and a tired looking Lord Hughes stood in the doorway. "What is the meaning of this?"

"Sir, we must see Christopher." I tried to use authority as I spoke but my voice shook with fright.

He looked us up and down with bags under his narrowed eyes. "Two ladies coming to the house at this hour? People will think it's improper."

"No one else is awake to see us. And we wouldn't care if they could—" I wasn't finished, but Lord Hughes cut me off.

"You wouldn't mind being mistaken for courtesans?"

Ordinarily, the word on his tongue would have made me blush, but my mind thought of little else besides Christopher's safety. "We need to speak to Christopher NOW. It's a matter of urgency."

"Please," Elenora added timidly.

"Hmph. Tie the horses there." He furrowed his brow but opened the door so we could step inside the foyer.

"Erm, we don't have anything to tie them with. I'm afraid we left in quite a hurry."

This received a long sigh. "I'll call for a footman. It seems you really are desperate to get inside."

"Very," Elenora added. He allowed us in where we stood like fools unsure of what to do next.

"We need to talk to Christopher," I repeated myself. Lord Hughes waved his hand.

"Yes, yes, I know. Christopher." He lit a light that

allowed him to see our faces clearly. His eyebrow raised. "Lady Anika. My son seems quite smitten with you."

I sucked in my breath. I'd almost forgotten that I'd yet to properly meet Christopher's father since our courtship began. This is not how I planned to impress him, showing up in a mess at his doorstep demanding to come inside. Unsure of what to say, I mumbled a thank you.

He staggered off to get his son while Elenora leaned over to me. "This is going really well."

I shot her a look.

"And, for the record," she continued. "I would have minded."

"What?"

"If we were mistaken for harlots? I would have minded very much."

I laughed. "I think we're safe. As long as Christopher is safe, we are safe."

Pictures flashed through my mind of Cera getting here first, climbing through his window and slicing his throat. I waited for Lord Hughes' scream as he found his son dead in a pool of blood.

Please, please be alive. Please.

"Anika."

Christopher rounded the corner in a navy robe and mishappen hair, and I began to weep.

"What's going on?" Though baffled, he came to me and wrapped his arms around me while I sobbed into his chest. Lord Hughes watched on, but I didn't care. Christopher was safe, and that's all that I cared about.

Lord Hughes cleared his throat. "Will you ladies be staying for the night?"

Elenora stepped up to answer. "Yes, I'll take my room now. They need a moment."

"Thank you, father. I'll see Lady Anika to a room." Christopher's voice vibrated from his chest against my cheek.

His father made a disapproving sound at leaving us alone, but he was too tired to argue. He left, with Elenora trailing behind and a footman scrambling to button his shirt as he ran past us to take care of the horses.

"Now," Christopher said as soon as they were gone. "Want to tell me what this is all about?"

I clutched to him, grateful for his warmth. Warmth meant life. "I thought you were dead." Amidst wet sniffles and the chocking sobs, my voice came out in a very unattractive way.

"You'd better start from the beginning."

CHAPTER THIRTY-FIVE

*L*ate into the night we stayed up, perched on the end of the guest bed while I told him my tale and held his hand tightly. A little too tightly—he had to ask me several times to take it easy.

"I'm sorry." I lessened my grip. "I really thought we might arrive to find you dead."

"I know, and I love seeing your concern for me, but I also like the use of my hand." He stroked mine with his thumb. "Everything is going to be fine."

He must not be listening to me. "Cera is planning to murder you."

His spare hand ran along his jaw and down to the back of his neck. "I don't see why, in truth there's nothing I know that an entire army doesn't know. I'm baffled that she knows I've been in touch with them and confused on why she'd still see me as a target."

"I think it has a lot to do with your association with me."

He was quiet for a few moments as he stared at our

hands intertwined. We left the bedroom door open for the sake of my honor, but it still felt borderline scandalous sitting in the guest bedchambers with him alone at night.

"What do you suppose Lady Claire is getting out of this?" Christopher asked suddenly. My eyebrows raised. So, caught in protecting Christopher from Cera, I hadn't thought about Lady Claire's involvement in this scandal.

"I can't claim to know. I've noticed she's been growing distant since the start of the season; we used to have lessons daily and nothing I did escaped her watch. But we haven't had a lesson in months; I'd assumed she'd given up on me. Maybe her time shifted to the Silver Raiders."

Christopher chuckled. "I can't picture you being trained as a lady. You would have broken my governess."

"I think I broke Lady Claire."

"But Ronin's never said anything about her to you?"

I thought through every conversation to see if I mentioned Lady Claire to Ronin and while I knew that her name came up a few times, he never claimed to know her. "No, I'm fairly positive he would tell me if she got involved with them. Since Cera is coming at night, I assume Lady Claire's involvement is limited. Besides, Ronin swore they didn't kill Lord Thames, so Cera is working around him."

Unless he was lying to me, something we were both thinking but neither of us said out loud.

Creaking from the hallway caused us to both pause as if we were about to be caught doing something wrong. Frozen in place, we waited to hear if the noise would repeat itself, but it didn't. I tried to predict what Lord Hughes would do if he found us in this room together, but I didn't know him well enough to guess.

Christopher let out a long breath that suggested he was

more worried about being caught than I was. By the state of my muddied clothes, red cheeks, and wild hair, no one could think my intentions in coming here were seductive.

"I don't know why I'm worried about being caught as if we're doing something wrong," I said, turning to look at Christopher. I was surprised to find his face close.

I was even more surprised when he kissed me. He took his hand from mine and wrapped it around my waist, sliding me closer to him. The kiss wasn't long, but it was deep enough to send warmth vibrating through me. Suddenly, I didn't think the redness on my face was from the tears anymore.

It was simple, but this kiss felt different than the other two we shared. A sense of urgency lingered behind his lips.

"Oh, perhaps I should be worried about being caught." I laughed as I pulled back.

He sighed and leaned his head into my shoulder, keeping us close. "You have no idea how happy I am that you're here. I thought I would lose you after I went behind your back to the crown."

"Hmm. Well a little fear is healthy for any relationship."

His head jolted up to look at me and I laughed and kissed him again. "I'm kidding."

"Fear is abundant right now, nevertheless. I think I should travel for a few weeks to keep from Cera." He rubbed his forehead as he spoke, and I saw real worry behind those lines.

As much as I hated the idea of him gone, it was better than dead. Though weeks might be generous. I guessed it would take more than a few weeks to ease Cera's vengeance.

"Where will you go?"

He didn't think before answering. "My grandfather's. I've been planning to visit him anyway. If anyone can tell us about Basiliea, he can. If she's already able to bring people back from the dead, then she's closer to escaping her banishment than I thought."

My eyes lit up. The eventful past few months took away my remembrance of the tale he told of his grandfather, and now I regretted not seeking him out sooner.

Come to think of it, perhaps I knew someone else who could help in this situation. It might've been time to write Rumpelstiltskin to see what he knew, though I dreaded my family knowing the mischief I'd been getting into. "Will your grandfather know how to destroy her?"

The side of his lip pulled back. "Likely not. But he may know something useful."

That didn't sound encouraging, and the little hope that I felt started to fade.

"Come with me." His hands took ahold of mine.

"What?"

"I don't trust Cera, or Ronin for that matter. Come with me and let's wait this whole ordeal out."

I knew I was asking Christopher to hide away somewhere he couldn't be found, but it felt like running away when I considered it for myself, especially since the target wasn't on my back and no one else could talk to Ronin like I could. The last time I tried to talk to him didn't go the way I'd hoped, but I wasn't ready to give up on him yet.

Ronin sought revenge, but he loved his son more than anything. Once the Vestalin army came after Basiliea he would see how dangerous it was and he would take his son somewhere safe. That was my hope, and I wanted to stay to help convince him of that.

Plus, I owed Elenora answers, and I couldn't do that if I ran. Then there was the matter of Lady Claire to deal with.

I planned to deal with her harshly.

"I have to stay."

Christopher frowned, thinking the situation over. That's what attracted me to him, his unwavering dedication to look at things logically. Often headstrong, I tended to jump into situations without inspecting them from every angle, where Christopher looked at angles I didn't even know existed.

He took a breath and opened his mouth, but shut it again quickly. After another pause, he spoke, "As much as I hate saying this," he let the words hang in the air before continuing, "I think sticking to Ronin is your best bet right now."

If Christopher was saying that, he must have really meant it, because not only was he logical, but he despised Ronin.

Now that he'd said it, I'm surprised I didn't think of it myself. Not only would sticking with the Silver Raiders keep me from Lady Claire, but it would also provide protection from Cera. Unless she had more audacity that we thought, she wouldn't dare strike me so near to Ronin.

There was a slight sense of deceit about it, hovering by Ronin for my own protection, as well as attempting to manipulate him away from the Silver Raiders, but I reminded myself of little Landon and it quelled my hesitation. That boy deserved to be as far from Basiliea as he could get.

One downfall stuck out to me, and I wondered if it occurred to Christopher. "It'll put me closer to Basiliea though."

He nodded to show me he already placed that. "At the first sign of trouble, run."

Not particularly gallant advice—it wasn't the same as 'stay and fight your ground'—but it was the advice I needed to take. While unsure to the extent, I was in over my head with Basiliea. My one goal at this point was to convince Ronin to take Landon as far away from trouble as he could before the trouble came.

Once the trouble came, I was afraid I would be useless.

"I won't make you promise me to stay safe," Christopher said as he kissed my forehead. When he spoke, his breath rippled over my eyelashes. "Just...stay safe."

CHAPTER THIRTY-SIX

The next afternoon after a delicious luncheon and a long conversation with his father, Christopher departed for his grandfather's home. Lord Hughes called upon some soldiers to stand guard around his manor to keep his household safe from a possible attack, and Elenora, after a grueling discussion with me that included a scolding about my endless bad decisions, bravely rode back to keep an eye on Lady Claire and to deliver a story about me visiting my family to explain my absence.

I wrote a letter to Rumpel to explain the situation. Then I rode back to the Woods of Silver and Light.

"Must say, wasn't expecting you back, 'least not so soon." Jack stood at the front of the camp with his arms crossed in a position that spoke anger, but his eyes didn't hold it. I'd forgotten I left the Woods on rough terms, but now I was just grateful Jack met me at the border instead of Cera.

"You heard about my argument with Ronin?"

"Aye. But for what it's worth, I've had the same conversation with him myself. In fact, I think I set you up for the reaction you got; he's quite put out about the topic."

My eyebrows arched. I hadn't thought Jack was against Basiliea. "You think he should leave the Woods?"

"Far as he can go. But I see his hesitation. He fears Basiliea coming after his son if he doesn't hold up his end of the bargain," Jack explained. Ronin hadn't voiced that same concern to me. When we spoke, it sounded like vengeance held him here, not fear.

Ronin didn't seem capable of fear.

"It's no good, you know. He won't leave, not as long as the people need him."

"Then I guess we'd better find a way to show him the people don't need him. And if it's all right with you, I'm moving in for a few weeks."

His brows shot up and his eyes widened before a smile stretched across his face. "Welcome to the Woods."

I decided arguing with Ronin would get me nowhere. Instead, I set aside our differences and focused on assisting Ronin with whatever he needed, including caring for Landon. Pleased at my sudden change of heart, Ronin eagerly agreed to let me stay with them in the camp for several nights, contented enough not to question my motives. If he had asked, I had an excuse prepared, for I remained unsure of how to deal with Cera.

She wasn't the only danger here: Basiliea's tent loomed in the trees, a constant reminder of the threat that lay ahead.

I felt trapped, caught in a story I knew wouldn't end well, but I couldn't figure out how to change what lay ahead. Taking Ronin and Landon away put them at the mercy of Basiliea's wrath once someone freed her, which would no doubt happen, and happen soon. But allowing them to stay and free her put us all at the mercy of her powers before we knew of a way to destroy her.

The safest bet remained convincing Ronin to abolish the Silver Raiders as soon as Basiliea returned and take Landon far away, but the scary reality was that I didn't have much say in the matter. Even if I knew how to keep everyone safe, my voice had little impact over anyone's actions, least of all Ronin's right now.

Maybe I could change that. Maybe I could get him to listen to me.

With nothing left to return home for, my days in the Woods stretched into weeks as I worked to gain back Ronin's trust in hopes of convincing him to leave the Woods. While the friendship rebuilt easily, each time I tried to steer the conversation toward Basiliea he shut down, making progress difficult.

Cera avoided me over those few weeks, but I kept my eye on her, making sure I spotted her each day. She wouldn't have time to find Christopher and come back in such a short time, so as long as I saw her once a day, Christopher remained safe. Part of me wanted to tell Ronin what I knew about Cera, both so he was aware and to soothe my fears that he might have known all along, but I suspected I held an advantage while Cera remained unaware of my knowledge, and I wanted to hold onto that.

"The heist at Hid'Nill Castle is coming up," Ronin said as we drew water together from the clear river. He filled his first bucket then set it down for the next. "I want you to come with me."

My bucket grew heavy in my arms as a small battle

raged within me. If I begged him to stay away from the castle he'd only get upset and be driven away, making it difficult to convince him to leave later. This ought to be the last heist until Basiliea returned. One more robbery before he freed her. Then I'd convince him to leave. Finally, I settled for saying, "I'd rather stay here with Landon."

Ronin didn't look bothered by my answer. In fact, a small smile crept to his lips. "Landon really likes you. Says you're funny. That's a huge compliment coming from him."

I couldn't think of one joke I told Landon, but the compliment made me smile. "He's a special boy."

Ronin looked like the proudest father there ever was. "He sure is. Smart lad—he gets his best qualities from me." A slight hesitation. "It's good for him to have a woman's influence in his life."

When I thought of a mother's touch, I thought of words like 'gentle' and 'soft spoken'. Neither of those things described me. I could sooner be described as brash and my manners were near those of a pirate. Landon deserved a mother, but Ronin hoped for something from me that I couldn't provide.

He ought to have a real mother, and I hoped Ronin found that someday.

Jack came from around the bend and strode quickly to Ronin, whispering something in his ear. When he pulled back, Ronin nodded and jogged away, leaving his buckets of water sitting by the lake's edge. Jack took over the work for him.

"What was that about?"

Jack debated answering for a second before shrugging his shoulders. "Basiliea requested his visit."

Intriguing. My eyes looked in the direction where Ronin

ran and debated running after him to eavesdrop on the conversation. Among other reasons, I came here for information, and I wouldn't get it by doing nothing. I set my bucket down but Jack stopped me.

"She specifically requested you not come."

I peeked at Jack to gauge how serious he was and found his stoic expression. Under my breath I cursed. If I sprinted after Ronin, I may be able to reach halfway to the tent, but Jack was faster than me and I wouldn't get much further than that. His loyalty to Ronin bound him to his wishes, and therefore to the will of Basiliea.

If I couldn't get information from Basiliea, maybe Jack would provide some help. Though loyal to Ronin, he'd already voiced his uneasiness concerning the situation, and I could use that uneasiness to convince him toward changing Ronin's mind.

"This mission to Hid'Nill Castle, is it dangerous?"

His face fell downcast as he chose his words. "It's certainly different from our other missions."

"Because it's at the castle?"

Again, he thought before he spoke. When he did speak, it wasn't more than one word. "Yes."

His hesitation brought worries to my mind that mingled with my other fears and made my stomach bubble. I clutched the handles of the buckets and lifted them to walk back into camp while mulling over his expression.

He knew more than he was saying.

As we approached the main huts, Landon ran by with some friends, laughing. He stopped to give me a hug and some water spilled from my buckets as I bent down to him. He didn't stay long before running back with his friends.

We set the water outside Ronin's hut just in time for him to step outside.

"I thought you were with Basiliea?"

Ronin raised an eyebrow at Jack and I realized I shouldn't have offered that he shared that information with me. "It's time."

Jack understood before I did.

"Time for what?"

Jack's eyes darkened, but Ronin's carried a circle of fire. His quiver strapped tight to his chest and his bow hung in his hand while his other rested on a sheathed knife. Color drained from my face as I realized what he meant.

"It's time to ambush the castle."

My breathing quickened as I stepped in toward Ronin. "Please don't do this," I begged him. All plans of biting my tongue until he'd returned vanished as fear flooded my veins. It was the same feeling I felt when Cera rode to kill Christopher, like something dreadful was about to happen. Like death was near. The dread sank deep in my bones until it consumed me, and I pleaded with Ronin to save his life. "You have your son; you can take him and go somewhere safe."

His voice was flat and his words hard. "I'm not leaving innocent people under the rule of tyrants with no heart and no morals." The fire stayed lit in his eyes.

I placed my hand over his bow. "This started because you wanted Landon back. You raised him back from the dead. It's time to stop. Ronin, if you continue, it stops being about your son and starts being about vengeance."

Jack took a step back, but Ronin took a step forward. "You have no idea what this is about! This is about me giving these people better lives and taking power from those who hurt innocent people like my son!"

He made it hard to argue when he invoked the injustice done to his son years ago, but I knew the nobles now in a way he'd never cared to. Some of them might be power hungry and ignorant to the struggles of the villagers, but most of them, including everyone I'd spoken to, cared for those under them with diligence befitting their title.

Ronin's anger was misplaced, and his judgement was blinded by resentment.

"Landon deserves better." I couldn't think of anything else to say to get him to see that his actions would lead to hurting his son. His eyes narrowed and Jack let out a low whistle.

Ronin pulled his bow from my hand and stepped around me. "Landon deserved a doctor. And Landon deserves a mother."

As if summoned by his name, Landon ran up to Ronin and tackled him. Ronin's bow fell to the ground as he picked his son up into a hug. I stepped back and lowered my head as Ronin set his son down and knelt next to him.

"I have to go on a trip," he began.

"To get the bad guys and save the people!" Landon yelled as if rehearsed. I could picture Ronin telling him stories at night of how he single-handedly saved the villagers from starvation, and Landon leaning on his knee to listen eagerly.

At his son's gusto, Ronin laughed. "That's right! You be good for me while I'm gone, okay?" In reply, Landon crossed his hand over his heart, then his head, then put his fingers to the air.

"Promise!" He kissed Ronin's cheek. Ronin gave him

one last squeeze before letting go. As he ran off, Ronin sighed.

"I love him so much."

My eyes closed for a moment as I bit back instinct to argue, knowing Ronin's mind wasn't going to be changed today. I wouldn't stop trying. Once he brought Basiliea back, I would push harder for him to leave.

Once Basiliea was back, the Vestalin army would come at her and a fight would break out. Basiliea's true intentions would be revealed, and I had no doubt that she had something terrible planned. Ronin, upon seeing the destruction he caused, would have greater motivation to flee with Landon.

Hope wasn't lost yet. I could convince Ronin to flee, and the Vestalin army could overtake Basiliea. I could still make this right.

Ronin didn't know that the Vestalin army knew he planned an attack on the castle. This was information I shared freely with Christopher a while ago, and while the army didn't know when Ronin planned to come, they knew it would happen. I should warn Ronin of the danger he planned to walk into.

"I don't want to hear anything more from you Anika. Not today." Ronin brushed past me and informed Jack to alert the other Silver Raiders.

"There's something you need to know."

"You've said everything before, and it's not going to change my mind." Ronin proved he could be as stubborn as I was. His hand ran along his neck. "You know I want you to marry me. I want you to stay here with me and Landon, live in the Woods and help the people along my side. But I'll never convince you to join me, will I?"

With tears in my eyes, my head turned slowly. He breathed out through his nose. "Then you'll never convince me to leave."

He pulled his bow over his shoulder and reached into his pocket for his mask. Once it was fastened, he looked back at me. "You can't be a part of both worlds."

With that, he ran off toward the edge of the camp where the other Silver Raiders collected, preparing for their biggest mission.

Jack reappeared by my side and I tilted my head. I'd yet to see Ronin ride out without his trusty mate. I brushed the tears from my face. "You aren't going?"

"No, I'll stay with Landon. Cera will watch after Ronin." That thought brought me no comfort.

I tore my eyes from Ronin to inspect Jack. His hands folded over his chest and his finger twitched. The frown on his face set deep, matching the shape of the wrinkles on his forehead.

"Either you aren't going because you trust they will be safe without you," I spoke. "Or you want nothing to do with this mission."

Jack didn't look to me as he watched the Silver Raiders mount their horses and ride off. Once out of sight, he dropped his head to me. "My morals bind me from this mission."

"Tell me, what is this mission they ride to?"

His eyes remained dark.

"Jack, what's their mark?"

Ronin told me they stole the thing that a person valued the most. These treasured items held an anchor of their owner's soul, which when put together served as an offering to bring back Basiliea. She believed the king's sacrifice would be enough to bring her back, but I didn't know what that sacrifice was. What did King Rinaldo love most of all?

Jack's voice deepened when he spoke. "They ride to kidnap the Crown Prince of Vestalin."

CHAPTER THIRTY-SEVEN

My heart roared in my ears as I rode toward Hid'Nill Castle. Wisps of a plan formed in my mind, but my desperation to find Ronin outweighed everything. He didn't know the Vestalin army waited for him, and with such a high-profile target, he'd never succeed.

While the Silver Raiders were restricted to back paths to get to the castle without being seen, I wasn't bound by the same constraints. This would allow me to beat them there, but I'd be left to guess which entry point they planned to use.

A golden hue covered the sky as the sun bid the day farewell. The grand castle stretched ahead, looking normal, though I wouldn't know what it would look like once the Silver Raiders were inside. No trumpets blared and no battle cries pierced the air, so that was a good sign that I'd beaten them here.

The gate held shut, and I trotted up to the guards at the post outside. Four men stood, two at each side, leaned against the wall. They straightened themselves as I rode up and put frowns across their faces. "We aren't accepting visitors tonight, madam."

My horse halted in front of them, and they shifted their bodies in front of us. My horse sniffed at their weapons. "I have business here."

"What sort of business requires a lone lady to come to the gate in the evening?" One gentleman asked, which brought snickers from the others. "The crown has no tolerance for such affairs; find another bed tonight."

I blushed at their assumption and held my back straight. In my riding pants, I didn't have the look of a lady, but I didn't think I carried the look of a courtesan. "I am Lady Anika of Wateredge Manor, and I have business with General Walter."

"You lie. Begone."

I pursed my lips. "I demand to see the General *now*."

One of the guards shrugged. "My shift is about over; I could escort her to the general myself to see no mischief happens." The other guards mulled over this for a few moments before consenting. I didn't like the victorious look that the guard gave as he gestured for me to follow. The gate opened for us, and I dismounted my horse to walk alongside the guard. Once inside, the guard whistled to a footman standing along the edge of the courtyard to come fetch my horse. I didn't fancy the idea of parting with her, but I saw little way around that.

The guard led me to a side door where he put his hand on my back and gently pushed me inside. I tried to turn the way I guessed General Walter would be based on his office location the last time I visited, but the guard turned me the other way.

"Follow me."

As I did, I slid my hand on my waist where a dagger lay hidden under the waistband. Injuring this man would bring me no joy, but I had no intention of seeing General Walter and blowing Ronin's cover.

The guard had no intention of me seeing General Walter either. He opened a door to a dark room and pushed me inside.

"Now," he said, breathing into my ear. "The general doesn't take ladies, but I'll give you a fair price and a warm bed for the evening." His tongue flickered against my ear and I yanked away.

In the cover of darkness, the man didn't see me pull out my dagger. The blade flipped into my hand and the hilt came down with all my force against the side of his head.

He grunted before collapsing to the ground, and I wiped my ear of his saliva and my dagger of his blood, not checking for a pulse before shutting him in the room.

Now inside the castle, I guessed where the Silver Raiders would enter from. Built into a tall hill, there were only three directions they could approach Hid'Nill Castle, but numerous entrances. I doubted they'd use the main gate, but the castle was lined with servant doors on both sides.

To increase my odds of seeing them enter, I wouldn't pick one door and wait by it, but find a high point and watch from above.

One side held the livery and training fields, the other held the chapel. The chapel seemed a barbaric way to enter for a planned kidnapping, but it was for that very reason that I felt certain it was their plan. I couldn't decide if I had a better chance of sneaking toward the west side or if I should walk like I belonged and hoped no one questioned. My end result turned into a mix of both, walking with confidence while no one was around, then waiting it out in a side room or around a pillar when someone came down the corridor. If I'd dressed differently, this might have been easier, but my clothes resembled neither a lady's nor a handmaid's, and that made blending in difficult.

I happened upon a set of stairs and climbed until a landing produced a window that overlooked most of the west side. I placed my sweaty hands against the sill as I stared out into the darkness.

Blast. I couldn't see anything.

Frustration mixed with anxiety as I flew back down the stairs and searched for a servant's exit to the outside. Under the stairs stood a narrow door, and I prayed as I pulled it open.

Cool air greeted me. I'd found a way out.

I slinked along the castle wall to the hill it was built into, climbing as high as I could to sit and watch. The building took so many twists and turns that I couldn't hope to see every entrance, but I kept my eyes fixed on the distance to watch for anyone coming in.

I waited, and waited, and waited.

No one came.

I felt certain I'd missed them, but I also felt certain that a trumpet would go off at the first sign of intruders, and I hadn't heard one yet. Either the Silver Raiders succeeded in their mission already, or they went through the east side, and were already in the castle.

Either way, there was nothing I could do.

A noise behind me caused me to jump up with cat-like speed and bring my dagger to my chest.

A figure moved in the darkness, then a second, and a third. Hope flickered inside as I pushed myself against the wall. Either Ronin was about to cross my path, or this was an unlucky night for the castle.

The familiar mask of the wolves eased my worries. I hadn't though they would curl up and come from above.

"Ronin," I called out into the night. All of the Silver Raiders froze when I peeled myself from the shadows.

One of them reached up and pulled off their mask. Ronin held up his hands to ask what I was doing.

"You're making a mistake."

The Silver Raiders joined me in the shadows and urged Ronin to make this quick, who looked annoyed.

"You told me that already. It didn't stop me then, it won't stop me now."

I placed a hand on his chest as he tried to walk by me. "They know you're coming."

His look turned from annoyance to betrayal. "You told them?"

My head was already shaking. "No, but they know anyway. They don't know when, but they know you plan to come to Hid'Nill Castle and they'll be prepared."

He laughed. "We'll be fine."

Now it was my turn to be annoyed. "You think the king's guards will be stopped by your band of fifty girls when they try to take the king's son?"

Surprise flickered in his eyes.

"That's right, I know what you're after here. Tell me, did you plan to kill him before you took him?"

"Depends on how willingly he comes."

"I'm going to guess not very. You'd seriously kill

another man's son after you lost your own? You'd inflict that pain on someone else?"

Ronin balled his fist up and slammed it into the wall, cursing. "He had his chance! I came here to ask him to save my son and he didn't! Do you think I'm the only one he turned away? His people starve and he doesn't care!"

"The whole country is shaken from the war; mine is broken too. That doesn't mean the king or the nobles deserve to have their children killed in the night by a man too proud to see what he is doing as wrong."

"We need to go," Cera's voice came.

My patience with her was gone. "Did you tell Ronin that you killed Lord Thames?" I asked her, causing her to curse.

With wide eyes, Ronin turned to her. "Cera?"

"Or that you tried to kill me? Multiple times?"

Her voice sounded unapologetic as she focused her eyes on Ronin. "I did it for the same reason you'd kill Bastian today. I did it for Landon, and for the other children of the village who deserve better."

Ronin's gaze flickered between the two of us as he shifted from foot to foot. This new information ought to be enough to shake him out of his mission today, but his stubbornness made him unpredictable and a battle raged in his expression.

Cera took advantage of his uncertainty to push further. "Think of Landon, and what Basiliea will do to him if you don't do this for her. Think of the king who sat by while your son died."

Blast. At her words, something in Ronin's eyes cleared and I knew he couldn't be persuaded now.

With a dry voice he spoke, "I'm sorry, Anika. They deserve to pay."

He slipped inside the castle with the rest of the Silver Raiders, closing the door behind him for extra effect. I huffed.

The situation was out of my control now.

CHAPTER THIRTY-EIGHT

*P**lease Ronin, forgive me for what I'm about to do.*

I knocked on the door with trembling hands while squirming in my shoes. Please be here. Another knock.

My hand lowered just as the door opened. General Walter stood in the crack peering down at me.

"Sir, you might not remember me, but I have important information," I said with a shaking voice.

"I remember you." He pulled the door open completely. "Would you like to come in? You aren't the only visitor on this dark night."

My mouth opened to ask what he meant, but it quickly closed again. Christopher stood behind his desk in his riding clothes with a tight grip on the chair in front of him and stress in his stance. As I came into view his shoulders relaxed and he crossed the room to crush me in an embrace before I found the words to ask what he was doing here.

"I just arrived this evening," he said, anticipating my question. His riding clothes smelled like dirt, but for a moment it was the sweetest smell in all the land. He was here.

"You were supposed to stay away. Safe." I buried my head in his shoulder for a moment before looking up at him. The bags under his eyes and wrinkles on his forehead made him appear several years older than he had when he left a few weeks ago.

"I did go, but after speaking with my grandfather I rode straight here."

What information did he find that would drive him here to the General of the Vestalin army?

Again anticipating my question, Christopher said, "Grandfather knew more about Basiliea than we thought he would, including the fact that once she gains enough sacrifices of people's souls from these objects, she can come back."

I nodded; we knew that much already.

Christopher wasn't finished. "When she comes back, her powers return at the same time, not before."

The color drained from my face and the room swayed beneath my feet. My voice felt distant as I breathed, "But she has her powers back."

He nodded. "If she really brought his son back, then yes. She's free."

My knees felt weak and I steered myself to a chair. "Then why would she send Ronin and the Silver Raiders here?"

Now it was the General's turn to speak. "My guess is to do away with them or have us do it for her. Sending them to Hid'Nill Castle is an easy way to get them killed."

I sucked in my breath. "Would you really kill them? Most of them are girls, and many of them are young."

He snorted. "Well they *are* outlaws." He stroked his chin. "But since some are young girls and I see how Basiliea has influenced them, I'd settle for prison."

"It'll be an easy capture; they won't stand a chance against the guards," Christopher said, taking ahold of my hand.

"We've put all of the king's personal items inside his room and filled it with guards, as well as surrounded his room."

"What?" I breathed.

"That's what you said they take, a favorite item. Do you know which one they are after?"

Oh no. They were stationed at the wrong spot. "They aren't coming for an item this time, Basiliea sent them to take Crown Prince Bastian."

General Walter moved to the door without hesitation. "Are you certain?" He asked me quickly.

"Positive."

"That room is guarded by only two men. Stay here." General Walter shut the door and we heard him running down the hallway. A few moments later an alarm sounded throughout the castle.

My hand almost reached for the door to open it and run after General Walter, but rationality stayed me. I would be no help to Ronin now.

I still planned to fight for his freedom, and I prayed the country would be too busy dealing with Basiliea to care if Ronin lived in a distant land as opposed to a cell. I was prepared to vouch for his character if it came to that.

"Are you mad that I came here instead of finding you first?" Christopher asked behind me. He must have mistaken my silence for anger.

I pushed a smile to my face and grabbed his hands. "Not at all, it was a smart decision. That's what I like about you; you're full of smart decisions. I always seem to make the wrong ones."

Obviously pleased, he wrapped a hand around my waist. "You're pretty smart yourself." He kissed me then as soldiers ran in the corridors, the siren rang through the air, and the musty smell of the castle filled our lungs.

He's here. He's safe. I'd worried endlessly for two weeks about his wellbeing, and now he was here in my arms. The stress of it raised from my shoulders and allowed me to breathe again.

For a moment, it all vanished, and all I could hear, see, or smell was Christopher, while the chaos in the air vanished like a vapor, drifting away at Christopher's touch.

But the vapor thickened again until it was a fog that I couldn't see through, and all the senses rushed back, crowding my mind: the deafening siren, the musty smell, the pounding of feet as soldiers marched in distant halls, the fear in my fast-beating chest, and it overwhelmed me. Just as I was freed from my worry for Christopher, I was thrust into dread for Ronin. "I'm scared," I admitted into Christopher's chest while he stroked my hair.

"He'll be okay," he said, and I appreciated that he knew why I was so afraid without having to say it.

His optimism didn't spread to me; even a mere shred of his hope would do my heart good, but I couldn't find the strength. When I looked inside my head, all I found was fear and hopelessness. "What does she want?"

"That I do know. She had a claim on the throne years ago when her older brother died, but the advisors saw her as unworthy and gave it to her cousin instead. She's claiming back her throne."

That was the information that should have been included in that history book. I pressed my hand to my head, imagining what was going on out there and fearing when Basiliea would make her move.

If Basiliea was back, her daughter was probably back too, and I could only imagine what sort of a child Basiliea raised.

"I don't think I can stay in this room." The room felt too small to hold my worries.

Sympathy dwelled in Christopher's eyes. "While I understand your desire to oversee the situation, there's nothing you could do to help. If anything, they'd mistake you for one of them with how you're dressed."

"You could come with me; they wouldn't mistake you for one. Besides, the Silver Raiders are dressed in their wolf attire, and we aren't wearing any masks."

"Without bearing their crest, I still think they'd be confused, and confusion is a dangerous thing when weapons are involved." Christopher thought for a moment before letting go of my hand and striding to the side of the room where a few doors stood. "Nothing in here but weapons, maybe a dagger wouldn't hurt... let's try this one...ah yes, here we are." He pulled out a guard's livery and held it up. "I'll put this on, and you stay by me."

"Shouldn't I wear one too?"

He gave me an apologetic look. "Likely if you wear one, they will think you're a Silver Raider attempting disguise. There are no female royal guards." Again, he thought things through more thoroughly than me.

"They're going to be surprised when almost the entirety

of the Silver Raiders is female." I huffed, bothered by the minor injustice.

"I'm sorry you can't enlist as a guard." Christopher snickered. "It bodes well for us that the Silver Raiders are girls; the guards will be less likely to strike down a female."

"They can kill Cera," I mumbled, surprising myself at the harshness of my comment. On the verge of taking back my words, I realized I meant them. Cera planned to kill Christopher, and I wouldn't feel safe until she was dead.

But, I remembered, she stood on Ronin's side, and as long as she remained alive it counted as one more person protecting him and Landon.

Christopher took a long sigh as he paused with his hand resting on the door latch. Before opening, he swiveled his head to look at me. "We aren't joining the fight; we are merely watching." He waited for my confirmation.

"Fine. No fighting," I said, but I duly noted the tight grip he kept on the dagger he borrowed that was fastened to his waist.

"One day you'll be the death of me," Christopher said as he opened the door and peered out. I heard nothing but the scream of the alarm.

He led me out into the corridor and down to the end where the hallway split three ways. Christopher hesitated as he glanced to me, but I could only shrug. After a moment of thought, he chose the middle path which quickly morphed a staircase. I wanted Christopher to climb faster but he kept calm and inspected every direction before moving. His ability to remain sensible in such a time astounded me while my own blood coursed like a raging river.

The blaring sound of the alarm mixed with shouts came

from the side. No horrified screams, I noted. And no indication of Ronin.

We traced the sound to a courtyard, but while we could hear soldiers, the area lay empty. Christopher pointed up, bringing my attention to a circular railing enclosing the upper perimeter of the courtyard. Gruff shouts and the clattering of chainmail vibrated off the stone walls directly above us. If we moved out further into the courtyard, we were sure to see the action taking place on that balcony.

Now faced with it, I lacked the bravery to reveal myself to the rest of the guards, even if this meant I couldn't see Ronin. By the way Christopher held his arm out in front of me showed he wouldn't allow me to throw myself into the middle of the courtyard even if I wanted. It made me smile that he thought me brave enough to do such a thing.

The mixture of sounds made it extremely difficult to discern what anyone said or to make a shred of sense about the situation. My feet shuffled nervously, and I saw Christopher's do the same.

Sticking under the cover of the landing, we treaded lightly around the bend to the other side of the courtyard. As we moved, the scene began to unfold.

The Silver Raiders clutched against the landing, occasionally glancing down to see how far the jump would be. They'd survive it, but not without an injury too great to allow them an escape. They knew this too, because none jumped.

The guards surrounded them, multiplying by the moment as reinforcements arrived. Just as we were watching, guards filed out from the exact place Christopher and I stood a few moments before. We pushed ourselves against the wall as they ran into the courtyard, guaranteeing that jumping would do nothing for the outlaws. A bow rested in each of the guards' hands.

Prince Bastian stood among the crowd with his sword in hand. He looked almost comical, standing in his nightclothes among the fully dressed guards, but the anger in his eyes left little opportunity to laugh at him. He shouted insults at the Silver Raiders, and I guessed which one was Ronin based on the insults he shouted back.

One of the guards stepped too close to the Silver Raiders, and they swung their knife at him. The guard retaliated by swinging their sword, but the stealthy Silver Raider ducked quickly enough to avoid the deadly blow.

This move led to three guards approaching the Silver Raiders to wrestle the knife away, but other Silver Raiders came to the aid of the first, leading to a mad rush of all the guards involved. Swords drew with immaculate speed, and the guards on the ground knelt before nocking an arrow and aiming into the madness. They had to be excellent shots to trust they wouldn't hit one of their own. Either none were such good shots, or they had orders to not shoot, because the guards held their position.

Before the fight could cause anyone harm, the sky lit up with golden vibrance and a shock sent us all to our knees.

At this point the entire landing filled with guards, all who shifted their attention from the Silver Raiders to something above the courtyard. A dark sound rippled throughout the air, but it took me a moment to identify it as laughter.

My curiosity outweighing my fears, I stepped forward to see what stood in the sky that held everyone so captivated.

Basiliea floated in the air dressed in a long gown of gold

with her white hair rippling outwards. She smiled as she looked upon the scrambling in the courtyard.

"Twenty-five years and mankind still looks so weak." Though she barely spoke in more than a whisper, all could hear her voice. She twisted and cast a slender arm over the century towers. This time she didn't whisper. She bellowed her words as a fierce warning.

"Look east. Look, and see my army coming to take your throne."

CHAPTER THIRTY-NINE

I couldn't see the army, but a trumpet blasted and sent the guards into further frenzy. General Walter shone in the midst of the chaos, yelling orders and looking like the definition of strength.

Basiliea laughed again. "You're trapped here. By morning all will be slaughtered."

I should have stayed home.

"My silver puppets, I give you a choice," Basiliea went on. "Join me or die with them."

That's why she had them come to the castle, to force them into being her first line of attack. I didn't know of a single Silver Raider who would turn down her invitation, but the fact that they already stood at the tip of the guard's swords made for an interesting twist.

The blasted alarm finally ended, but the air was anything but silent.

"Silver Raiders," General Walter spoke this time. "All who join us will be granted freedom at the end of the battle." I didn't think he had the authority to forgive their injustices, but he hardly had time to confer with the king first. I silently begged Ronin to take the offer.

The Silver Raiders looked to each other for a moment, before Ronin raised his bow in the air. "For freedom!"

Something told me he wasn't talking about the freedom that General Walter offered, but freedom from the oppression of the crown. Still, the call was sneaky enough to convince the guards they accepted their offer, while clever enough that the Silver Raiders recognized the meaning. As the guards cried out in the small victory, they ran together from my sight, preparing to meet the army on the hill.

I wondered how long it would take Ronin to turn on the guards.

I also wondered who Basiliea brought back to life for her army.

But mostly, I wondered how the blast we were going to get out of this alive.

Christopher was wondering that too, and he grabbed my hand. "Go west," he hissed in my ear.

"West?"

"She said her army is in the east, so we go west. We climb high, exit above the hill, and move west." His plan sounded better than my plan, which was to stand frozen in fear.

Still uncertain of the way, we ran through the endless corridors and maze of rooms, climbing each staircase we could find. The members of the castle household pushed against us, each moving lower to some safe room that they yelled for us to follow them to, but we ignored them. We didn't want to hide within the castle; we wanted to get as far away as we could. We no longer took slow, methodical steps. We, like everyone around us, ran full speed.

"I think we're getting close," Christopher huffed.

"Good." If I wanted to maintain my breath, that was the only word I could manage.

Christopher found a window and stuck his head out. The sky remained lit at Basiliea's bidding and the gruesome sounds of fresh battle raged on. Christopher's head dropped down suddenly in a way that scared me, but it popped up just as quickly again.

"It's a bit of a jump, but there's feeding hay under this window. There's a trellis down a way, but it's a further drop and there's no guarantee it holds."

"Let me see." I ducked out to peer down. An unpleasantly damp stack of hay sat on the ground, but I wouldn't say it was under the window. We'd have to jump at an angle to reach it, but the trellis was under the window by the stairs, which would be a much harder window to mount, and he was right that we'd have to fall a ways before grabbing the trellis, and the force would bring it crumbling.

"Hay it is."

If we managed the jump with no injuries, this was the perfect place to exit the castle and run the last distance up the hill and down the other side to safety. A tall watchtower stood at the top of the hill, though I saw no sentries in the lookout.

"I'll go first, so I can help catch you at the bottom." Christopher didn't hesitate before hoisting himself out the window and lunging to the side. He landed awkwardly and rolled down the hay, but he appeared fine. I liked my odds of rolling in the hay better than him attempting to catch me, so I quickly followed suit.

Surprise filled Christopher's face when I rolled into him. "You were supposed to wait."

"I'm not waiting in a castle that's under attack."

"Fair enough," he grunted. "Come on then."

The height of the castle kept the battle from us, but when I turned my head I saw Basiliea still in the air, watching the scene unfold. The sight of her made me run faster.

We reached the watch tower and I peeked back over my shoulder. From this vantage point, we could see a large part of the battlefield where the men and Silver Raiders fought against each other. I tried to turn back to continue running but my muscles froze in place as my eyes searched wildly for Ronin. Did he stay loyal to Basiliea? Was he okay?

Looking at the watch tower, I heard myself say, "Let's go up."

"For what possible reason?" Christopher looked itching to continue running.

"To watch the battle."

"Anika, you are the only girl I know who'd rather watch the battle than run from it."

"I want to make sure Ronin's okay," I confessed. He sighed heavily.

"We are far enough away that we can look for a moment. But we are only climbing as high as that window there," he pointed to the window closest to the ground and I wanted to argue about what better view we'd have from the top, but the lower window meant easier escape if it came to that, so I agreed. All I needed was to see Ronin.

In the tower we found narrow stairs leading up to a wide window where a table was knocked over as the guards left in a hurry.

"For goodness sakes girl, keep your head down." Christopher said as I leaned out the window. I wanted to see everything.

The army Basiliea came up with impressed me in size, but there was no order to their formation and no obvious leader they followed. The entire army moved on foot, while half our men rode on horseback. Their only upside was Basiliea, who raised back up the fallen soldiers to continue fighting against our score of men.

"Who do you think she raised to fight for her?" A glimmer of hope stirred in me that she'd raised the men who'd recently fallen in war, and while I couldn't guess how she turned them loyal to her, I had no doubt we could sway them back to our side. Perhaps this battle could be over soon if we did so.

"Grandfather said she had an army of her own; I'm guessing we are looking at them."

My chest fell. "Where have they been this whole time?"

"Dead."

Her army spread as far back as I could see until the scattered trees and dip of the hill took them from my view. Our own army came from within the castle to valiantly push the resurrected army back. A new trumpet sounded, drawing our eyes to the south where the trees stirred. "There they are," Christopher breathed.

"Who?"

"The reinforcements General Walter told me about. They've been preparing for Basiliea."

"Do they have magic?"

Christopher hesitated. "No."

I peeked at Christopher. "I'm fairly positive killing Basiliea requires magic."

"I'm not privy to the general's war plans. All I know is he had reinforcements and a meager group of the few magicians he could find who aren't certain what spell will kill Basiliea."

I wanted to watch for the army, but if I waited too long to search for Ronin then he would be lost in the abundance of men.

The Silver Raiders stood out as the only ones not dressed in armor, and they'd already switched sides to Basiliea's. Disappointment sunk in me. I kept waiting for them to realize that they were unprotected against the blow of a sword and to run, but none did. I had to admire their courage.

The scene was partly hidden behind the castle, and though I could spot the small figures of the Silver Raiders, I couldn't tell which one was Ronin. Christopher searched with me, but we had little chance of spotting him.

"There!" Christopher's sudden voice made me jump, but I regathered myself quickly and looked where he pointed to the side nearest us. I'd been looking into the thick of the battle, but Ronin stood toward the edge of the fight, utilizing his skill with the bow while his long dagger remained sheathed. While he proved an excellent shot, taking down man after man, his quiver treaded toward empty.

A soldier kept Ronin in his sights and once he used his last arrow, the soldier rushed at him.

Coward.

Ronin saw the attack coming and threw down his bow to grab the short blade at his side. The soldier sliced downward in a thrust that Ronin deflected, then brought his sword to the side. Defending against a sword with a dagger required a lot of strength on Ronin's part, and each time I thought his blade wouldn't withstand the blow, but it did. The soldier swung again, but this time Ronin was faster. He knocked the blow to the side with a heavy force, then twisted his blade and thrust it forward in the same motion, driving it into the armpit of the unsuspecting soldier.

The soldier went down to his knees as blood flowed from the wound. Ronin pushed him to his back and stood over him triumphantly, with a darkness in his eyes that I didn't recognize.

"For justice!" he cried, lifting his dagger into the air and pumping his fist. A few around him roared.

I saw the attacker come from behind, but my cry got lost in the air.

The victory on Ronin's face quickly turned to shock as he dropped to his knees. Pain spread over his face and his mouth dropped open. I screamed, but I knew he couldn't hear me. Even if I had been on the battlefield, my voice would be lost in the noise of battle.

Slowly, Ronin's head tipped down to look at his wound. Erupting from his belly was the tip of a sword.

The sword disappeared as the man who'd crept behind him pulled the blade out and wiped it clean on the ground while Ronin collapsed on his back. He wrapped his hands around his stomach and pushed tight, the motion bringing a new rush of pain to his face. When he eased his grip on the wound, blood rushed through his fingers.

Cera came to his defense and slayed his attacker before dropping to Ronin's side. Anger blurred with my sadness as I blamed Cera for Ronin's wound. She'd pushed him to come here. She looked frantic, jumping up then dropping down. Ronin remained lifeless at her feet and I strained to hear her cries.

"Bring him back! You told me he wouldn't die!"

I closed my eyes for a moment as a tear fell down my cheek. If Cera ever came near me again I swore I would kill her.

Christopher wrapped his arms around me, and I saw tears in his eyes too.

"We can't stay here," he whispered into my hair.

"I need to see her bring him back."

Christopher's lips pulled tight as he looked back out the window. Cera cried out to Basiliea, but she didn't answer her pleas. She continued to fight her way closer to Basiliea until Cera found herself facing multiple foes who disarmed her.

Despite my hatred for Cera, I didn't want to see anymore death today, so I turned my eyes away before one of the soldiers could raise their sword.

"Anika, it isn't safe for us here."

Quieted, but still shaking, I nodded.

We had to go; there was nothing here for us anymore.

CHAPTER FORTY

We traveled until morning when we came upon a home large enough to have horses. Christopher knocked on the door. "We would like to borrow your horses, Sir." He poured coins into the man's hand. "I'll pay you twice this upon returning."

The man stared at the coins and nodded eagerly. Then he looked up at me. "What's wrong with the maiden? Is she ill?"

Christopher stepped in front of me while I hid my face. "Our business is private."

The man looked at the money again and shrugged. He led us to his small stables and helped us load the horses. Then we rode hard out of town.

Uncertain on where we should ride to, we decided it best to travel to Christopher's manor so we could wash and regather ourselves before deciding our next move. With Ronin dead, Basiliea alive, and the battle going on, I saw nothing we could do to make a difference, but we were both too tired and worn down to think clearly.

All I could think about was Ronin's death.

I thought of little Landon and how someone would have to tell him his father died. I found it ironic how Ronin once had to learn how to live without his son, and now his son would have to live without his father. It almost would have been better if Landon stayed dead than to be brought back into a world with no parents.

My stomach growled ferociously by the time we reached Christopher's manor, but I wanted to wash up before doing anything else. The footman looked at the two of us strangely while asking how our trip was, to which Christopher gave a short reply. We entered through a side door and Christopher found a maid who promised to take care of me and rushed to start a bath.

Outside my door, Christopher pulled me in for a hug. "I'm so sorry," he repeated. He'd repeated the sentiment so many times during the ride here that the words lost all value. They couldn't bring back Ronin.

"I know." I left him with those words as I closed my door behind me.

I dismissed the maid as soon as the bath was drawn and waited until I'd submerged in the water to cry. In the privacy of the room, I allowed my body to shake with tears until my eyes ran dry and my throat was hoarse with each sob.

Once I'd properly cried, I pulled myself together. I wouldn't give Basiliea the satisfaction of breaking me.

I dressed in the simpler of the two dresses laid out for me and brushed through my hair before heading down to face Christopher and figure out our plan. Surprised, I found Christopher wasn't alone. In the same sitting room where Christopher and I spoke the first night I came, I found

Christopher in deep conversation next to his father and a third gentleman with a full head of gray hair.

They each stood up as I arrived. "I didn't think you'd be down so fast," Christopher said as he moved over on the couch to offer a place for me.

"If there's anything we can do, I want to do it."

"You can eat, for starters." Lord Hughes motioned to the platter of food before Christopher and insisted I nourish myself. I wanted to repeat that I'd rather take action, but my stomach interrupted my thoughts with a demand of its own.

"This is my grandfather." Christopher motioned to the man next to his father on the couch.

"Turns out, my father was one of the magicians who'd helped capture Basiliea the first go around," Lord Hughes said in a way that suggested he wasn't pleased with the information. I looked at his grandfather with wide eyes.

He was a thin man; it was difficult to believe he held any power that could help us now, but his smile was filled with mischief. He wore a blue suit with tails and a fancy broach pinned to his chest depicting two snakes fighting. No, I was wrong. As I looked closer, it appeared to be three snakes.

"Basiliea found someone to break her banishment I see."

I blushed, embarrassed as if I'd personally released Basiliea from her prison. "I tried to stop them," I said pathetically. He smiled at me.

"I know you did. My grandson told me all about you. The girl with fire, he calls you."

My brow furrowed. "Why didn't you come with Christopher to the castle where they need you?"

Christopher nudged me while his grandfather chuckled. "I needed to find the spell first, so Christopher rode ahead."

"Why didn't you ride straight to the castle?"

Christopher nudged me harder.

"Because I needed rest." His grandfather didn't seem bothered by my constant questions, but Lord Hughes cleared his throat and set down his cup.

"The question is, can you banish her again?"

"Or kill her," I added.

"She does have fire!" He smiled wide at his son, revealing a mouth of uneven teeth. Then he bobbed his head. "Yes, I could banish Basiliea again, but that requires many magicians to cast a powerful spell and I'm afraid I can't do it alone."

"You won't have to," Christopher said. "I spoke with General Walter and he's already prepared a band of magicians, but they aren't certain what spell will hold her. If we can get you to Hid'Nill Castle, can you work with them?" We looked to his grandfather eagerly.

He clucked. "Magicians never play nice together, rowdy bunch they are, but if he thinks they'll cooperate, then yes. I'll come."

"I don't like the idea of sending you into a battle," Lord Hughes frowned.

"Because I'm old?" his father accused.

Lord Hughes grunted. "Yes, that's precisely why."

"I can go with him," Christopher offered. "The battle must rest at some time, and while they stop to regroup, we'll sneak in through the same route we snuck out."

"You can't jump up to that window," I pointed out.

His eyes rolled. "Alright, not exactly like how we got out, but the same idea."

"I know a cloaking spell or two that'll keep us safe." His grandfather spoke with an optimism that encouraged me.

"Well I'm not letting you two have all the fun," Lord Hughes said with his lips pulled tight. "I'll come too." He cast a worried look over his father, who bounced eagerly in his seat.

A small plan began to form. Christopher voiced his concern over me coming again, but I shook my head. I had other matters to deal with, and I knew a full army and band of magicians had no use for me.

Once the plans were set, they decided it was best to leave right away. I hated seeing them leave but hoped this would be over soon.

"Remember," I said to his grandfather before they left. "Kill her if you can."

"Yes ma'am."

"Where should I meet you?" Christopher sat on the borrowed horse to return to the farmer and his father used the second one, while his grandfather rode one of their own fine stallions.

I held the reins to another one of their horses as I pointed him east. "Meet me at my manor when this is over."

"I'll see you then," Christopher promised, then they rode off.

I waited until they had gone a distance to turn my horse northwest and ride back to the Woods of Silver and Light.

CHAPTER FORTY-ONE

ack knew something was wrong the moment I entered camp.

The rest of camp knew it too, and I soon found myself surrounded by nervous children and fathers left behind, wondering why their loved ones didn't return last night.

Landon slid his hand into mine, breaking my heart. I couldn't meet his eyes.

"Jack, I need to speak with you," my voice wavered but I resisted tears.

Part of me hoped I'd walk into camp to find the Silver Raider's returned, spared by Basiliea's mercy and enlightened to the errors of their ways. I'd pictured the camp packing up their belongings to move elsewhere and start a new life. I pictured Ronin laughing with his son, telling him the story of how he died and came back to life.

But things never seemed to go the way I hoped. People died, families got torn apart, children starved, and widows sat on the porch waiting for their lost husbands to return.

Wishing for anything different wouldn't bring back the fallen.

Jack nodded somberly and led me to a tent. Inside, he crossed his arms and closed his eyes. "What happened?"

A shaky breath escaped my lips. "The guards knew they were coming. They were surrounded before they could get to the Crown Prince."

Jack opened his eyes slowly, and I saw the question lingering behind his eyes. "Did they slaughter them?"

I wished for an easy answer to give him. "No, Basiliea came back first."

His shoulders dropped with relief.

"But, Basiliea brought an army with her, and the Silver Raiders joined her in a fight against the castle."

Jack sat down in a chair and leaned forward on his arms. "She raises her fallen soldiers once they die. They should all be alive, right?"

I wouldn't have ridden into camp looking somber if they were alright, and Jack knew this. He waited for me to tell him the problem.

"I don't know if she chose to raise the Silver Raiders once dead." I sucked in my breath; the words caught on my tongue. It took all my effort to force out the sentence. "I know she chose not to raise Ronin."

Jack buried his head in his hands and stayed that way for a long time. When he finally looked at me again, his eyes were red. "Why didn't they ride back with you?"

"I wasn't in the fight; I came back before the end."

"You ran?"

My hands settled on my waist as I raised my eyebrows. "I had no sword or bow to fight with, and which side would I stand by?"

"Ours!" he said as if the answer was obvious.

"This is not my fight."

"Coward." Jack stood up and turned away from me. A comment came to my lips, but I caught it before it escaped. I'm certain Jack felt the guilt of staying behind instead of riding with them, and he didn't need me to point it out to him.

Quietly, I waited for him to process the information, watching as his back moved gently with each deep breath. Finally, he turned back to me.

"I'm sorry; I didn't mean to lash out at you."

"I know."

His shoulders raised with his hands before dropping in a helpless gesture. "What do we do now?"

The answer I'd prepared caught in my throat, and I found myself debating it. I wanted to tell him to take the children and head for a new life free of banditry and evil sorceresses, leaving behind a note for any returning Silver Raiders to find and follow them. I wanted to tell him to take care of Landon as his own, telling him only the best stories of his brave papa.

That is what I wanted to say. I wanted him to run.

But when I spoke, a different answer came out. "Mount a horse, and we'll go bring back the rest of the Silver Raiders."

As soon as I said it, I knew this was the right answer.

Jack straightened his back at the command. "Yes ma'am."

THE SKY TURNED DARK BY THE TIME WE REACHED Hid'Nill Castle. We left the best explanation we could to the rest of the camp, riding the line between giving them hope and letting them know things looked bleak. I didn't want to tell them that their family members were dead, in the case that they weren't, but it didn't feel right to deceive them with pleasantries just to return in the morning with the news that they were gone.

"Look." Jack pulled his horse up to the hill and stared over the way.

The top of the castle came into view first, starting with the watchtower, then the rounded turrets. Over the battlements of the castle we saw the field where the fight took place last night. It lay clean, as if men hadn't died on that grass hours before. Across the field started a scattering of trees which continued as far as we could see. At the edge of the horizon, smoke pillars drifted into the sky.

Christopher guessed correctly; the fight paused, and the teams withdrew to regroup.

Now prepared, the battlements lined with guards, each watching the distance to see if the enemy moved. The Vestalin army spread to the southwest in tents, resting as the night stood still. A few sentries wandered the border keeping watch.

Between the sentries and the watchtowers, I knew we had little chance of moving unseen. If we tried to sneak in, we risked being killed on spot.

"We need to give ourselves up," I said. Jack looked at me like I was crazy. "If you don't offer up who you are, they won't know. Stick to me and you'll be fine." Jack tried to bring his mask, but I forced him to leave it behind, and now I was glad I had. He nodded, but his lowered eyebrows told me he wasn't pleased.

Slowly we nudged the horses forward out in the open

toward a door, so while we made our target clear, we didn't look like we were trying to sneak in.

Within moments guards burst through another door and ran toward us. Jack shifted in the saddle, but I kept a calm face as I pulled up on my reigns and waited for the guards to surround us.

"What is your business here?" one guard asked in a gruff voice. Each kept a hand on their sword, but none drew. Their horses moved to form a half-circle around us, causing Jack to shift more. Sweat formed on his brow.

"We are here to speak to General Walter," I said.

Multiple guards laughed. "He's a very busy man and doesn't have time right now."

Jack peeked at me, but my voice remained strong. "He had time for me last night when I told him about the attack. Trust me, he wants to see us."

They looked between each other while Jack glared at me for my deceit. He could yell at me later.

Just when I thought they would send us away, Christopher burst through the door and held up his hands. "Let them through! They are with the magicians."

At the word *magicians*, each guard straightened up. "Yes, yes, of course, let us take your horses." They spoke with fear, and I realized they must think us to be magicians as well. I didn't make the correction as I let them take the horse.

"What are you doing here?" Christopher asked as soon as we were inside. "And who is this?" he whispered the question, so the guards didn't hear. I waited until the guards walked far enough away to answer, but Jack, who had been waiting for the same thing, spoke first.

"You told them about the attack?" He looked like he

might punch me, and if he was a less kind man, I think he would have.

"They knew already; I told them not to kill them." I held up my hands.

Jack looked furious, but Christopher stepped up. "She caused you no harm, I assure you. In truth, she's brought much danger upon herself by her association with you." He correctly assumed Jack was with the Silver Raiders. Jack backed down but the fire in his eyes remained.

"I need to find my people, and in order to do that, I think I'm in the wrong camp." He turned as if he was ready to walk out on his own, but Christopher cleared his throat.

"You're in the right place, mate. Your crew sits in the dungeon below us."

"Then take me to them," Jack said without missing a beat.

"Can't. There's no explanation for me to be down there. Now, unless you want to draw attention to yourselves, I suggest we join the magicians."

Christopher walked without checking if Jack followed, who looked between Christopher and the other end of the corridor for a few moments before following reluctantly. A few guards had just rounded the far corner, and I think that influenced his decision to remain in our company. Christopher led us up a stairway and into a room with a window that looked out by the watchtower, which explained how he'd seen me coming.

The room held eight people sitting in a circle talking over each other with animated voices. Christopher's grandfather sat among them, and he gave me a kind wave before turning back to argue with the young girl sitting next to him. These must be the magicians. They looked different than I thought they would. Besides Christopher's grandfather, whose proper name I'd yet to learn, only one other magician appeared as old. Most looked between my age and my parents', and two looked younger than me.

I assumed they'd dress in colorful scarves and big amulets, but while most boasted markings on their skin, their appearances were otherwise disappointingly normal.

"Where's your father?" Lord Hughes was nowhere to be seen.

Christopher smirked. "He insisted on suiting up with the other soldiers like a war hero. I got stuck serving these loons."

Jack stayed close to the door as he watched the magicians argue with no apparent purpose.

"Are they close to something?" I asked.

"Honestly? I have no idea."

I peeked at Jack before inching closer to Christopher. "How did the Silver Raider's get captured?"

He glanced at Jack as well. "The soldiers were under orders to capture, not kill them." He knew my question before I asked it and shook his head. "Ronin was not among them."

Part of me hoped Basiliea changed her mind and brought Ronin back after I'd left. The tiny piece of hope I'd been holding on to died down until it was nothing more than a flicker of my own foolish wish.

To distract myself from my disappointment and keep my anger at bay, I fixated my eyes on the arguing magicians.

"Thyme will not do that!" A man with an impressive beard argued.

"T'will! I'm certain of it!" A hefty woman crossed her arms.

"Hmm. Boy!" The man snapped toward Christopher. "Go get me some thyme!"

Without hesitation Christopher darted from the room. A few minutes later he reappeared with the thyme in hand.

"Give it here, alright let's see this." The man took the thyme and held it in the air. The woman said a few words over it, then the man let it go.

"Ha! See! It fell."

The woman drew in her eyebrows. "Erm, rosemary then. Yes, I remember now! It's rosemary."

"Boy, fetch rosemary."

Christopher looked like he might argue, but he ended up closing his mouth and obeying.

This time, when he let go of the rosemary, it didn't fall.

"What do you know?"

They just as quickly began arguing about something else, and I put my hand to my head. "We're all going to die." Beside me, Christopher nodded.

Just as I finished my sentence, Christopher's grandfather spoke up. He rubbed his hands eagerly as his words filled the air.

"Magicians, I think we're ready. Let's kill her this time."

CHAPTER FORTY-TWO

Christopher fetched General Walter who arrived with two guards all looking like they hadn't slept in days.

"Are you confident?" he asked the magicians, who each gave a different answer running between 'extremely confident' and 'we'll see what happens.'

"It's the best we can do in such a short time, General," Christopher's grandfather said.

"General." Beside me, Jack fell to his knees. I puzzled over his sudden respect for the hierarchy, but it made sense when Jack raised his head. "I am Jack Ollands, a leader of the Silver Raiders, and I would like to give my word that we will leave these lands alone, as well as offer my life as sacrifice, if you let the others go."

Without Ronin, Jack was the closest thing Landon had to a father. "No, Jack don't," I started to say, but General Walter interrupted.

"You Silver Raiders continue to surprise me." He stroked his chin. "Alright, if it pleases you. Bring him to the dungeon." One of the guards bowed and went to grab Jack's hands, but he pulled them away.

"I will walk on my own."

"No, please!" I cried out, but General Walter turned back to the magicians.

"If you're ready, let's not waste time."

Christopher held me back as General Walter exited the room, the magicians trailing behind. "You can't save everyone," Christopher whispered in my ear. I nodded but planned to fight for Jack's freedom later. Landon needed someone.

Curious, we followed the magicians at a safe distance to watch them perform their spell. General Walter showed them to a battlement where they ducked behind the merlons and waited.

After a long while, General Walter said, "Well?"

They looked at each other. "Where is she?"

General Walter sighed. "In the camp over there." He pointed across the way, and they peeked around the merlons to look.

"Oh that's no good, she needs to be closer."

General Walter's face showed little faith in the band of magicians. "Well how do you suggest we do that?"

"We don't know, what have you been doing this whole time, twiddling your thumbs? You figure it out."

Another loud sigh. "I've been getting my army ready in case you can't do this!" He turned to Christopher. "I've put a lot of faith in you, son. This better work. In the meantime, I'm going to converse with my commanders and get them ready for a fight."

He left as the magicians began to argue again on the best way to bait her out without using magic, which would alert her to the magician's presence and right now her ignorance was the only hope we had.

"How'd you do it last time?" I raised my voice above their arguing.

"Her daughter helped us, but Basiliea killed her so we can't use her again."

My mouth snapped shut and my eyes grew wide as Christopher and I exchanged glances. Like an ignorant fool I'd been worried about Basiliea returning and bringing back her daughter and her fiancé who would take back their lands, leaving me homeless. I never considered that Basiliea didn't want her daughter back.

The magician's continued debating. "Someone could go in the field and challenge her? That'd get her close enough."

"No, no, they'd be killed."

"Not by us."

"We don't want anyone to die at all."

"Except her," one pointed out.

"She doesn't count."

They continued in this fashion while an idea came to mind. Christopher wouldn't approve. I almost went anyway, but so much of our relationship consisted of doing things without telling the other person, and I didn't want to set precedent. "Trust me?" I whispered to Christopher. A warning crossed his eyes as he looked at me, and I knew he wanted to say no, not because he didn't trust me but because he knew whatever I wanted to do would be dangerous.

A long pause, then the nod. I mulled over the idea some more until I'd worked up the confidence to go through with it. Then, when Christopher stepped forward to offer his own ideas to the magicians, I peeled back and fled down the stairway.

At the bottom, I rested my hand on the latch, aware that this would be my last chance to turn away. If I didn't go now, my courage would fail me, so I flung open the door and ran across the field, not allowing my mind to share its warnings. If I ran fast enough, I could outrun my fears.

A few moments later I thought I heard someone call my name but I didn't look back to check who. I'd already showed myself to both sides, turning back now would surely label me a coward.

If they needed someone to bait Basiliea, I could do it.

The quarrel between us served as adequate distraction so she shouldn't suspect ulterior motives when I called for her. In truth, my plan served two purposes, and only one of them aided the magicians. Besides luring her into the field, I desperately wanted to bargain to get Ronin back. Now would be my last chance.

Tentatively, I allowed the hope within me to burn again.

"Basiliea!" I yelled into the night, praying she heard me. "Basiliea!" My steps led me further from the protective castle and closer to the camp where Basiliea awaited our next move. Sentries from the Vestalin army lined the side to watch but stayed back at their general's command. The camp slowly began to wake up as riders went through, preparing them for the battle in case we didn't defeat Basiliea.

I didn't know if she could see me, and I doubted my voice carried as far as their camp, but there must be a sentry posted who would see me and report to her. I would run into their camp to see her if I needed, but the magicians depended on her coming to the field.

As I yelled her name for a third time, a light appeared in the sky.

Suddenly, where a void of darkness rested only a moment before, she was there, standing before me wearing a satin dress and a wicked smile.

"Anika. You wish to join Ronin in death?" Her voice carried a tone of mockery and she looked at me like she'd won. She wouldn't scare me. I rushed, praying the magicians spotted her and that they could do their spell at this distance, but not before I talked with Basiliea first.

"I want you to bring Ronin back."

She floated around me in a small circle, inspecting me from every angle. I wondered if she was looking for a dagger, which I did wear, and if it would hurt her if I used it.

She settled back on her feet in front of me. "No."

"He has a son, who is now alone." I tried to appeal to her motherly side, forgetting that her daughter had turned her in.

No sympathy showed in her eyes. "Landon will recover."

"Ronin fought for you; he's the reason you came back. Why can't you give him back his life?"

Her laughter cut my ears. "The boy is too unpredictable. I can't count on his allegiance. Ronin will stay dead."

Anger burned within me as I thought of all the times I told Ronin he couldn't trust Basiliea, and now how she used him to come back to life then didn't save him when she could. My breaths quickened, desperate to get Ronin back and aware that my time was running out. Basiliea watched me shake as I clenched my fists.

"If you bring him back, I can convince him to leave. He won't be a threat to you." At this point, I didn't know of anything to say to change her mind. The air around us remained still, and I wondered what held the magicians back. I wouldn't turn to look and risk exposing them. I hoped the spell was working, but I needed one more minute.

She leaned forward. "I don't want to bring him back. His heart is too torn." She straightened. "But you're right, I am in debt to him. To pay that debt, I'll spare you. Leave before I change my mind."

At that very moment, a high-pitched sound cut through the sky. Her head whirled back, sending her white hair trailing over her shoulder as she looked past me to the battlement. "No," she breathed. "No, magic won't take me this time." In panic, her hands bent together, and she started to mutter words I couldn't discern.

I hoped the magician's spell would be instantaneous, but it didn't look that way. The sound died out as soon as it began, but in its place light blasted from the sky straight to Basiliea, engulfing her in red rays. Still working frantically, her hands circled each other, and a light flicked between.

Without thinking, I grabbed my dagger and sliced at her hands to stop her spell.

Satisfaction filled me as deep red ran from her wrist. The emotion quickly turned to fear as the light in her hands burst forth, slamming into me and sending me flying. My legs curled over my head as I rolled to the ground tangled in the fabric of my own dress, and I struggled for breath. My stomach burned, and for a moment I understood the pain Ronin felt when he died. The fire quickly spread to my head, until my whole body felt engulfed in flames, and my head pushed against the ground to block out the pain.

My hands fumbled beneath my knees to lift me up, and that's when I realized I'd lost my dagger in the blast. Hopefully I'd left a wound on Basiliea. Above her, the red light flickered with white, flashing bright enough to make seeing Basiliea difficult. At one point, I wasn't convinced she was in the beam anymore.

The sound blasted again, and the light died. In its place, Basiliea lay on the ground motionless. Willing my tired legs to move, I managed to crawl back to her. Behind me I heard horses stampeding as loud as thunder, but I didn't turn to look.

Basiliea lay with both hands over her chest as she stared at the sky.

"Ronin," I breathed. "Please."

Her head turned toward me, and she let out a small smile, raising her hand. Blood trickled from the wound on her arm.

Just as she flicked her wrist, her body began to shimmer until it vanished completely. I collapsed into the space, crying out, cursing at the ground to give me Ronin back.

Vestalin's cavalry surrounded me and one of the men offered me his hand. "Come with me; you'll be trampled here." Behind him, the army continued coming over the hill as a mighty force, but too late for the battle.

"She's gone; the fight is over," I yelled through my tears.

He pointed across the field. "She might be, but they aren't."

Basiliea's army moved across the field, bold even in

their new mortality. Basiliea's power couldn't save them now.

Seeing the approaching army gave me newfound strength, and I used it to get to my feet and mount the horse in front of the soldier. He steered us through the flurry of horsemen toward the tower where I'd first ran from to meet Basiliea. I wiped my tears against my shoulder, mad at myself for believing I could convince Basiliea to bring back Ronin. The soldier set me down and turned to join his men.

Inside the safety of the tower, I collapsed back against the wall and buried my head in my knees, overcome with disappointment. As I sobbed, a hand reached over my shoulder and pulled me close to their body.

"She wouldn't bring him back?" Christopher's voice breathed into my hair.

I shook my head. "He's gone forever."

I knew how hard it was for him to comfort me over the loss of another man, and I wished I could explain it to him. I didn't mourn simply Ronin. I mourned my friend who taught me to shoot a bow and made me laugh without trying. I mourned Landon, the boy who lost his father. I mourned Jack, who'd die so the Silver Raiders could go free. And I mourned the other lives taken while I watched helplessly.

This feeling burned inside me, and I hated the very essence of it. Helplessness. I'd never felt more helpless than I did in this moment with my only chance at saving Ronin gone and the sounds of battle raging behind me.

We stayed crouched in the dark against the wall for what felt like hours until Christopher's grandfather came down the stairs.

"It's done. The battle is over."

With no way to know how much time had passed, I took a guess based on the sliver of light coming through the window. The roaring sounds that once filled the sky now dulled into the sporadic clang of metal and talk of men.

"Did we win?" I asked.

The corners by his eyes wrinkled. "You'd know if we lost."

"And her army?"

He hesitated, glancing at Christopher before replying, "Returned to the earth of which they came."

My eyes fell to the floor. "Did none of them surrender?"

"The army she raised wasn't any army, it was her army, the men she used to call upon to fight for her. These men are barbarians with a love of nothing besides war and power and death. They surrender to nothing."

I tried not to think of the slaughter that went on behind the door as I stood up with Christopher who said, "At least Basiliea is dead."

His grandfather paled, causing my stomach to drop. "She is dead, isn't she?"

His words came slowly. "I'm afraid not. She's greatly wounded, and stripped from her powers, but she's not dead."

My head shook, not wanting to believe it. It didn't seem fair that Ronin died while Basiliea got to live. "How did she vanish if she's powerless?"

"That was me, I sent her away to a far land where she can't bother anyone. We used all our power to hurt her, but couldn't kill her. With luck, the cold will do that for us, but if not, she won't soon find her way back here. And she'll never have magic again."

I stared at him. "We could have killed her with a sword if she was powerless!"

His nimble finger tapped his chin. "Ah yes, it seems that would have done it as well, but I, for one, felt much better knowing she's far away from here and couldn't pull any further tricks."

His words brought no comfort. Basiliea being alive meant she could come back, and that terrified me. Either Christopher didn't fear her as much or he trusted his grandfather more, but he didn't look worried. Maybe it was a difference in our personality that I feared the worst, or maybe I was more aware of the dangers of the world, but the thought of Basiliea caused my hand to tremble in a way that I feared would never stop. My other hand clasped over my first to control the tremor as I sucked in a breath until my lungs filled my chest.

"Okay." I blew the air out. "We have to find her. We have to know that she will die. I can't rest if she's still out there."

Christopher's grandfather didn't hesitate. "Then I will go after her and make certain that the cold killed her. If it didn't, I'll be reenergized enough to finish the job myself."

I'd never felt more grateful than I did in that moment, but as I looked him over, taking in the thin arms and heavy bags under his eyes, I knew it wasn't fair of me to ask this of him. "You shouldn't have to go. Let us do it for you."

Christopher glanced at me, but then he shrugged. "Sure, why not?"

Christopher's grandfather chuckled as he straightened his vest. "Without magic, you two won't be able to keep up! I'll take the magicians with me, it's about time we bonded together."

Christopher's entire body relaxed as he thanked his grandfather.

"Are you ready to go home?"

I gave his grandfather a hug, then laced my hand in Christopher's. "Almost."

CHAPTER FORTY-THREE

General Walter allowed the Silver Raiders to go free the on the condition that they signed the contract they'd created and moved to another country. Cera, with red eyes and a tongue of rage, put up the most fight, but upon threat of death she stuck her hand out to sign the papers. Some Silver Raiders fell in battle, but most had been captured and their life spared. Now their heads hung low as they signed the contracts and agreed.

"Good. Have guards follow them to be sure they leave," General Walter said to the man next to him, who nodded.

With a deep sigh he crossed the room to see us. "I'm greatly in debt to you all." He looked around at the magicians and to Christopher and me. "Let me know if I can be of help in the future."

I cleared my throat and stepped forward. Sadness still dwelled within me, but rage fueled my decision in this moment. I looked to Cera, ready to leave and be free when she'd caused this destruction that brought upon Ronin's death, and the sight of her made me furious. "Sir? I hope I've earned some of your trust."

General Walter raised a bushy eyebrow at me. "You have. Is there something you need?"

"Have you heard of the death of a Lord Thames?"

His face fell. "Aye, I've heard of it."

I pointed across the room to Cera. "That is the girl responsible for his murder."

His head swung to Cera and he yelled at his guards to capture her. Then he turned back to me. "Are you certain of this?"

I nodded. "She and the Lady Claire Coengburr of Vestalin schemed together with Basiliea, and Lord Thames's death was a part of it." Beside me, Christopher nodded as confirmation.

Recognition crossed General Walters's eyes. "Those were the two who approached me with the information that you were with the Silver Raiders. Guards, bring that girl here!" Cera's eyes grew wide as the guards yanked her toward us. The other Silver Raiders hesitated to watch what would unfold, while I debated if I should stay or not. Cera's feet tripped beneath her, and she fumbled to keep up with the stiff guards who pulled her toward us.

Before they reached us, General Walters asked, "Do you have proof?"

I bowed my head. "I can get another witness who overheard them say this, if you need. That is all the proof I have."

"Thank you Anika. We will send guards for Lady Claire right away. If they are found guilty, both she and Cera will be punished for their crime."

The guards with Cera halted before us, her hair falling

over her face as they jolted her upright. General Walters faced them. "You will be sent back to the dungeon to await your sentence for the murder of Lord Thames."

She denied it repeatedly, releasing dramatic sobs and shaking her head and begging for them to listen to her. As it became clear that her pleas would not release her, her mood shifted, her eyebrows drew in, and her head swung to me where she said something that pierced my heart. "Ronin is dead because of you."

Christopher squeezed my hand sharply, and I squeezed it back to release some of my anger. I might have yelled at Cera, but Christopher spoke first. "Ronin is dead because of *you*; you brought him to Basiliea."

Her eyes held fire, and she spat at his feet. "You don't remember me, do you? The girl who used to play with you when we were little? Do you remember how my family's title got stripped away, and we were thrown on the streets? This king did that! Basiliea was meant to save us all. She was going to restore this kingdom after the war, give us back our wealth and me back a title! You alerted the castle against it and because of that, Ronin died, and we failed." She pulled on her arms to free herself from the guard's grip, but they held tight.

General Walters shifted in front of us in case Cera managed to break free. "Take her away."

I still had more questions and more I wanted to say to her, but I held my tongue as she got dragged back to the dungeons while the Silver Raiders watched, each with a questioning look on their face. The only one who didn't look surprised was Jack.

Once Cera had vanished, and General Walters strode off, Jack crossed the room to give me a firm hug.

"I promise Annabeth and I will watch after Landon as our own."

Remembrance of the orphaned boy softened the anger in my chest. There wasn't a better fit for parents than Jack and Annabeth. Jack was sensible in a way where Ronin was reckless, and Annabeth carried as much kindness in her heart as Ronin ever did.

He tipped his head at us before leaving with the rest of the Silver Raiders.

I redirected my focus to something I could do—confront Lady Claire.

"Do you know what you'll do?" Christopher asked.

"Not yet," I admitted. "But I want to get answers before the guards get there."

Upon returning home, Lady Claire was found in the front sitting room with her legs crossed and knitting on her lap, a small smile on her face as if today was no different than any other day. That same face that I once found so gentle and polite now stirred up vicious thoughts in my mind. Before rationality could take hold, my words came out all at one, shouting in a manner that made her drop her knitting and widen her eyes. Elenora rushed down the stairs at the sound of my voice and planted herself next to me with her arms crossed and her eyes glaring at Lady Claire, nodding periodically to let both me and Lady Claire know that I was not alone. Christopher, kind as always, fetched me water, but the fear of squishing the glass into shards kept me from drinking.

"I want to know why you killed Lord Thames." I started with my demands.

"I didn't kill him." Lady Claire clarified as she picked up the blue yarn from the floor and smoothed out her stitches. "And I didn't know what she planned to do." She put a dainty hand to her forehead as though the thought of his death still made her weak.

"That doesn't make you innocent in that man's death. Why did she do it?"

"Really Anika, that tone is not needed."

My lips pursed. "You agreed to her killing Christopher! You knew about Basiliea! You will give me answers or I will deliver you to General Walter myself!" Elenora nodded eagerly beside me, though she had no idea who General Walter was.

"Fine, I'll tell you. Lord Thames's father created the spell that banished Basiliea in the first place. Basiliea feared his son carried magic and would be strong enough to banish her again. From how easy it was for Cera to kill him, I don't think he carried any magic at all."

I expected tears or a fight. I hadn't expected her still face and smooth voice in the face of getting caught. An innocent, helpless man was slaughtered, and Lady Claire showed no remorse over the fact. I remembered how she'd gasped when we first heard the news of his death, pretending to go into mourning for days, and I shook my head; she was either cold-hearted and felt no guilt for her actions, or she was far more evil-minded than I'd anticipated. "How did Basiliea get you on her side anyway?"

"She didn't. Cera did." When she stopped talking, I raised my eyebrows and motioned for her to go on. She sighed. "I owed Cera for something that happened when she was little. This is how I was repaying her."

I glanced out the window where guards on black horses

decorated in king's livery approached the wide path to the manor. "What happened to make you owe her?"

She set down the cup a little harder than usual, and a drop of tea spilled out. "Now Lady Anika, just because you're so smart, doesn't mean I now have to tell you all my secrets. I hurt her family, they lost their title, she's very bitter over the whole thing, and Basiliea promised to give her title back once she took over the kingdom."

New anger curled in my chest. While Cera repeatedly attacked me for my title, claiming it made me different from them, she actively sought one for herself, and wanted it badly enough that she called upon Basiliea to get it. Her actions led to destruction and the death of Ronin.

"Are you planning to kick her out, or shall I?" Elenora looked at me.

"Neither," I said, and I relished the smile on Lady Claire's face before I continued. "Guards are here to escort Lady Claire to the castle where she will be punished for her crimes."

Her eyes grew wide and she scrambled to the window. The guards knocked at the door before Christopher opened it.

"Here she is."

"Lady Claire, you are to come with us to Hid'Nill Castle to report before the king."

She looked between Elenora and I, then at the four guards, who put their hands on their sword for good measure. After a long pause, she sighed dramatically. "Alright."

I resisted cheering. The guards took her arms and led her outside the manor with them, not giving her a chance to fetch any of her things. I would box them up and donate them later; she'd have no more use of them.

She asked to pause in the doorway and cast a look over her shoulder to hold my gaze.

"This world holds far more dangerous things than Basiliea. I suggest you think of that before awakening the magic within people, Anika. This land is not prepared to hold magic again."

Her words were meant to frighten me. Her words were meant to take away some of the power I'd found for our village through the Gifts and make me feel weak. Helpless. But her words meant nothing to me, and her warning fell on deaf ears. "Goodbye, Lady Claire."

The door closed with a slam.

We all shared a sigh of relief when she left. Already the manor felt better, as if she took a foul feeling with her and that now the manor would be better off. No more lessons, no more pretending to be proper, no more strict meal times and forced attendance to balls. From now on, I ran this manor the way I saw fit, and would be turning her old chambers into a card room.

It was time to turn this stuffy manor into a proper home.

The door swung wide and we whirled around to see Lady Claire, but someone else stood in the doorway. Someone who made my heart jump from my chest with joy and tears form in my eyes.

"Cosette! Rumpel!" I threw myself into my sister's arms while she stared at us with wide eyes. She wore a brown riding dress with black gloves, and her hair was twisted into a knot just like the day she'd left. Rumpel's curls were longer, and he tied them back with a black ribbon, while holding a stack of books in his hands. With them here, things felt somewhat normal again, as if the last few months hadn't happened. As if Lady Claire wasn't still outside being arrested. My sister's warm hug comforted me all the way to my bones.

Rumpel squeezed my shoulders with affection, but his eyes were tight with worry and his voice strained. "We've come to warn you against Basiliea. If we'd known the Silver Raiders were dealing with her, we never would have left you alone."

"And what happened to Lady Claire?" Cosette pulled me back at arm's length to look over me.

"It's been handled. All of it. Oh, how I missed your faces." I hugged her tight again, even as she cast a concerned look out the window.

At our side, Elenora whispered to Christopher as she pointed to Cosette and Rumpel, and he nodded his head. Rumpel paid them little mind as he set the books down and crossed his arms.

"What happened with Basiliea? And what of the Silver Raiders?"

I separated from my sister and took a deep breath. "It's quite the long story, I'm afraid."

Cosette's eyes narrowed before gasping. "You got involved with those raiders, didn't you!" She wagged a finger at me then moved it to Rumpel. "I knew we should have come sooner! She's gotten into all sorts of trouble!"

"That doesn't surprise me in the least, but I'd really like to hear about Basiliea please. Is everyone alright?" He still looked worried as he glanced between us all. "Elenora? Anika? What's been going on?"

"Well," Elenora sat down and rubbed her feet. "This has

been quite the exciting few days. And I thought wedding planning would prove stressful."

A laugh escaped my lips as I crossed toward Christopher. "I imagine a wedding can prove equally eventful."

"Let's get married in some quiet way to avoid all the fuss in the future," Christopher said with a long sigh as he leaned against the wall and squeezed my hand. A moment later his eyes opened wide as we looked at him in shock.

"Oh," Cosette wiggled her eyebrows at me and Christopher. "Tell me more about your wedding?"

"Erm I just mean, if we get married. Someday."

A smile pulled at my lips. "Quiet sounds nice. Would you have a small reception afterward?"

Pleasantly surprised, Christopher bobbed his head. "Whatever you want."

"With a card table present?"

Less enthusiastic, he still nodded. "If it'll make you happy."

I slid away from him and settled into the couch. "That sounds very nice. Whoever you marry will be a lucky girl." His face fell for a moment, but the playfulness in my eyes cheered him up again and he winked at me.

"Very lucky, indeed."

Rumpel coughed. "I hate to be like this, but I must know about Basiliea."

Cosette watched me with an amused face. "I'd rather know about that." She pointed to Christopher.

"Then you'd better unpack. Because it's quite the tale."

CHAPTER FORTY-FOUR

he clouds formed in a way that suggested a storm brewed within, casting a grey hue over the land as they warned us of the coming weather. I rested in the sitting room, waiting for the storm to be upon me. The view out my window showed my gardens, which looked better than ever thanks to the villagers. One by one they'd accepted their Gifts, and now they used them daily, even the ones that weren't practical. It was almost humorous to watch some of them navigate their newfound talents, but however inexperienced they were, they made up for it in generosity.

Thanks to the Gifts, the towns thrived once again.

Not all accepted the change, however, especially towns on the Vestalin side of the border where folks didn't have Gifts, but none seemed to mind when crates of food were sent over out of the generosity of Westfallen towns. The townsfolk who thought they couldn't survive without Ronin's assistance pulled together to get by, and they were one of the first towns who didn't originally attend the festival of talents to begin using Gifts.

They didn't need Ronin to survive after all.

If I looked beyond the beautiful garden, I could see the pile of stones I'd set up as a memorial to Ronin. I didn't need the shrine to remember him by, but it felt wrong not to do something. He deserved more than a collection of stones that visitors rode past and squirrels climbed atop of; but this was the best I could put together. I'm sure Jack and Annabeth found their own way to honor him, and I took comfort in the fact that I would not be remembering him alone.

The thought of Ronin didn't release a river of tears anymore, but occasionally I still felt overcome with sadness at the friend I'd lost. I suspected it would always be that way.

Rumpel and Cosette couldn't stay long. And with Elenora gone and Lady Claire exiled, Wateredge Manor felt lonelier than ever. The silence echoed through the walls where dust now settled and rooms went untouched. I had enough money now to afford a lady's maid but decided to wait until after my trip to hire one.

Without knocking, Christopher came through the front door holding a letter in hand.

"Just made it in before the rain," he said, shivering in his overcoat. He handed the letter to me. "This was under your door."

The scribbles on the front told me who posted the letter, and I tore it open.

Christopher started carrying my bags to the carriage for our trip while I read the letter. When I finished, I pressed it to my chest.

"How are they doing?" Christopher closed the door behind him and shook off tiny droplets of water from his coat. Behind him the storm began with a strike of lightning and a loud clap of thunder that vibrated through the house.

"They've settled into a small town in Aurrinn where Jack works as a carpenter and Landon is studying under him." I smiled at the image.

Christopher grinned too. "I'm glad they are well. We can go visit them someday." He plucked my coat from the couch and brought it to me, wrapping it around my shoulders. "We won't make it to Autumn Leaf Village by nightfall if we don't leave now."

"Are you sure we shouldn't wait out this storm?" I leaned up to kiss him softly before he could answer.

The front door flew open and interrupted our kiss. We both jumped to see who came to visit in this treacherous storm and found Joshua standing at the doorstep with his hat and coat dripping water on the floor. His lower lip quivered, and his knees wobbled against each other. It was a wonder he managed to travel in such a condition.

"Joshua, good man, come in and sit by the fire." Christopher took his appearance in stride, ushering him forward and out of the cold air. Joshua stood frozen on the doorstep while the rain beat down behind him.

His tongue forked out to wet his lips before speaking. "The north."

"Come again?"

"The north," Joshua said, louder this time. His wild eyes looked between us. "Something moves in the north. A great power has awoken."

Greetings from this side of my laptop!! I hope you enjoyed reading the second book in the Storyteller's series! There was something so fun about the magic of the Woods that I loved writing, and at several points through the process I was ready to pack up and move to a cabin in the woods to be like the Silver Raiders.

As an indie author, for a book to be successful, reviews mean EVERYTHING. If you could take a moment to leave a review on Goodreads or Amazon, it would help my career immensely. I'll read every review posted so I can hear your thoughts on my book! I love hearing from readers and am grateful for your time. You are also welcome to find me on social media (Instagram: victoria_mccombs) to connect further! My inbox is always open to readers.

For my third book, we are travelling north to ice palace in Elenvérs. I'll include the first few pages as a sneak peek for you!

Thank you, readers! Your support is invaluable to me.

-VM

ACKNOWLEDGMENTS

My deepest gratitude goes out to all my readers. All the early morning messages, posts about the book, and support for this series warm my heart. Thank you so much!

Thank you to my kids who played so nicely (sometimes) while momma was writing. And thanks to my incredible husband who sacrificed precious kid-free time with me so I could write. I appreciate everything you do for our family so that I'm able to pursue this dream. To my parents, sister, and Oma—this book wouldn't be the same without you. Thank you for always being there to listen and help me work through plot holes, and for being my first readers. I'm so blessed to be a part of this family.

A huge thank you to my in-laws, who welcomed a book nerd into the family of sport-lovers. You have all been so supporting and loving and I'm so so grateful for you all. I also can't wait to beat you in fantasy football this year.

For Parliament House Press—I can't thank you enough for everything you do for me. I'll never stop bragging about how wonderful of a publishing house you are.

And thank you to Jesus for everything.

A SNEAK PEEK AT BOOK
THREE: THE WINTER
CHARLATAN

CHAPTER ONE

After frost bites your fingertips, you have two hours until it circulates to your heart, freezing it forever; that's what the cave mages say. That, and that belliberries make the best pies.

I believed them when I was younger, until a treacherous snowstorm caught our family on the outskirts of the Wandering Mountains with little protection from the unrelenting snow that surrounded us through the bleak night. Though my fingers froze, my heart didn't, and I never believed the cave mages again.

Except about the belliberries. Those pies were divine.

Still, frozen heart or not, I pulled my parka closer around my neck and nuzzled into the thick fur as a harsh wind lashed across my red nose.

It was the strongest winter we'd had in ages, though they say that every year. Elenvérs hadn't seen the heat of summer in hundreds of years since the kingdom moved to the ice palace nestled between the calm Northern Mountains and the enchanting Wandering Mountains. While the snow lessened during half the year, the ice never melted and the flowers never bloomed. We lived too far north for heat to find us now, and the court that once overlooked autumn colors now saw nothing but white mountaintops and endless icicles, until those who remembered warmth were gone and replaced by those who knew nothing but the heat of a mage's magic.

The snow whipped up from banks along the rocks, swirling in the air and funneling through trees before settling back on the ground as the wind travelled to find a new playmate. Crystals draped from frosted trees, casting the glow of the morning sun into tiny fragments around me. White flakes rested on green pines that grew along the mountainside. The occasional cluster of snow fell from the trees with a soft sound as wind interrupted their slumber.

For a moment, the beauty captivated me.

The Wandering Mountains might carry a fair amount of uncertainty, but they were far more beautiful than the predicable Northern Mountains. The crystallized trees. The calm snow. The frozen lakes. The peaceful air.

Focus.

It'd be easy to get lost in these mountains, but I had to stay alert. This was my one chance. If this didn't work, I didn't know what else I'd do. This was already a long shot.

My mind banished the doubt. I had to break the curse.

The White Bear only revealed itself to the pure of soul, and I'd washed my soul in the spring of refinement three times this morning to be certain the tricky creature showed itself to me. My plan was foolproof.

With my bow and arrow, I'd bring down the bear. An anxious finger rested on the relaxed string, rubbing nervously against the fletching while Elis gave my hand a sideways glance.

"Stop your fidgeting, you're making me nervous."

I peeked to my side. Elis looked anything but nervous, though I hardly knew what nervous looked like on her. Wolf's fur lined her sharp face while subtle snowflakes rested against her brown hair and the tip of her eyelashes. She kept her frame hidden behind a large tree, utilizing the low pine branches as cover. Our vision was partly blocked, but we were equally concealed from the eyes of any who passed by if they didn't look closely. Elis already mapped out our path up the tree if we needed to hide, putting a lot of faith in my ability as an archer to protect us once stuck in the tree.

No one should pass by. The only ones who travelled into these frozen woods were aspiring knights looking for the White Bear to prove their value to their king.

"It's just a bear, we'll be fine," my voice came as a whisper.

Elis whispered back, "I don't think you understand what a bear is."

A grunt escaped my lips. "I've seen some of the knights who bring back the bear's paw; I'm just as strong as them. It can't be that ferocious."

When Elis didn't reply, I glanced her direction, but her hazel eyes remained fixated on our surroundings as she slowly scanned the area. Large pine trees made it difficult to see much, but I appreciated the change in color that would hopefully provide an easier background to spot the White Bear.

We'd travelled out early this morning before the sun peaked over the mountain tops. I'd always valued Elis for her reliability as a sister, but I'd never loved her more than when she agreed to join me this morning with no questions asked. Even still, as we'd crouched in the snow for hours seeking out the mysterious White Bear, she didn't ask what I planned to do once we acquired its paw. Her unwavering loyalty amazed me, and I ranked it as one of her highest attributes.

I didn't tell her that enough. "I really appreciate you being here."

She glanced my direction. "Your nose is the same color as your hair. You look terrible."

Her candor was another one of her attributes that I enjoyed. Still, the corner of her mouth twitched upward as she repositioned herself. Her own nose carried a tint of redness to it as she sniffed.

Red was good. Red was not blue. We might come out of this with frostbite, but we were not frozen. Not yet.

I'd stay here until I froze beyond thawing if it meant I caught that bear. I needed this.

I took a moment to bury my nose into the hood of my parka as the frosted fibers rubbed against my skin, providing little relief from the chill. This had already taken longer than predicted, and my stomach complained of hunger while my skin complained of the crippling cold. *Where was that blasted bear?*

"Are you certain Briggs said he came here?" I asked Elis, whose suitor, Briggs, told her where he found the White Bear on his quest to become a knight. After retrieving the bear's paw, he snuck past King Olin's personal guards to hide it under the king's pillow. The queen wasn't amused but King Olin was impressed. Briggs was knighted the next day and began pursuing Elis a week later.

His instructions to the bear sounded clear. *Travel east from the caves of the people, down the Lost Man Trail to the edge of the Wandering Mountains. Go to the second mountain on the left, then travel halfway until you find a stream—free flowing despite the frozen temperature. Follow the stream to the source. The bear will be nearby.*

Besides the stream, there was little to distinguish this part of the Wandering Mountains from the rest of the range. Every inch of the rocks was coated in the same layer of snow and ice and pine trees. If it weren't for the stream that flowed with clear water while the rest of the mountain stood frozen, I wouldn't know this valley from the next.

Travelers often got lost here, and it was easy to see why. It wasn't marked with the mines and the civilization like the Northern Mountains were. The Wandering Mountains were large and uncharted and lifeless. Mostly lifeless.

Perhaps we were lost. Crossing another mountain would take too much time; we must return to Elenvérs castle before anyone questioned our absence. It wasn't unusual for me and Elis to take off for a week at a time, but whenever we left, trouble usually found us. After a few days the king would send a few knights looking for us. It was his way of showing he cared.

Elis gave me one of her famous sighs. "Of course I'm not certain, but I'm fairly sure. Why are we here anyway?"

Ah, she finally asked. I wasn't ready to share the answer. Instead, I mumbled in reply, and she frowned.

Customarily, these parts of the Wandering Mountains were only ventured into by brave men and women aspiring to knighthood, which could be achieved if they found the White Bear, cut off its paw, and returned it to the king. The way the paw was given mattered. King Olin didn't see aspiring knights on request, so instead they had to find a unique and clever way to present the paw to him before he'd grant knighthood.

I enjoyed seeing the different ways knights offered the paw, like when Briggs snuck it into the king's chambers, but my favorite was under the silver platter at dinner one evening. Even the cook was surprised.

It was a tradition that continued from before I was born, and the idea behind the ritual hadn't changed. Knights proved their soul's purity by their ability to spot the White Bear, then proved their skill by acquiring the beast's paw, then their cleverness in how they got the paw before their king.

Pure, skilled, and clever. The three markings of an Elenvérs knight.

As far as I knew, no one ever sought out the bear unless aspiring for knighthood.

My legs tingled, and I shifted my crouched position from my feet to my knees to allow better blood flow. This position made it difficult to move quickly if needed, but it didn't look like we'd be going anywhere any time soon. The snow started melting into my pants, and I instantly regretting the change in posture. I was about to shift back when Elis let out a sharp gasp.

My head sprang up and eyes skirted across the terrain to see the White Bear. My fingers pulled back the bow string slightly, ready to fire.

I saw nothing.

To my side, Elis aimed her bow through the tree with a steady hand. "Finally," she whispered. She slid her foot down quietly and moved her knee up, giving her a balanced base to shoot from.

The trees must be blocking my sight. With as much stealth as I could muster, I tipped slightly to my left to find the same angle as Elis, whose eyes remained straight on the opening in the trees several meters ahead. Her arrow tracked some hidden movement.

From my new position, I could see more than before. I saw the mass of pine trees, most with layers of snow reaching to their tops and small icicles hanging from periodic branches. I saw the mouth of the stream bursting from the heart of the mountain, the water flowing from the rocks as they carved their path downward, meeting to form the stream. I saw the sparkle in the air as the sunlight gleamed off the endless snow and reflected with a blinding white.

I saw it all.

There was no bear.

Some of the things I love most in this world are peppermint hot chocolate, peanut butter ice cream, golfing dates, Jesus, and game nights with family. And of course, books.

Fairytales were my first love. I became obsessed with the idea that if one was brave enough, they could defeat dragons, and that true love was real. I met my true love in college, and together we raise our two boys. I have my dad to thank for teaching me to love writing, and my mom to thank for allowing us to keep a wall of medieval weapons in the house, which curated my love for that time period.

My dream is to write vivid worlds and charming characters that will leave an imprint on my readers hearts, the way that so many books have done for me.